CRAIG MARTELLE

STARSHIP LOST

CONFRONTATION

aethonbooks.com

CONFRONTATION
©2024 CRAIG MARTELLE

This book is protected under the copyright laws of the United States of America. No part of this publication may be reproduced, stored in a retrieval system, or transmitted, in any form or by any means, without the prior permission in writing of the publisher, nor be otherwise circulated in any form of binding or cover other than that in which it is published and without a similar condition including this condition being imposed on the subsequent purchaser. Any reproduction or unauthorized use of the material or artwork contained herein is prohibited without the express written permission of the authors.

Aethon Books supports the right to free expression and the value of copyright. The purpose of copyright is to encourage writers and artists to produce the creative works that enrich our culture.

The scanning, uploading, and distribution of this book without permission is a theft of the author's intellectual property. If you would like to use material from the book (other than for review purposes), please contact editor@aethonbooks.com. Thank you for your support of the author's rights.

Aethon Books
www.aethonbooks.com

Print and eBook design and formatting by Josh Hayes. Artwork provided by Vivid Covers.

Published by Aethon Books LLC.

Aethon Books is not responsible for websites (or their content) that are not owned by the publisher.

This book is a work of fiction. Names, characters, places, and incidents are the product of the author's imagination or are used fictitiously. Any resemblance to actual events, locales, or persons, living or dead is coincidental.

All rights reserved.

ALSO IN STARSHIP LOST

Starship Lost

The Return

Primacy

Confrontation

Fallacy

Engagement

Check out the entire series here! (Tap or scan)

SOCIAL MEDIA

Craig Martelle Social
Website & Newsletter:
https://www.craigmartelle.com

Facebook:
https://www.facebook.com/ AuthorCraigMartelle/

Always to my wife, who loves me even though I work every day writing stories.

STARSHIP LOST TEAM

Beta Readers and Proofreaders - with my deepest gratitude!
James Caplan
Kelly O'Donnell
John Ashmore
Rita Whinfield

Get ***The Human Experiment*** for free when you join my newsletter. There's a zoo, but the humans are the ones being studied.
https://craigmartelle.com

PREVIOUSLY FROM STARSHIP LOST

When will we be out of the woods?

Brad found his ship filled with children. He chased the smallest out of the captain's seat, but then caught her when she tried to scurry away. He put her in his lap and activated the sensor systems. They didn't work inside the cargo bay. He shut them down.

He activated the radio. "*Cornucopia*, this is *Starstrider*, status please."

"*Starstrider*, *Cornucopia*. We've been trying to reach *Chrysalis*. It's been hours. What is going on?"

"*Starstrider* is on board *Chrysalis*. We've taken heavy damage and are on emergency power with barely enough for life support. If you're available, we could use a tactical assist."

"We'll be there in twenty minutes," the voice replied. "But there's one problem. The troopship is right behind us. They're slowing down with us. Do you have any weapons?"

"Negative, *Cornucopia*. We are lucky to be breathing. We are capable of nothing else."

"We will dock with you, *Chrysalis*, port-side roller airlock, but be prepared to repel boarders because they're coming in behind us."

"Roger. We'll take your assistance, and we'll pay your price," Brad replied. "Brad out."

He leaned back for a moment and then decided what he needed to do. He plopped the child down in the captain's seat and ran from the cargo bay straight to Engineering.

"Teo," he interrupted her mid-bite, "I need power to one missile tube for a manual launch."

Teo shook her head but capped her food bag and stuffed it into a thigh pocket.

"Bec, I'm going to need you for this, and you, too." She pointed at Vantraub. The three left Engineering.

"I'll be at the manual launch station, Deck Three."

Teo waved before she disappeared into the central shaft.

Brad headed up the ladder until there was no gravity and kept going until it pulled him the other way. He found it odd to stand on the ceiling of Deck Three, but that was what it came to.

He activated his magnetic boots and got into position. The station had no power whatsoever. He had to wait. He verified that the cables and couplings were intact before returning to find that there was still no power.

Brad could do nothing but wait. He had twenty minutes from when he contacted the cargo ship.

He clomped to the ladder and headed down. He pulled himself out of the shaft when he reached the command deck.

He knocked gently on Jaq's door. She didn't answer. He went in and found her asleep.

The second-last thing he wanted to do was wake her. The last thing he wanted was to die.

But Jaq didn't have to be the one. He left the captain's quarters and flew to the bridge, where he found Alby doodling around. "Come with me. We have a troopship to kill."

"With what?" Alby asked.

"From the Malibor we receive, to the Malibor we send. We're going to return one of their missiles."

"How?" Alby followed but was still surprised that they could do anything, not until they reached the magic ten percent.

"Teo is going to bypass everything to feed *Starstrider's* power to the launch tube."

"How do we know where it is?"

"*Cornucopia* is going to tell us. They'll be here any minute."

"We have help?"

"We have help," Brad confirmed. They reached Deck Three and walked down the ceiling until they arrived at the manual launch station.

The power had not yet come on.

The time suggested *Cornucopia* should have arrived. "You have it," Brad said. "I'll be right back."

Without the relays active, the portable comm units were nearly useless. Brad had tried his once and stuffed it back into his pocket when no one answered.

Brad had to descend seven decks, but after the first

couple, it was zero-gee. He flew down the corridor to the airlock, where he found the space beyond the window had turned dark. Brad opened the inner hatch and used the manual lever to crank the outer hatch open. A quick rush of air showed the pressure in *Cornucopia* was higher than what was in *Chrysalis*.

"Am I happy to see you," Brad told Godbolt and Nokes. "But I need targeting data on that troopship. We are trying to fire a missile."

Godbolt grinned and headed inside the cargo hauler. "Gangway!" she shouted on her way down the corridor with Brad close behind.

The tactical screen was active. The troopship was less than thirty minutes away. Brad repeated the coordinates three times to make sure he'd remember them.

"Gangway," Godbolt repeated. "We got us a troopship to destroy!"

Brad led the way to the manual station where Alby waited. He brightened immeasurably with Godbolt's arrival. The two hugged like more than old friends.

The power appeared on the panel. "Alby?"

Brad didn't know how the system worked. Alby dove in with great zeal and asked for rough coordinates. Brad stated them, and Godbolt confirmed that was what she had seen.

The missile tube powered up, and the outer hatch opened. The tube capacitors energized to send the missile out on an electromagnetic launch-rail. "Go forth and conquer!" Alby pressed the button the second it turned green.

The sound of the capacitors discharge signaled the missile's launch. The panel exploded beneath Alby's hands, spraying him with tiny shards. He stumbled, and his boots disconnected from the floor. He fell to the ceiling. Godbolt joined him.

A thousand cuts on his arms and face. "Take him to Medical." Brad took one arm and Godbolt took the other. They walked him toward the central shaft.

"Nokes, check on my missile. See where it went," Brad directed.

Nokes was off like a shot.

Going down the ladder was tough with the injuries to his hands, but Alby made it, leaving bloody handprints nearly the whole way.

"Take him to Medical. If we didn't kill that ship, I'm going to be real busy, real soon."

Brad bounded into the shaft and hurried down until he grabbed the ladder for the last three decks. He found himself alone in Engineering. He turned to run to the cargo bay, but Bec, Teo, and Vantraub staggered in, looking defeated.

"What happened?"

"We couldn't do it. We ended up shorting the whole system. I'm sorry, Dad."

"But it worked. The missile is on its way."

"It did?" Bec was the first to be skeptical.

"You said you shorted the system." Brad looked to his daughter for an answer.

"We have to run cabling and bypass everything. The system inside the bulkhead is destroyed. We can't open the cargo bay doors at present, so we might as well use *Starstrider* for power production. Only we can't until we run a direct line from there to here."

"I'll help you carry the spool of wire," Brad offered. "But let's wait until after we find out where my missile went. I don't want to work harder than I have to. I'll be right back."

He headed up the ladder and to the port-side airlock. The crew from *Butterfly* carried spare parts to a growing line of damage control personnel.

"That's how you do it. In the old days, we called this an unrep for underway replenishment. Coming through." He squeezed past those working and found his way to the bridge. "Please tell me good news."

"See for yourself, Captain." Nokes pointed at the screen.

A pink cloud was heading toward them. "Looks like we might get some debris impacts."

"No doubt. I wonder if their power plant is intact."

"I wouldn't risk it. Does this tub have any extra power plants around?"

"Now that you mention it, the one Bec had running on *Butterfly* is in the hold and looking for a new home."

Brad smiled. "It's hard not to love you guys. I seem to be surrounded by the best people. I need to check on my girlfriend, and don't you tell her I called her that or she'll be pretty mad."

"I hear you, Captain. I'll work with Teo. We'll get that plant installed right quick and in a hurry. As soon as we can help you stop spinning, that is. It'll be much easier to move that thing in zero-gee."

"Shouldn't we have heard from Crip by now?" Jaq groused.

Brad nodded. She was still in her quarters under Doc Teller's orders. The energy gauge on her monitor showed eighty-one percent and climbing.

"We're out of the woods, Jaq. We have time."

"We never have enough time," she scoffed. "Are you the only person left on my ship? Why does no one else visit me?"

"They think we're naked," Brad replied.

Jaq's mouth fell open. "They better not think that."

"I'm just a pawn in the game of life," Brad replied.

"What did you say?" Jaq nearly came out of her cubicle. Brad laughed. "I'm getting up."

"Doc Teller said later today. I guess this is late enough. And I said nothing to the crew besides your proclamation of enduring love while in your concussed delirium."

"I didn't. Did I?"

"No. I'll wait outside."

He left the room so she could dress. She bent over too quickly to pull her jumpsuit on, making her head swim. She stopped, grabbed the mid-rail, and forced herself to breathe slowly. She recovered enough to finish dressing. *Don't overdo it,* she warned herself.

Brad gestured for her to lead the way.

She returned to the bridge quietly, not as part of a triumphant procession. The command crew clapped softly and welcomed her back. It had only been two days.

"Message from the combat team?"

"Not yet. We have sent our message to *Starbound* for transmission to the combat team."

Jaq nodded. The board had an alarming number of red lights.

Alby held up a bandaged hand. "I have the enemy order of battle reduced to two cruisers and ten gunships. The Malibor fleet is almost finished."

"That's good news, Alby. Nothing against the old girl, but I'm not sure how much more *Chrysalis* can take."

Brad added, "Nothing against her at all. The finest ship and the greatest crew."

"Victory is ours," Jaq said softly. She found the louder the noise and the brighter the lights, the more her head ached. The lights on the bridge had been dimmed and the ambient sound kept to a low roar.

Jaq stopped to talk with Mary. Her leg was bandaged, but they were at zero-gee because they were on a ballistic trajectory away from Farslor, not actively engaging in anything other than repairs. She didn't need to be there, but she insisted.

"I'm fine. It was a flesh wound, as Doc Teller labeled it."

"How many stitches for a flesh wound?" Jaq asked.

"Fifteen. My lucky number."

"Fifteen is your lucky number?"

"It is now." Mary winked. Jaq gripped her shoulder for a moment before moving on.

Donal was off helping the damage control teams rebuild one of the primary junction boxes. Slade was working on a sensor receiver. Dolly was the only one present from that section on the bridge. Jaq eased over to her.

"Good work on the targeting interface. Without it, we wouldn't be here."

"It was important to get right."

"If we keep getting things right, then one day soon, we'll be standing on Septimus, celebrating life."

"I look forward to it. Donal talks of blue skies and green lands. I want to experience it myself."

"You will," Jaq promised.

"Message coming in," Amie reported.

Jaq pulled herself across the bridge and waited.

"Crip here. We've found the Borwyn who are actively fighting the Malibor. We are going to join them and open the gates of Septiman's wrath."

"That's it?" Jaq asked.

"There is no more. It was a short transmission. Your message regarding the delay in our return has been sent."

"Thanks." Jaq frowned deeply. It was a cryptic message but one that carried promise. "Let the Borwyn rise against the enemy."

"It's what we'll do until the Malibor stop fighting or we can rise no more," Brad said.

CHAPTER 1

The ship is life. Save the ship.

Jaqueline "Jaq" Hunter chewed on the inside of her lip. She tried to stand, but her head swam. It forced her back into her seat. Captain Brad Yelchin, her deputy in Crip Castle's absence, watched her closely.

"We should get you back to bed," he suggested.

She looked for the innuendo, but his expression showed concern, not opportunity. Crow's feet at the corners of his eyes hinted at his age, but he looked nowhere near as old as he really was.

The bad-tasting water on New Septimus helped to extend the lives of the survivors who had hidden there. Maybe it was the protection from solar radiation since they lived inside a moon. Regardless, he was over seventy Septimus years old. He was considered an original, one of the few survivors from before the war. None of the survivors who had saved Chrysalis were still alive. Space's radiation and the chemical leaks within the ship had taken their toll. The last generation had made it possible for the future generation to live free of the unseen elements that would attack their flesh.

"I'll relax, I promise, but I'm staying here." With her finger, Jaq drew an X across her chest.

"Then stop trying to get out of your seat," Brad replied. He perched on the edge of his gel-infused station, hanging on to the harness to keep from floating free. He kept his boots detached from the metal deck plates in case he had to intercept Jaq.

Annie pressed her communications headset to her ear. "Report coming in from Deck Twelve. The emergency bulkheads have activated, and we have four crew trapped in a space that is venting atmosphere through a microfracture in the hull."

Jaq came out of her seat. Brad caught her before she made it one step. "I'll take care of it, Jaq. You stay here."

Her concussion would only get worse with activity, but being the captain, she felt the weight of the crew on her shoulders. Jaq had never been capable of sitting back to let others handle emergencies she saw as her responsibility.

"I'll have you restrained," Brad threatened.

Her eyes flared angrily. The fire behind them quickly died with what little energy the surge in adrenaline brought. She was on the verge of exhaustion. Brad was right. She should be in her bunk.

"Just stay here." Brad signaled to Alby. "Keep an eye on her. Make sure she sits right there. Get her something hot to drink. I'll be on Deck Twelve."

Brad kicked off the deck, caught the mid-rail and pulled

hard to propel himself toward the open hatch and corridor beyond. He used zero-gee to accelerate toward the central shaft, pulling down the mid-rail until he needed to slow, but he didn't slow down. Deck Twelve was three decks below the command deck.

He hit the opposite side of the shaft, coiled his legs against the far bulkhead, and kicked off at an angle that took him to the Deck Twelve exit. In zero-gee, the access doors to the central shaft remained open. They closed when acceleration replicated gravity and the crew could fall down the shaft. The elevator was the primary method to move from the bow to the stern or anywhere in between when the ship was under acceleration.

The rest of the time, the crew operated in zero-gee and the central shaft provided an opportunity for them to demonstrate their aerobatic skills, like Brad had done for expediency's sake. He was new to a ship the size of *Chrysalis*. He'd flown on small recon craft for the previous fifty years.

He reveled in the space and support systems. He didn't have to do everything like he did in the scout vessel.

Brad raced down Deck Twelve's corridor to the emergency bulkhead, gripping the mid-rail to slow himself and stop before running into the small group gathered there.

"Report," he said, clamping his boots to the deck and walking the last few steps to join them.

"My son's in there," the ship's premier welder said, stabbing his finger repeatedly at the bulkhead. He clutched the plasma welder in his other hand.

"Don't cut through that bulkhead," Brad said.

The man started shaking.

A plan came to Brad. "Get on a spacesuit. We're going outside. We'll fix the breach from that side, then the bulkhead should open automatically."

"Yeah, that should work," the man agreed.

"What's your name?"

"Phillips, sir."

Brad gestured toward the central shaft. "We better get going if we're to save your son. Head to Deck One and find a suit. Bring your welding gear."

"Just me?"

"No. I'm going with you, Phillips. I welded the plates into the breach on Deck One."

"Shoddy work, sir, but it'll do." With a quick nod, Phillips bolted down the corridor.

"What's his son's name?" Brad asked a woman standing and looking concerned but doing nothing.

"Junior, as in Phillips, Junior."

"What do you propose doing while we're outside?"

"Working on the manual override for the bulkhead. The leak is from a microfracture. It shouldn't seal the bulkhead so we can't get people out. It wasn't designed with a singular function."

Brad was sure none of the current crew knew the original design details. It was before his time, even. "Sounds like a plan. If you can open it up, go ahead and let's get our people out of there. We'll still need to seal the breach. What do you think Junior is doing in there? Wouldn't he be trying to weld the breach closed from the inside?"

She pointed at the central shaft. "Phillips was bringing the welder. They don't have one in there."

"Understand. See if you can get a second unit from *Cornucopia*, but only after you've figured out how to override the controls on this thing and get it open. Stay in touch. I'll be on an open channel."

"Departing from Airlock Four to seal the breach on Deck Twelve," Brad announced using his suit's comm unit.

"Negative," Jaq replied. "There's a lot of debris out there from the destruction of the Malibor troop transport. Whatever you want to do, you have to do it from inside the ship."

"Not possible at present, Jaq. Roll the ship to keep this side away from the debris cloud. We'll be fine with the whole ship between us and the bits and pieces of the transport."

"That's a good idea. Standby."

Phillips fidgeted incessantly. He was used to working with his hands. He wasn't the patient type, and with his son trapped, that made it even worse.

Two minutes passed before the comm crackled to life. "Permission granted. Do not stray from that side of the ship or you might find Septiman accepting you through your suit filled with holes, a holy transposition."

"Funny. Heading outside. Keep the lights on. This shouldn't take long," Brad replied. He cycled the air to equalize with space, and the hatch light stopped flashing and turned solid red. He punched the button and the hatch opened inward. He stepped out with Phillips close behind. They clomped down the hull to find the leak.

Jaq settled into her seat. Her head throbbed and body felt like it had been slammed around her cubicle during high-speed maneuvers. The bridge started to spin. She closed her eyes and gripped her seat, but the spinning only got faster.

Her stomach rebelled. She spewed into the vortex of the centrifuge dominating her existence. Jaq fought it, refusing to surrender, but it was too much. The spinning ended with the darkness.

"Captain?" Alby asked. He took one step before she delivered a sparkling technicolor yawn into the zero-gee of the bridge. "Bags!"

"I'll help." Taurus launched herself to the upper rail and pulled herself across the bridge.

Alby unbuckled the captain.

"Call Medical and let Doc Teller know that we're inbound," Taurus directed.

Amie gave the thumbs-up while already talking.

"Notify Brad," Alby added.

Carrying an unconscious person in zero-gee involved little more than controlling momentum. Alby pulled on Jaq's boots while Taurus pushed her shoulders. They kept her from bouncing off the walls while they hurried toward the central shaft, up one level, and to Medical, where Doc Teller met them in the corridor.

"She yacked," Alby stated, "and passed out."

"I shouldn't have let her leave sickbay, but we're still swamped. Can you secure her inside her quarters? What she needs is rest amid no stimulus. Don't tell me she was on the bridge." Doc Teller looked from Alby to Taurus and back again.

"Okay, we won't tell you then," Alby said. "Come on, Taurus. You have captain watch."

"Why me?"

"I have the bridge," Alby said, not to sound important or to hold it over her head, but it was a valid point.

She nodded. Together, they guided the captain to her quarters. When they opened the door, Jaq roused.

"What happened?" She rubbed her eyes, wincing with the pain of moving.

"You spewed most ingloriously and passed out. We've been down to see the doc and he said lock you in your quarters for at least a week."

"Nonsense. I'm going to the bridge," she said, not looking stable enough to take one step to get into her own quarters.

"Afraid not, Captain," Taurus said. "Your cubicle. It's sleepy time."

"But..." Jaq had no fight left. Her head drooped. Taurus caught her under the arm and pulled her into her quarters.

"I'll leave you to it." Alby leaned toward the bridge. "We need to find a stable orbit. We need to free our trapped crew. We need to get power back. I could go on."

Taurus waved him away. She needed both hands to guide the captain the rest of the way. She closed the door behind them.

Alby didn't wait. He used the mid-rail to pull himself the

rest of the way. The air handlers were not working at full capacity, but enough to have removed the smell. The puke capture bags had done their job. They were already on their way to recycling to get cleaned up and returned to service, the contents turned into fertilizer for the hydroponics bay.

"Status," he requested.

Amie was the first to speak. "Notifications made. Brad would like to talk with you."

Alby nodded his receipt of the message. He faced the sensor pod. "Chief Ping, anything?"

"I just got back and have no idea. All my people are still with Damage Control. The ship is kind of screwed up, Alby."

Alby smiled at the sensor chief. "We still need whatever eyeballs we can get looking out for us. Let us know if you get a sniff of a Malibor vessel."

"Of course, but I don't have any systems operational right now. I'm looking at blank screens."

"Go on then. Back to damage control." Alby waved toward the hatch.

Chief Ping was off like a shot. He wanted his systems up as much as anyone and he couldn't do it from the command deck.

Alby settled into the captain's seat and checked through the systems. The power gauge showed nothing. The ship was operating on the backup provided by Brad's scout ship. It was barely enough to keep the lights on.

Auxiliary power units were still being setup by the engineering team formerly of *Butterfly* and fresh off *Cornucopia* that was still attached to the port roller airlock. The cargo ship would be wired into *Chrysalis* soon, too.

"We're in much better shape than our ancestors," Alby said to no one in particular. "We'll get through this. The captain will get better. Bec and Teo will get the engines repaired so we can get back to Septimus. It'll just take time."

Alby found he was on the bridge with Amie and no one else. The rest of the command team had left, even Dolly Norton, the thirteen-year-old prodigy. They were trying to save the ship. Alby had nothing to do besides stare at the red lights on the system status board and the blank energy gauge.

He'd never seen the ship in this bad of shape. "Amie, contact *Starbound* and let them know our return is delayed for the foreseeable future, for further transmission to Crip and the team on the ground."

CHAPTER 2

Not all walks in the sun are a walk in the sun.

Commander Crip Castle stood tall with his gear arranged ergonomically across his back and in his load-bearing vest. He carried a pulse rifle and three supplemental power packs. That gave the rifles roughly eighty shots.

The outskirts of a primitive Borwyn village in the forest east of Pridal on Septimus, the Borwyn home planet, were quiet with rich air. Birds flitted through the trees while a slight breeze whisked by. The other members of the combat team along with the two unwitting recruits of Tram Stamper, the former battle commander, and Kelvis, an original who was a nuclear engineer. They had flown the Malibor gunship that had brought the team to the planet surface, but it had burned too much fuel.

It wouldn't get them into orbit. They'd had to abandon the craft.

But they had a new plan. Fly it low through the mountains to the west side where the Borwyn were actively engaged in combat operations against the Malibor. On the east side, the locals didn't have the stomach to fight.

Sergeant Max Tremayne checked the team's packs one last time. He'd already put Danzig on point. "Binfall, Barrington, Hammer, and Larson on the left flank. Johns, Zurig, Anvil, and Tomans on the right. Crip will ride the center with Kelvis, Tram, and Deena. Finley and I will take Tail-End Charlie."

Crip asked their host, Paulus Hunter of Free Septimus, once more if he would accompany them.

"I'm afraid not. My place is here. I won't ask for one of your weapons, which would greatly increase our ability to hunt for our village." Paulus looked hopeful.

"We need all of our firepower if we're to fight the Malibor on their terms." Crip shook his head slowly to reinforce his words.

"You don't want to fight them on their terms," Paulus replied.

Crip smiled. "Exactly."

The two men shook hands. When Crip faced the combat team, he saw nothing but sad faces.

"What's wrong with you guys?" Crip demanded.

"The Borwyn village," Danzig said and pointed as if Crip didn't know that the village was behind him.

"So? We have a war to win. The battle is joined, gentlemen!"

"But they have two ladies to every man. Maybe some of them can come with us?"

Crip closed his eyes and rubbed his temples. After a few

moments of uncomfortable silence, he looked to Paulus for support.

"It's not a bad idea," Paulus said.

"We're going out there to fight our lifelong enemy." Crip pointed using his whole arm and a knife hand. "There's no place for girlfriends."

The entire team turned their heads to look at Deena.

"I'm the only one who's been in the city! I'm here to provide intelligence support to the mission." She held her arms up.

"And technically, she's not my girlfriend," Max added. She gave him the side-eye.

They had gotten married before the Septimus infiltration.

"How long will it take you knuckleheads to find the right *volunteers*?" Crip restrained himself from using air quotes around 'volunteers' since no one in their right mind would come with them and run headlong into a combat zone.

"Fifteen minutes?" Danzig ventured.

Crip trooped the line, studying one face after the next. Their hopes and desires were reflected in their expressions. *Chrysalis* had limited personnel and restrictions because of a static amount of available space and resources. That was not the case on Septimus. The planet exuded freedom, at least in the forest away from the city.

"One hour. They carry their own loads, but that doesn't appear to be a problem. And they go armed because we don't know what we'll run into. And they're going to have to get real cozy on the gunship. Tram, we can take the extra weight, can't we?"

"Since we're flying only a hundred kilometers, we'll be

fine. We're not going to orbit, whether we have two people or thirty, but with thirty, about a hundred klicks is all we'll manage."

Crip looked at Danzig, who had already dropped his pack. His pulse rifle was balanced across the top of it.

"Keep your rifles on you. I don't want one to go missing. One hour, then we go fast, back to the ship. It'll take less than two days to get there. We'll fly with the sunrise two days from now."

"What if the Malibor have found the ship?" Tram asked.

"Then we'll adjust, develop a plan, and take it back. Any other questions?" Crip waited a moment while scanning the group. "Go on now, find your future ex-girlfriends."

"Hey!" Danzig shouted at Crip and ran off with a purpose. Most of the group made beelines for various hovels and huts.

"What have I done?" Crip said to the sky. "May Septiman grant my troubled mind peace."

"You're in for it," Paulus said and sidled up next to Crip. "Your people seemed to like the feisty ones."

"I don't know what that means, but I'm amazed they had time to meet anyone, let alone form a bond."

"Your people were extremely efficient and our people, shall we say, were aggressively engaging."

Crip knew what it was like. "My Taurus is on the ship. It took me nearly forty years to wear her down, and she only caved because of us almost dying. No one wants to die alone, Paulus."

"Good luck, Crip." Paulus offered his hand. "If you're able to liberate Septimus, I think we might still stay here, but it would be nice to establish real trade and not get the Malibor castoffs as if they were the most valuable items in the city."

"We all compromise, but you haven't completely caved. And now the Malibor are on notice. They know that we're coming, but they can't tell their people. That should be an eyeopener, make their buttholes pucker."

"They think they're still driving this ship. I doubt we'll see them again, especially once the shooting starts." Paulus chewed on a sprig of grass. "When I say good luck, I mean it. I've lived my whole life with the Malibor as our masters and betters. I know they're not, but they have everything that we don't."

"Except mastery of the sky." Crip tipped his head back to look at the blue overhead. Wisps of clouds danced on the cerulean palate. It was something he was growing used to. The Malibor wouldn't be willing to give it up. Like the Borwyn were willing to do anything to get it back. "We're going to keep reducing their ability to fight until they can no longer resist. And then we're going to dictate the terms of their surrender. That's the strategy."

"Like I said, good luck." Paulus waved over his shoulder as he walked away. A small group of hunters waited for him. Together, they disappeared into the woods without a sound. They were gone as soon as the last one passed into the foliage.

Crip marveled at their ability to blend with the surroundings.

Max and Deena eased up next to him. "Am I going to regret this?" Crip asked.

"Oh, yeah." Max snickered. "A lot."

"Maybe next time, lie."

"I wouldn't do that to you, my friend. You should probably request they get married and be done with it."

"How is that going to take care of anything? I caved to the pressure. They were giving me sad eyes. Every single one of them."

Max chuckled. "They are probably better at woodcraft than any of us. We could learn a great deal from a closer relationship."

"Are you being facetious? I can't tell." Crip kicked at the dirt.

Deena chuckled softly, enjoying the situation far more than Crip. With the influx of the villagers, she wouldn't be the only woman on the team. That was possibly an added benefit. Crip couldn't be sure. The team treated her as an equal. They gave her privacy without giving her any grief.

"Not in the least," Max replied. "Consider it an expanded team. We're bigger *and* better. More eyeballs to watch out for the enemy. More opportunities to stuff a blade into a Malibor soldier. We have a couple days of walking to figure it out. You'll still regret it, but we'll be better for it."

"Sometimes, you make the most sense when you're not making any at all," Crip said. He clapped Max on the shoulder. "What do you think?"

Deena shrugged one shoulder. "I don't know. Sometimes you need someone to lean on, someone to confide in. I see how you talk to each other. Knuckleheads indeed. These soldiers need a soft voice and a shoulder to cry on."

A pain started behind his eyes and radiated through his head. "I think they need to train harder," Crip replied.

"Because you have your soft shoulder and someone to think about." Deena tapped her nose. "It looks different to you but not to them." She looked toward the village.

"You both are making too much sense. Where do we put the newcomers, Max?"

"If we put them with their new best friends, they'll be so distracted, no one will be looking out for the enemy. If we don't put them together, they'll be so distracted, no one will be looking out for the enemy. In either case, we'll be like a ship that's dead in space. Anyone can take us out with a single shot from an electromagnetic railgun," Max replied.

"I say we make the soldiers carry the locals' gear. They'll be far more alert than the guys who will focus all their efforts on the physical strain of hauling too much gear," Deena suggested.

Crip gave them the thumb's up. "I think we have our plan, at least to get us through today. We'll reevaluate on the fly if needs dictate. I'm regretting this, Max, but I know it's the right thing to do."

"Why don't you drop your pack and relax. Have some water, the good stuff. Maybe a little venison jerky." Max pointed at the ground with his chin.

Crip put down his pack and then sat down, leaning against it. "Wake me when they're back and ready to go. I better not hear any giggling, especially from our people."

The group made little noise as they formed up. They didn't want to live down to Crip's expectations of them, but they were definitely distracted, judging by the number of furtive glances cast back and forth.

Crip looked to Max, who was no help at all. He'd said his piece. Max was at the rear of the formation with Deena and Finley. They were joined by a young, willowy woman who walked too close to Finley and looked angrily about as if seeking to fend off competing suitors with her fierce determination alone.

"Why me?" Crip whined. He drifted to the back of the formation. "Ma'am. The enemy is out there, not in here."

Her face twitched after she stopped glancing around the formation. She tried to smile. She motioned for Crip to lean close. He stayed on his guard, worried that she might knife him.

"I'm sorry. I've never had a boyfriend before, and I don't want to lose him."

Crip held up his fist for a halt, but they hadn't even stepped off yet.

"Listen up, people," he said forcefully so all could hear without him having to shout. "No one is stealing anyone's boyfriend. It's been suggested that we get the marriages over and done with so everyone can relax. I see the wisdom in that course of action, but also the challenge. None of you people know each other!"

Crip's voice rose more than he wanted. Tram and Kelvis also had company, women who would have been called spinsters. Their peers had children who were old enough to join the combat team and find their own partners.

"The enemy is out there! They are the Malibor, and we are going to fight them, boys and girls, with everything in our power, with our last breaths, if need be. Until then, focus out there." He stabbed a finger at the woods. "When you have down time, enjoy it to the utmost getting to know each other. When you're ready, I'll conduct the ceremony, but don't rush into it. I don't want to deal with that situation!"

Max clapped.

"I'm ready," Finley said. He took the young woman by the waist and pulled her in for a kiss. She melted into his arms.

"Okay, stand up straight, and for the record, this is completely ridiculous, and I'm only doing it so we can get out of here." He pointed at the happy couple. "Raise your right hands. Do you?" Crip nodded at Finley.

"I do."

"Do you?" Crip looked to the young woman.

"I do!" she all but squealed.

"With Septiman's concurrence and good grace, I pronounce Mr. and Mrs. Finley. You may kiss the bride."

They kissed longer than Crip was willing to accept.

"That's enough! Everyone back in your place. Look out, not in. See the enemy before he sees us. If you spot food, don't be afraid to let us know."

"Crip?" one of the other soldiers interrupted.

"No!" He found the speaker. "Zurig, is that you? You'll wait your turn. Tonight, after we stop, we'll round up the rest of you miscreants and condemn your souls to fate's dark embrace. Ma'am. No disrespect intended." Crip tipped his helmet to the woman at Zurig's side.

Danny Johns, an original, stood by himself. He had gone to the village but came back alone. Crip waved his arm in a circle over his head and brought it down on the line of travel. Danzig stepped off.

Crip worked his way to Danny Johns. "You and me, Danny. We're the only ones with our wits about us."

"Not for lack of trying," Danny replied. "I accept my fate as the oldest here. I'll help you shepherd the young'uns, Crip. Do you want me on point?"

"Not yet. I figure the area around the village is as clear as anything will be. Probably tomorrow we'll need your keen eye unfettered by womanflesh."

Danny shook his head. "You know you'd be one of them if Taurus hadn't surrendered to your charms."

The group walked at an easy pace. Crip pumped his arm in the air. The signal was passed up the line until Danzig picked up the pace.

"Too true, Danny Johns, but I had my business in order before leaving the ship so I can be clearheaded down here. You, me, Max, and Deena have to look out for the rest of them. You and me, my man."

"You can count on me, Crip. I'm starting to feel my age down here with you young bucks. It's so much easier in zero-gee."

"I wonder how they're doing." It was a question that wouldn't be answered until the next time they were to check in, when they'd be with the Borwyn on the far side of Pridal.

CHAPTER 3

One step at a time, no matter how small, must always be forward.

Alby left the bridge in Amie's hands. With limited power and issues throughout the ship, he wasn't doing any good sitting and waiting. He headed for Deck Twelve.

He made it to the emergency bulkhead in less than a minute, where he found two crew with the panels along both sides of the corridor dismantled and parts floating in mesh bags attached to the side bulkheads with magnets.

"Any luck?" he asked.

"Can't override the bulkhead. It's probably as much to do with minimal power as it is to do with the controls. The default is closed, and we haven't been able to convince the equipment otherwise."

"How much atmosphere is on the other side?" Alby asked.

The crew shook their heads. "Don't know."

Alby punched the comm unit on the wall nearby. "Amie, give me a direct line to Brad's spacesuit, please."

"Connected," she replied.

"Brad, tell me it's fixed."

"We can't find it, Alby. We've been over that section three times and there is nothing that looks like it is venting atmosphere. We can't find the damage to the hull. If it's no longer venting…" He didn't finish his thought.

"Cut it open!" Alby shouted down the corridor. "Abandon caution, and get it open now."

Alby flew down the corridor to join the crew.

"Roger." They put on welding helmets and lined up their plasma torch. It hissed to life and sizzled as they touched the stream to the center of the bulkhead.

Alby returned to the comm panel to contact Brad. "They're cutting into it now. Efforts to override the emergency automation have failed."

"Understood. We'll finish this last pass and then come inside. Phillips is ready to chew through the bulkhead if needed."

"Roger. Come on back and let's get this door open."

Alby stared at the comm unit on the bulkhead. They were scattered throughout the ship and helped provide contact with anyone at any time. It was the backup to the backup. They stopped carrying small comm units because most were fifty years past their useful service life and inoperable now. Those that worked were best left in a single spot and not carried around to eliminate the risk of damaging them.

Which defeated the purpose of having them. There was no greater emergency than this.

Alby returned to his attempt to cut into the emergency bulkhead. He didn't want to interrupt them. When Brad and Phillips arrived, they'd let them know.

"We need power," he said aloud. That meant Engineering.

He flew down the corridor and grabbed the last mid-rail to slow himself to turn downward. He caught the structure that supported the elevator and stopped himself fully before accelerating toward the lower decks. He hit the bottom going much faster than he wanted, but this wasn't his usual routine.

He deftly coiled his legs when he hit the bottom of and gently kicked toward the ladder running up the inside of the central shaft. He needed to climb toward the bow one level to get to Engineering. He followed the cabling that came from the lower-level cargo bay where *Starstrider* was running wide open to bring power to the cruiser.

The hatch from the central shaft was open, like most of the hatches that weren't subject to automatic control. During general quarters, they'd be closed manually by crew assigned to the area.

Emergency bulkheads in the outer sections were not manually operated. They needed power.

The hatch to Engineering was open. Work lights had been added and cast odd beams across the space, leaving shadows across the walls and overhead where there were usually none.

"Status," Alby said to announce his arrival.

"Eat me," Bec called from inside the ion drive.

"We need power before we need engines." Alby clomped across the engineering space. "What are you doing?"

Bec leaned out of the access hatch. "I work on the engines. Other people work on the power systems. Go talk to them about that stuff."

"You're the chief engineer!"

"I'm not," Bec replied. "Now go away and leave me alone."

"I am," Proteus "Teo" Yelchin called from the neighboring space where the power plants were located. A low din said she wasn't alone.

"I knew that," Alby replied. "Status."

"We've got a long ways to go and we're crawling through broken glass to get there."

"Later today, then? Tomorrow before we have main propulsion?" Alby wasn't kidding with his quips, but they were jokes, nonetheless.

"By tomorrow, we should have *most* of the lights back on. Best we can do. We won't be moving in the near future. Better tell my men Crip and Max that we're not coming for them."

Alby stepped back to regroup. "We are coming for them," he countered. "We have to. We can't surrender Septimus."

"We're not surrendering anything, but it's going to take time, a long time, to get operational."

"What are we talking, a week?"

"We need to rebuild the engines and the power plants. We don't have the parts because there are no spare parts for this stuff."

"Not even from *Butterfly*?" Alby knew that they'd moved critical spares from *Chrysalis's* sister ship.

"Those will eventually be adapted and installed, but they've been modified over time. We need to return them to their original configuration. I'm thinking the timeline is going to be closer to six months."

Alby's face fell. He shivered from the shock of the revelation. "I better not hold you up, then. The captain is down hard. You have a day or two before you'll have to update her."

"How about you update her. We're busy down here installing auxiliary power that will keep us from dying. That's going to be our focus for the next week, and then we'll relook the timeline."

"Can we maneuver with one engine?"

"Of course. When will we have one power plant operational to generate the juice it needs? That's the question. We have a whole lot of nothing right now. We need to tackle things one at a time. There is so much to do, I can't see it all. Let me work on this stuff in the best order I can think of."

"Whatever you need, personnel, equipment, parts. You are the focus of this ship."

"Can we have some meals brought down?" Teo asked. "We've been working solid since the last engagement."

"I'll take care of it myself and set up deliveries at regular intervals. The good Malibor packs. Like I said, anything you need." Alby lowered his voice. "Why is Bec working on the engines?"

"Because they're down hard. If we brought the power plants online in a week, we might be six months out from driving this ship with anything other than thrusters. He needs to concurrently fix one ion drive and then build a second from scratch."

"He can't fix the second drive?" Alby was incredulous. He maintained the belief that Bec could fix anything. But when it came to the ion drives, those were his babies. He was the genius behind them. The ship wasn't going anywhere without Bec Draper.

"You know Bec. Better to let him do what he does best without any distractions. We'll take care of this other stuff, but don't expect any miracles. We'll get there. And you know as well as anyone that when we move out of Farslor's shadow, we better be able to maneuver and fire because the Malibor are going to attack us with everything they have. You see, Alby, we can't just cobble the engines together and take off. We have to be at nearly one hundred percent in all areas."

"You're making too much sense, Teo. That's why you have the job. DC teams are taking care of the punch list items throughout the ship, but we're held up while we work to open that emergency bulkhead that trapped some of our people, the boy welder being one of them. His dad is helping us to get them out. Saving our people takes priority over everything else." Alby retreated toward the hatch. He planned on going to the mess deck first and getting a load of meals to bring to Engineering.

"If we don't get the power on, then we'll lose what we have of life support, even with *Starstrider* and *Cornucopia* supplying us. *Chrysalis* is a big old energy hog. I've never seen a hog, but if I did, I expect it would look like this ship."

Alby waved from the hatch. "I'll be right back with food and water."

Why Alby? Because everyone else was occupied. As much as he was uncomfortable with reality, it didn't change the truth. He could be in Engineering the second Brad was back on the bridge. Otherwise, he had to wish people well wherever they were working and be nothing more than a runner.

Which reminded him that he needed to stop by Deck Twelve on the way to the mess deck.

Phillips pulled himself hand-over-hand, faster and faster from the airlock to Deck Twelve.

He reached the emergency bulkhead and fairly elbowed the others out of the way so he could take over with the plasma torch. Despite his skill, he couldn't speed the process.

Brad banged on the bulkhead with a spanner in the hopes of eliciting a response from the other side.

"This section is fairly large, and those inside could be out of earshot," Alby explained unnecessarily when no one answered the banging. He was trying to give hope when panic and fear were starting to overwhelm those on the outside.

Phillips was nearly frantic.

"Slow down," Brad cautioned. "It'll go faster."

"We've sent for two more plasma cutters. That's all we have," one of the damage control personnel said. They had taken too long trying to override the system to get it open.

"Get out of the way," Phillips bellowed, even though no one was near him.

Alby choked back a tear at the tone of the welder's voice.

"Come on. Cut!" He steadied his hand to focus the entirety of the cut on a single small hole.

A small sound, little more than a single tink of metal on metal. "Listen!" Alby cried out.

But the plasma torch raged and filled the corridor with the white noise of its fury. Phillips wouldn't let go.

Alby pounded on the shoulder of Phillips's spacesuit. The welder angrily shrugged him away.

Brad pressed his head to the side of the emergency bulkhead, away from the torch's fire. The heat radiated from it, but Brad stayed close. He held up his hand. "I hear it!"

Phillips changed nothing. He remained oblivious to the sounds from the other side.

The sound of the cutting torch changed as it punched through and the plasma flowed. Phillips powered the torch down. "Water!" he shouted.

Alby hadn't gone to the mess deck yet to get food and water for the engineering team. Alby pointed at one of the others, who bolted down the corridor. She was gone for a total of twenty seconds before she returned with a bag that she handed to Phillips. He squirted the water on the hole, making it sizzle and pop. A little at a time. Then a little more.

He hovered a bare hand over the hole. He tapped it but jerked his finger away. He leaned close. "Junior!" he shouted into the hole, barely the size of his pinkie finger. Air whistled as it was pulled into the space.

"Hey!" a voice called back. "We could use some air in here. Can you make the hole bigger?"

"Is everyone okay?" Brad yelled.

"All okay but loopy. Only Junior can function in low oxygen. He's still working on the patch."

"Stand back." Phillips reengaged with the plasma torch. With the first hole, the process sped up. In five minutes, there was a line drawn a finger length away. "At this rate, it'll still be a couple hours before we can make a hole big enough for everyone to get out."

"No need," Alby replied. "Once the air equalizes and there's no breach on the other side…"

The actuators inside the casing engaged and the emergency bulkhead retracted, showing six people lying in the corridor beyond.

Phillips looked for his son but didn't see him.

Vantraub from Engineering stood and pointed down the corridor. "He's that way," she said. The panels on the inside had been torn apart, too, as the engineer looked for a way to disengage the bulkhead's locking mechanism.

Phillips clomped down the corridor. Alby, Brad, and the two damage control personnel moved in to help the others up.

Vantraub shook Alby's hand.

"What I see here is that we need a manual override on both sides of the bulkhead," Alby said.

Vantraub agreed. "Within reason. We can't lose the ship because a desperate individual is trying to save themselves."

"Which puts us back into this situation. How do we stop this from happening?"

"Have a manual air access. We only need to breathe and keep warm until help arrives."

They both knew why the ship didn't have spare environmental suits and blankets pre-positioned throughout the ship. There weren't any spares, but with the arrival of *Cornucopia*, that problem wasn't going to be a problem.

Phillips and Phillips, Junior strolled down the corridor together, relief and joy on both their faces.

Alby laughed. "I'm going to need you to fill that hole you cut in the emergency bulkhead, and Vantraub—" He turned to the engineer. "—I need to you put those panels back together. Look at putting air into the outer sections. *Cornucopia* has to have valves that we can use to bypass the automated systems."

"That's a lot of valves and a lot of spaces. Something like one hundred different sections can be isolated by emergency bulkheads."

Alby frowned. "Sometimes, facts get in the way of what we want and need. Belay that. Get back to fixing the ship. We're dead in space right now, and a lot has to happen for us to not be, you know, dead."

"Only too well, Alby. We'll get this cleaned up and move to the next job." She stopped Alby from leaving by grabbing his arm. "Before I forget, Junior saved us all. He was the only one with the skill and wits to seal the breach. He stayed coherent while the rest of us were face down in our own drool."

Alby nodded. Before he forgot... He had been on his way to the mess deck. He'd lost track of time. "Thank you. I have to go." He flew down the corridor and hurried to fulfill his promise to the engineering team.

CHAPTER 4

Freedom comes at a high cost.

A day of movement through the woods. As Paulus suggested, the women from the village were far better at woodcraft than the combat team. They settled into an easy pace with the locals watching and moving silently while the soldiers tried to mirror their movements.

Learning while avoiding getting waylaid by the Malibor.

Crip was happy to make it halfway through the day. They hadn't covered as much ground as he wanted, but that was due to the late start. Once they were underway, they traveled quickly enough.

"We'll get to the ship in the early morning, after daybreak," Crip complained.

Max replied, "So? Then we dig in and wait a day before finishing that last run straight up the slope. We pile in, fire it up, and fly to the new location under cover of darkness. They don't need daylight to fly the ship, do they?"

Crip raised his eyebrows. "I don't think so." He strolled over to Tram and Kelvis. "Can you fly the ship at night?"

"Of course, but landing will be blind. It would be nice to see the ground so we can set it down in a clearing."

"You can't use radar?"

Tram sighed. "This is a Malibor gunship made for combat in space. It just so happens to have a limited ability to fly intra-atmospheric. As long as the radar is looking up, we're good, but it doesn't do ground mapping so well."

"Night flying is fine, but night landing is bad. Got it. We fly at dawn!" Crip thrust his fist toward the sky. "Septiman shares His light with each new day to guide us closer to His glory and the freedom we will realize in His name." Crip smiled and then shrugged one shoulder. "Not tomorrow but the day after."

Max snorted and spoke softly, "Since when did you become a holy roller?"

"Since I started marrying your team off."

Max sobered. "The way I see it, we just doubled the number on our team. We need more weapons to arm them properly. The family that fights together stays together."

"Is that a real saying?"

"Sergeant Max Tremayne, the eleventh day of the Borwyn return to Septimus."

"It has legs. You should write it down, memorialize it. Someone may think our memoirs will be interesting—as long as we win, that is. Winners write the history books. I'm sure the Malibor's version of the last fifty years is, shall we say, somewhat distorted."

"I can confirm that," Deena added. "The Borwyn are the root cause of all the Malibor troubles."

"Are they?" Max snaked his arm around her waist and pulled her close.

"No, but the Malibor won the war and wrote the history. Five civil wars suggest the Malibor are the cause of the Malibor's problems. Being with you shed the light on the dichotomy between what I was told and the truth. The two could not have been further apart."

Crip sat down to rest his feet. He removed his boots and changed his socks even though he didn't think the first pair were wet. Ground operations manuals from the before time suggested changing socks was important for greater combat effectiveness. Crip conceded that soldiers needed their feet but figured they could power through adversity when they had to.

He rested his feet on his pack and reclined just for a moment.

Until someone kicked him in the ribs. Crip startled upright to find Max staring down at him. "We're burning daylight, Crip. How long are you going to sleep?"

Crip rolled to his knees and worked his way upward to wobble and fight to remain upright. "How long was I out?"

"An hour. Looked like you needed the sleep so the rest of us made out with our wives and girlfriends. It was glorious."

"Tell me you're kidding?"

Max stared into the distance wearing a blank expression.

"I shan't sleep again. Someone has to watch over you reprobates." He crooked a finger for Max to come closer. "Even the old guys?"

"You mean Kelvis and Tram? I thought Danny Johns was going to punch Kelvis in the face after an argument about the corruption of youth."

"Did he?" Crip asked, stretching his shoulders and reaching for his pack.

"I don't think Kelvis corrupted anyone," Max replied. "Are we ready to go? The team is up and oriented."

"Why is my head so thick?"

"Bad genes?" Max joked. "You need to drink more water. We're not on the ship where you have to conserve. We're sweating far more than normal."

Crip downed his water and held out his hand for some of Max's.

"What am I going to drink?"

"The endless bounty of Septimus?" Crip replied, already feeling better. "Way to go, Max. Maybe your head is clearer than mine. I'm letting the locals distract me, exactly what I told everyone else not to do."

Crip returned Max's mostly empty water bag and waved his arm in a circle over his head.

"Move out," Max called. He took Deena's hand and strolled to the center of the formation. The locals moved quietly deeper into the wood with the soldiers trailing after them.

Crip moved to the middle and pushed forward to the front of the formation, where he found Danzig and a young Borwyn woman on point.

"How old are you?" Crip asked.

"Eighteen," she said, not sounding confident.

"Are you sure?" Crip worked his way next to Danzig. "Are *you* sure?"

"What?" Danzig risked a glance at the woman. "Mom approved and nearly kicked her out of their home. I'm not so keen but couldn't leave her back there. Don't worry. I'll be her big brother. I've got a girlfriend on *Chrysalis*."

"That's good to hear. Don't make me beat you into next week."

Danzig put his hand on his heart. "As Septiman is my witness, Crip. I'll watch out for her, but watch her. She moves quieter than the breeze and disappears into the brush within two steps. She could be the best point we'll ever have."

"I'll consider it. Probably any of them. We move through the woods like we were raised on a spaceship," Crip joked.

"And don't you forget it. Move her out front to keep a wary eye."

Danzig closed with the young woman and she hurried ahead. He was right in that she disappeared quickly, popping up every ten steps to make eye contact with Danzig.

Crip waited where he was until the formation passed him by. He picked up and walked with the one person bringing up the rear. Danny Johns.

"What do you think, Danny?" Crip wondered.

"I think we better train hard before we engage with the Malibor."

"Words of wisdom, DJ, and I couldn't agree more. If we're going to double the team size, we better figure out how best to use a dozen unarmed civilians." He tapped Danny on the shoulder. "Any ideas?"

"Arm them."

"With slingshots?" Crip had already mentioned wanting to arm the women, but they didn't have the weapons. "Maybe our western Borwyn will have extra firearms. Otherwise, they'll be stuck with spears since their families didn't send any bows and arrows. Do you think they know how to make bows and arrows?"

Danny Johns nodded. "I'd ask them to be sure."

Crip didn't dignify that with an answer. He moved forward until he found the nearest villager.

"Do you know how to make a bow and arrows?" he asked.

"Of course. We all do."

"How long does it take?" Crip pressed.

"If we can find the right wood, bark, birds, and deer, then it will only take a few days."

"A few days? And that's after you have the right stuff?"

"Yes, three or four days after we have the right materials," she confirmed.

Crip nodded and returned to the squad leader in the middle of the formation. "We may have to delay our plans by another week. It's going to take a while to arm our people, but it's not going to be impossible. It's a good news, bad news situation. When we check in with *Chrysalis*, we'll let them know."

"I agree that's the best course of action. A dozen locals armed with silent weapons. It'll give us some serious punch. You have to admit, the pulse rifles make a world-ending amount of noise."

Crip contemplated their way ahead. The chance of the Malibor stumbling across the gunship reduced with time. Anyone who saw it descend would forget about it after two or three weeks. They'd think it was nothing more than a ghost.

Extending the timeline gave the Malibor a chance to repair ships damaged in battles with *Chrysalis*, but most of the ships had been destroyed outright. There weren't any to fix that Crip remembered. He'd ask *Chrysalis* for a timeline. He figured the captain would be impatient and want it sooner rather than later.

He'd have to talk her out of it. The ground team needed time. He estimated two weeks to a month, because once they had the weapons, they'd have to train in how to integrate the archers into the team.

Crip wondered how well they could climb trees.

———

The night passed to the new day. Crip managed little sleep. He checked each watch section of three couples every two hours. Most of the combat team managed six hours of sleep. The women didn't sleep well at all.

Another challenge for Crip to work through.

But he didn't have to have all the answers. He only had to know who to ask.

"Deena, can you wrangle our new additions and figure out what their major malfunction is? Why are they not sleeping when they're supposed to? I think it's a combination of excitement and anxiety. Whatever it is, we need them to be more than walking dead."

Deena nodded. "I can try, but I'm not sure they trust me, being half-Malibor."

"You're probably their cousin. Unlike two decades ago when the women weren't given a choice and the Malibor took them, they all volunteered to become soldiers."

"Is that what you think?" Deena asked.

Crip ground his teeth together. "We're here to end the war and that means starting a battle that the Malibor have to lose. Yes, I need to believe that we recruited a dozen new soldiers."

Deena sobered. "I'll do my best."

Crip called for the newcomers to gather in one area. He gave a short speech on the importance of sleeping when they're supposed to sleep and turned them over to Deena for a heart to heart. He collected the combat team, ready to give them a piece of his mind, but they looked alert and happy.

"Crip, we're on Septimus. The sun is shining. We've got solid ground beneath our feet. We have food and water. And then we have fine company who can hold their own. What else do you want from us? The only one out of sorts is you," Tram stated. He stifled a laugh. "You don't know any of their names, do you?"

The group snickered and snorted. They were well rested. Crip felt like he was under three gees of acceleration. He removed his helmet and scratched his head.

"Okay. You win. I may have been hasty in my judgment that adding the locals to the team was a bad idea." He regrouped his thoughts and looked forward to stop lamenting his self-inflicted woes. "We're going to move most of the way to the ship and then we're going to establish a base camp. We'll need to find wood, deer, and whatever else our new recruits need to make bows. That could take a week. We'll help as much as possible, but we'll also need four on watch at all times. Keep your pulse rifles with you. Never take a step without one. Although we are on Septimus, we are in the enemy's embrace. They aren't going to easily give this up."

After a series of nods, Max spoke for the group. "Sounds like a good plan. Will the men be able to get some private time with their new partners?"

Crip hadn't wanted to hear the question, but he knew it was coming. The soldiers looked hopeful. "Of course. What kind of ogre do you think I am? But don't push it. I think they may be a little naïve in the way of love. If I see one of them crying, I'm sending the purveyor of their pain into the wood on a million-kilometer hike. Do you get me?"

"Why would they cry? They're Borwyn!" Hammer said.

Captain Brad Yelchin's sons had been extremely quiet during their time on Septimus. Hammer and Anvil, burly young men from New Septimus. They came along for their ability to carry more than the others and their willingness to learn what it meant to be soldiers. They were fitting in, possibly for the first time in their lives. They couldn't lean on their dad for top cover, and importantly, they embraced it.

They also had gained girlfriends from the Borwyn village.

"Explain." Crip rolled his finger, calling for more.

"These women are hard. They hunt to survive. They're not squeamish. They cut the living guts out of their kills. They can sleep on the ground or in a tree. These are the best women ever!" Hammer looked down.

"Someone is smitten," Anvil offered.

"Sparring partners for everyone," Max blurted.

"Thanks, Hammer. That helps. It puts my mind at ease." Crip looked at Max. "*Sparring* partners. You are a piece of work, my friend."

"Everyone needs a friend like me." He nodded toward the other group that was breaking up.

"Hang on," Crip called and strode to them. "I'm not sure I properly welcomed you to the group. I'm sorry for being brusque. Your presence makes us better." The group's spirit lifted with Crip's declaration. "I need to rectify a shortcoming. What are your names?"

The youngest one stepped forward, the one who had been shadowing Danzig. "I'm Fantasia, and that's what I'll be called. For the others, they'll take their husbands' names."

"Don't they have first names?" Crip asked, looking at their faces. None of them looked him in the eye. "No. I don't know how you guys do it, but that's not our way. Everyone is their own person first. I'll have your names, your given names."

"But we're to be married," a taller woman said. She was young, but not as young as the others, barely out of their teen years.

"Until then, what's your names?" Crip pressed. One by one, they said them behind furtive smiles. Charlotte. Amelia. Ava. Sophia. Isabella. Mia. Evelyn. Harper. Pistora.

Along with Fantasia, that made eleven locals, not a dozen, but Crip counted Deena in the group. She wasn't a soldier. A dozen non-soldiers joining the eleven carrying pulse rifles and the two crew of *Matador*, the Malibor gunship.

Crip straightened. "The battle is joined."

They stared back.

"You're supposed to answer 'victory is ours'."

They mumbled the response.

Crip rolled his eyes. "You'll get better at it." He stabbed a thumb over his shoulder. "When we stop today, it'll be to establish a base camp from which we'll do what we need to begin our bow-making operation. We'll stay there until you are properly armed. Now, get in formation."

They hurried past him, smiling and waving.

Deena waited until they were alone. "I'm glad you came around. They're good people, Crip, despite how they look to an old man like you."

"If you had used a spear to stab me in the heart, you couldn't have hurt me worse."

"You are old," she stated, crossing her arms and raising her chin in defiance.

Crip had no witty comeback. "Go on. Join Max and keep your eyes peeled. We have a way to go before we can take a break."

Deena slapped Crip on the shoulder and rushed off to find Max.

"At least morale is good," Crip grumbled. "The next thing we do is not going to be fun at all." He took a step. "Let's make some bows and a lot of arrows."

CHAPTER 5

There comes a time when your body tells you it's had enough.

Jaq tried to get out of her cubicle. She fumbled and would have fallen had the ship not been in zero-gee. She drifted for a while, free of the restraints within the sleeping space.

When her hand tapped the bulkhead, she roused.

"I need to get back to the bridge," she mumbled. But first, a shower.

She undressed and stepped into the capsule that was a zero-gee, water shower, but no water came. Power had not been restored to many of the ship's systems. Life support functioned. The air moved within her cabin. She took a deep breath to confirm it was fresh.

Her body enjoyed the rush of oxygen. She dressed and moved slowly to her desk, where she strapped in. Her computer system was online, but those ran with minimal power and were considered a critical system, wired independently and redundantly to maintain control when other systems were down. But not all computers were operational.

The status screen showed more than half the integrated computers as not connected.

She should have expected that, but her brain remained foggy. Thoughts didn't come easily. She had to make an effort to focus on a single idea. She wondered if she'd ever return to her old self. That thought scared her. She descended into a dark place, staring at the screen, which told her only one thing. The ship was broken.

It was damaged nearly as badly as when the last active Borwyn ship had been driven from its home and sent spinning toward deep space.

But this time, they had *Cornucopia* to provide support. They had spare parts from *Butterfly*. And they hadn't lost half their crew. Jaq checked the casualty list. Eight crew dead and a laundry list of injured, including herself.

Reinforcements from New Septimus were already on board, having come from *Cornucopia*.

"Your sacrifices were not in vain." She touched her fingers to her screen and the names of the deceased. One original from New Septimus and seven who were born and raised on *Chrysalis*.

She tapped her comm button to talk with Brad, but he didn't answer. He wasn't on the bridge. Jaq selected the ship-wide setting. "This is the captain speaking. Brad, can you come to my quarters, please?"

Jaq unstrapped herself and floated free so she could focus her energy on thinking, although the result hammered at her like a new and growing headache.

The captain lost track of everything by the time a gentle knock jerked her from her half-lidded wakefulness.

"Come!" she said softly, yet in her ears and head, it sounded like the drone of a bad air handler.

Jaq gripped her head in both hands while Brad eased into her quarters.

"Why aren't you lying down?" he asked more forcefully than intended. "Jaq. You need to do nothing."

"That's simply not possible for me. In my forty years on this ship, I've never relaxed."

"Never?" Brad raised his eyebrows and made a face. Jaq stared at him for all of four seconds before she had to close her eyes.

"You're hurting my brain," she said.

"You called me, Jaq. What do you need? Anything for you, future lover."

Jaq chuckled. "Don't make me laugh. It hurts." She pushed off her desk toward her sleeping cubicle. "I'm going to need you to take over, and I don't know for how long. I might never feel like the old me. I'm worse than useless. I'm taking up space. I'm not an oxygen thief."

"Get in bed, Jaq. We're not repeating any of that nonsense. You have a bruised brain. Let it heal before you try to make big girl decisions."

"Are you being intentionally demeaning?" Jaq turned to look at him.

"You picked up on that, did you? Good. Your brain isn't complete mush. We're not changing anything. I'm your deputy while Crip's celebrating life on Septimus. Maybe he won't return, and we'll get to join him. Isn't that the plan?"

Jaq refrained from nodding. "That is what I envisioned. Unfortunately, we have more battles to fight out here. The Malibor will fight to their last ship, and even with as much as we've hurt them, they still have a couple cruisers and ten gunships to throw at us. We wouldn't survive a determined attack by a lone soldier in a lifeboat right now."

Brad pushed her into her cubicle. "That is plenty lucid, Jaq. Rest, and you'll be fine. Stop with the doom and gloom. We're working on things. People are throwing themselves into getting this ship operational."

"What about the engines? Are they fixed?" Jaq looked hopeful.

Brad stared at her. "I don't know why you're not back in your cubicle. We should be getting underway sometime soon. We'll let you know well in advance so you can get to the bridge and into your seat." He nodded vigorously.

"You don't know when they'll be fixed, do you?"

"Not a clue," Brad admitted. "They're in bad shape, Jaq. The good news is that we're establishing a fabrication facility on *Cornucopia*. Alby and Godbolt will have that up before the end of the week. With a fabrication facility, we can start manufacturing parts and pieces to replace what was destroyed by the Malibor railguns. It's one step after another, and there are a lot of steps, Jaq."

"I know. I was hopeful. You're the captain, Brad. Make us proud. Deliver us from Septiman's final song."

"The final song? You mean death!" Brad strapped her into her cubicle. "We're not dead and we're not going to die. This old girl has a lot of life left."

"Why is my ship an old girl? Why can't he be a bronze god?"

"Bronze isn't very good against impacts or heat, for that matter. It's not a metal of the modern age."

"Don't be so literal, you big-shouldered tough guy."

Brad laughed. "If I didn't know better, I'd say you were taking too many painkillers. Sleep, Jaq. We'll get your ship back to you in prime condition as soon as possible."

Jaq closed her eyes and drifted away. She never heard Brad leave.

"It's deplorable," Bec stated in his haughtiest tone. "I will not use biomass on my engines."

"It solves the circuit board problems," Teo replied.

"It's not been proven," Bec argued.

"It'll work," the chief engineer insisted. "What's the worst thing that could happen?"

"It overloads the intact systems and takes the ion drive to its base components, or in other words, it turns my drive into a pile of useless metal alloys." Bec crossed his arms and frowned his grumpiest.

Teo threw her hands up. "Pulling rank on the special projects officer. We're doing it. We're installing the biomass pack, but in deference to you, we'll install it outside the drive while we test it. Can you be satisfied with that?"

"Of course not. It makes me queasy thinking about that abomination defiling my engines."

Teo nodded. "You would be sensationalizing this, would

you? I mean, it's not an epic struggle between good and evil. It's a physics problem. Nothing more."

"Physics using detritus from hydroponics? I don't believe in your theocracy masquerading as physics."

"It's not quite detritus. It's highly charged particles contained in a viscous suspension. It needs to be maintained at a constant fifteen volts. No more. No less. It's simple. I'm hooking it up. Why don't you go and check on one of your special projects?"

"Because the only thing that matters right now is the engines. The power plants are coming around, but these are my engines. Mine!"

"You are their creator, but it's time you let them leave the nest," Teo countered. "Bio-pack. I'm hooking it up. You better stand clear for when it creates a black hole and sucks us into the abyss." Teo smacked her lips, slowly.

Bec's arms started to shake from clenching his fists. But he stayed where he was, his magnetic books locked to the deck.

Teo moved to the outside of the ion drive, the place she worked months earlier when she first joined the engineering team, when the power recovery system was causing problems. She'd disconnected it and not caused a calamity. Bec was still upset about her work to fix it, even though she'd been right.

Teo connected the tool bag to the outside of the ion drive. The system was already in place, although she'd have to reroute four of the internal processes, bypassing them in entirety, but it started on the outside. She attached the pack within a protective casing and clipped four leads to it. She double-checked the colors and stuffed the wires through an access. The engine cover was off to the side, held in place by two magnetic clips. Teo crawled in through the opening, refraining from making faces at Bec.

She quickly attached the leads, but she took more time bypassing the circuits. The result was a more streamlined process. The safety protocols from multiple redundant systems were no more.

Bec was right that a power anomaly or spike could result in serious damage, if not the complete destruction of the engine. The circuit boards that needed replacing were already with Alby and his team to build replacements.

Teo climbed out of the ion drive. She moved the cover into place and started reinstalling the bolts. Bec joined her, wrenching them in opposite her, torquing them in without overtightening.

"You're right, you know," Teo said, "while also being wrong. If we take another hit on the drives, we're going to suffer mightily. But they won't simply self-destruct if someone looks at them wrong. You built a better system than that."

"I'd like to think so," Bec said. "I know I'm right."

"But it's going to work," Teo said. She winked at Bec, but he didn't respond. "To test it, we're going to have to run some aux cables from the power plants, feed the engines directly until we can recharge the power storage system."

"Another bypass. How many does that make?" Bec asked. "The only time constraints we're under are the ones we put on ourselves."

"You're sounding un-Bec-like. I'm not embracing the new you."

"Special projects has made me calm," Bec replied.

Teo shook her head while smirking. "I'll be right back. Don't touch anything." She headed for the neighboring space where the power plants were located. The space was filled with auxiliary generators cranking away to maintain minimum power to the systems. There wasn't any surplus that could be used to charge the power storage. They needed the power plants to generate.

Fixing the ion drives wasn't first priority, but the bio-pack solution had come to her while she was doing the mind-numbing task for rewinding a copper coil. It needed to be done and she was out of helpers. She found the coil exactly as she'd left it. No one had picked up for her even though four people worked in the space, but they were working on their own mind-numbing tasks. They had to rebuild both power plants from the ground up.

She disconnected the lead to the water purification system, knowing that she had an hour before she needed to reenergize it.

Teo plugged into the ion drive and returned to Main Engineering.

Bec hadn't moved. If there was going to be a blast area, he was still within it. Teo took that as a vote of confidence that it wasn't going to explode.

She accessed the operations panel and tapped buttons to bring it online. The ion drive powered up, one system after another, until it showed available at ten percent power due to the restricted amount of energy flowing into the engine.

"Good," she muttered. "Not just nominal but optimal." She tapped a couple more buttons. "Preparing to test with a one one-hundredth of a second burn."

She finished her programming and hung her head while her finger hovered one last time. She looked up at the overhead.

"What are you waiting for?" Bec taunted.

"Running through it one last time in my mind to make sure I didn't forget anything."

"You didn't. The only question is about whether the pack will weather the load. If not, we'll know very soon. Press the button, Teo."

She tapped it before she could overthink it.

It was over before they knew it started. The computer started it and ended it. They couldn't tell if anything happened, but a great thump vibrated throughout the ship.

"What the hell!" came Brad's frantic cry from the bridge. "We almost ripped *Cornucopia* off the airlock. Our power cables are tied through there. The port roller took the brunt of it, thank the heavens. It was you, wasn't it, Bec?"

Teo replied, "No, Dad. It was me. Sorry about that, but the good news is that the ion drives are online. We can move as soon as we've restored power."

"I have to say I'm surprised, because the ion drives weren't anywhere near the top of the priority list. This ship is still damaged beyond recognition, but, and this is an important but, it's nice to know that we can move if we have to. What do you say we get the power plants fixed and start banking energy. Good work, Teo. Now, don't do it again. Acting Captain of *Chrysalis*, out."

"He blamed me. Do you believe that?" Bec continued without giving Teo a chance to answer. "Of course you agree with blaming me first. You do it all the time."

"I only blame you when it's your fault, Bec, which is often because you're the one who creates the majority of your problems by being such an abrasive ass. I'll admit that you've gotten better since moving into the special projects role. Why don't you focus your considerable intellect on repairing the power plants?"

"Why don't you use the ion drives to generate power?" Bec countered with a smug expression that made Teo want to punch him in the face.

But once again, he wasn't necessarily wrong, just a jagoff about it.

"Open the plate," he said as if she hadn't understood. "Send the ions into space instead of off the plate to create thrust."

Teo lifted her hands and held them out in the perfect shape to wrap around Bec's throat. "That will still create thrust, and regardless, we can't go someplace and be torn between moving and generating power. If the Malibor find us in that state, they will easily kill us. Two things contribute to our survivability. Our speed and our firepower. We need both if we're to go into open space."

"As you wish. Maybe run them for a little to build power enough to defend ourselves and maybe get the showers running. I could use a good steamer."

"Bec," Teo exclaimed. "I never took you for being self indulgent, not in the personal body treatment sense. Look at you. Appearance is not your first concern."

"You talk about me being mean. What are you doing?" Bec asked. He turned and clomped away.

Teo had gained a level of verbal acidity since joining Bec in engineering. Had she developed it as a self-defense mechanism or was she growing more acerbic? She hoped not. She didn't want to be the female version of Bec.

"I'm sorry, Bec. You're right. I was just being mean to be mean and there was no call for it," she called after his retreating form.

He waved over his shoulder and shut the hatch to engineering on his way out.

Teo stared after him before activating the comm to the bridge. Brad answered.

"Dad, I'm going to run up the ion drive to start building our power reserve, but I can only do it for an hour at a time because I'm stealing power from the water purification system."

"That's a lot to unpack, but let me condense it to the basics. You run the engine, we build power, we can energize the systems we need to protect the ship, like the sensors and weapons. The price is we don't get clean water. We'll make do. When will the power plants be online?"

"A month," Teo ventured. "We need to rebuild them from the deck up. They were damaged beyond repair. You could say we're fixing them, but we're doing a complete rebuild. That's the real price of failure. We'll bank some power so we can see and also defend ourselves, but then, we need to get back to work repairing this ship. It has too many problems to take into space. A month, Dad. You have to give me a month."

"I have to give you what it takes. If that's a month, so be it. You know you have the whole ship to draw from as you see fit. You're the chief engineer and the focus of our efforts. As you go, the ship goes."

"No pressure, then. Thanks, Dad. How's Jaq?"

"Tired of working for your old man already?"

"Jaq. The captain of this ship. The apple of your eye. How is she?"

"Concussion. I think she'll get better after a few days of imprisonment, because that's what it's taking to keep her in bed." After a pause, he added, "Oh, look, here she is on the bridge. Gotta go, pudding."

Teo rolled her eyes. Chief engineer responsible for two hundred and fifty lives and she was called *pudding*.

She turned on the control panel. She had forty-five minutes remaining of the one hour she allocated for her experiment. She accessed the actuators and rotated the panels that the ion bounced off to generate thrust and sent the ion stream into space. At a ten-percent feed, the ion drives still generated enough power to feed the energy storage system.

After thirty minutes, the display ticked over to one percent. After fifteen more minutes, it remained at one percent. Teo shut down the engine and hurried back to the power plant space, where she reconnected the water purification system. It immediately kicked on and started processing the water that had backed up during the previous hour.

If it wasn't one thing, it was another. The ship was broken. They had one percent energy banked.

One percent. But it wasn't zero.

CHAPTER 6

A team is more than a group of people.

It was already dark when Crip called a halt upon Fantasia's advice. The young girl had guided them expertly to a hollow surrounded by tall trees standing in the shadow of the mountain that loomed over the gunship. They had a hill to climb to get to the ship, but they would in due time.

For the present, they needed to fabricate bows and arrows. Crip called them together into a tight group that smelled of sweat.

"Max, get the duty schedule implemented, four on watch at all times. Come morning, we're going to train. Rudimentary hand-to-hand combat. Then we'll break into asset obtainment groups. Hunters. Woodcutters. Carvers. Fletch fabricators. We're going to make some bows and lots of arrows."

"There's a grinder on the gunship for arrow tips. I'm sure

I can find metal that will do the job," Kelvis offered, his arm wrapped around the waist of his middle-aged friend.

"We passed good wood on the route here. No more than two hours' walk," the woman named Sophia said.

"Arrows and deer?" Crip asked. No one answered. "Then we go in search. Who is our best hunter?"

The women pointed at Kelvis's friend.

"Who is our best shot?"

"I think that would be me," Max said.

"Max and, you, what's your name?"

"Evelyn."

"Max and Evelyn are our hunting party. Just them to minimize the noise. Kelvis and Tram, you guys check out the ship. It shouldn't be more than a few hours away."

Tram stepped forward. "We'll take our time getting there to make sure the ship hasn't been discovered and they're waiting to ambush us. I'd like Fantasia to go with us, lead the way."

Crip looked to the youngest member of the group. She nodded vigorously, the starlight catching the sweat of her face with each lift of her chin.

"We'll dig a pit for toileting and clear an access to the creek."

A small creek flowed not far away, which was one of the main reasons for setting up camp where they did. It had everything they needed for a week of work.

"Sharpen your knives, people. We're going to do a lot of cutting and trimming." Crip nodded to Max, who dutifully delivered the news on shifts. With four people on two hours each, that meant only sixteen would have to lose two hours of sleep each night. Crip and Max were not included because they'd be up and checking with those on watch more than once.

Deena volunteered for a watch and Max put her with Danny Johns, who he trusted implicitly. Not that he didn't trust the others, but Danny had been instrumental in saving Max's life along with Tram's and Kelvis's. He was an original, but spry and had the wary eye of a career soldier even though he'd worked as a botanist the last fifty years.

His roots were as a soldier, and he never forgot. Now was his time to pay the Malibor back for the harm they inflicted on his friends and his family. He was ready to inflict pain on the enemy, measured and lethal.

"Okay, people. Get some shuteye." Crip waved the soldiers away. They spread out more than the previous night, the couples pairing off and cozying up to each other. Crip wanted to tell them no funny business, but as long as they didn't bother anyone else, who cared. "Max, when did I become a prude?"

"When you assumed the role of father to these wayward souls, but, Crip, they're warriors. You've seen that over the past two days. We're better with them."

"The men are happier," Crip conceded. "We'll see tomorrow what kind of fighters we have. You two, get some sleep."

"I'll tell you the same thing," Max said, holding out his hand for Crip. "We're doing well, Crip. Don't tell yourself anything different. We've been on Septimus for thirteen days. We'll contact the ship tomorrow and tell them we need more time."

"Do you feel any different? Weaker? Stronger?"

"I feel a lot stronger. It's Septimus standard, a single gee. We usually operate at one-point-two on the ship. It was less than a gee inside the moon of Rondovan. It was a little heavier on Farslor. All in all, it's nice to have the exact same gravity every moment of every day. Those who live here are spoiled."

"You're talking about the future wives of our soldiers."

"If only we had alcohol for a drunken party." Max winked and strolled away with his arm wrapped tightly around Deena's waist.

Crip stood by himself and looked up at the stars. "I'm doing the best I can, Jaq, believe me," he whispered as if praying. "When we hit the Malibor, they'll know it. Their time is coming to a close. They'll submit to Borwyn rule or they'll die."

He thought about his words, which probably sounded the same as what the Malibor said when they landed on Septimus.

"You'll find our terms better than what you offered us," he restated by way of a compromise. "We're not Malibor. We're Borwyn, and this is our home."

The welcome sunrise showed a cloudless sky and the promise of a beautiful day.

Before they ate, they set up an area in the middle of a clearing protected by an arboreal arch overhead.

"Pickets on the flanks, fore, and aft," Crip ordered. The

next group of four moved out. Crip waited for those coming off watch before he and Max started the training session with defensive moves. Hand and arm blocks plus learning how to fall. They made everyone do it, even the supposed old hands.

After two hours of back and forth, Crip called it a morning. They ate and then separated into their various groups. They set off to collect wood for bows, to look for wood that could be used for arrow shafts, a place where birds could be trapped, and finally, the small group that was going to the ship. If it had been discovered, then that would change their plan and make their next couple weeks painful and hard going as they crossed a hundred to a hundred and fifty kilometers to find the western Borwyn.

The gunship played a key role in their new plan.

"Take care," Crip told Tram.

"I'm going with you," Max interjected. "In case we run into any trouble. Maybe you should give Tram or Kelvis your rifle."

Crip would have handed his rifle over, but with Max going to the ship, Crip would have to be the hunter. "I'll be shooting deer," Crip replied. "Take Hammer and Anvil, too."

Max nodded. The group looked each other over and stepped out. Tram, Kelvis, Hammer, Anvil, and Fantasia. Two of the young women stepped up to join Hammer and Anvil.

"Do you need an army, Max?"

"Better to have one and not need it. Give us three pulse rifles and three scouts."

"What about..."

Max held up his hand. "No more. Evelyn is hunting. Ava

and Mia can go, but we can't completely empty the camp. You guys need to move fast."

Tram pointed at himself and Kelvis. "We're the long pole in that tent, Max." Tram twirled his finger in the air. "Time to go." He blew a kiss at Pistora. "We should be back tonight."

"If you can't, hunker down and wait until morning. We won't expect you until tomorrow."

"Let's go," Fantasia said without humor. She walked off without waiting. The others stepped in line and followed her out.

"Septimus said the children shall lead them," Crip intoned like he'd heard the shepherd speak and waved to the group. When he turned back, he found Evelyn waiting for him.

She had a sling that she removed from her pack. She checked round pebbles in her belt pouch, took one, bounced it in her hand and once satisfied, loaded it into the sling.

"What are you going to do with that?" Crip asked.

She twirled it over her head and let go, launching the rock at what seemed like light speed. It cracked against a nearby tree trunk. She watched it bounce and roll, then recovered it.

"Well done." Crip gave her the thumbs-up.

"In case we see any birds. Some might have feathers that make better fletching than others."

Crip believed she could hit a bird on a branch with her sling weapon, just like he could shoot a deer from long range. They each had their expertise and specialties.

The woodcutting group and arrow groups headed out.

The bird hunters scattered into the wood to sit in trees and wait.

Last off were Crip and Evelyn, going in a direction away from the others to follow the stream as far as it took to find sign of a herd. They knew they'd find one, but what they didn't know was how far they would have to travel. They left their packs behind and traveled light to also travel quietly.

Crip creaked and caught on the brush while Evelyn moved as quiet as a light breeze passing through old growth trees. Crip stayed back and let her lead the way through the woods, stopping when she stopped and moving when she moved.

One hour passed and then two. They'd seen signs of deer but nothing fresh.

Crip was starting to lose hope. The farther they traveled, the farther he'd have to carry a deer carcass back to camp. He snorted. He'd do what he had to do.

Evelyn pulled up and flashed a fist raised over her shoulder.

Crip dropped to a knee and worked his way behind the nearest tree.

Eventually, Evelyn crawled to where Crip waited. She covered her mouth and whispered, "Malibor hunting party up ahead. Three and a guide."

"What is that?" Crip asked.

"Private hunters on an exotic trip into the deep woods. They didn't see me."

"They're the enemy," Crip said. "And we could use their weapons."

"You want to kill them?" Evelyn asked, eyes wide. The

Borwyn of her world would run and hide. They never engaged the Malibor because they feared the Malibor.

Crip wasn't afraid of them.

"We have surprise on our side. Let's see if we can get a good angle on them."

Evelyn moved forward, crouched below nearby growth to remain out of their line of sight. Crip crawled after her and grabbed an arm to stop her.

"Maybe not. Let's lie low and hope they go away, but if they head in the direction of the camp, we'll have to stop them."

Evelyn breathed a sigh of relief. "Concur," she whispered back.

The woods were light, and the Malibor were talking. No wonder they didn't see any game. They were being scared away.

They meandered, three wide, with long rifles, propellant-based projectile launchers. These were so old they had to pre-date the start of hostilities between the Malibor and the Borwyn. They were deadly, but nothing like a pulse rifle.

Crip took aim as an exercise in dominance. He could kill them if he wanted, and they would have no clue. But Evelyn said there were four of them.

He could only see three. He lowered his weapon and scanned the woods.

"Where's the fourth?" he whispered.

Evelyn peered through the foliage and shook her head. "It's the guide. He's somewhere out there."

One of the Malibor spoke.

"Hey, I thought I heard something over here." He started

walking toward Crip and Evelyn. They raised their rifles.

Crip couldn't take on three at a time.

"Run," he told her. She bolted at a low crouch, dodging behind tree trunks to put as many of them between her and the Malibor. Crip took off on a parallel course, dodging and zigzagging.

"Woohoo! We got us some Borwyn," one of the hunters called. It enraged Crip, but getting away was more important than getting in a fight where one of the Malibor escaped and shared that there were armed Borwyn in the woods. It would put all of the Borwyn in danger, like those from the village where Evelyn and the others came from.

"Much better than deer. I see one!"

The report of a round being fired and a bullet ripped through the leaves over Crip's head.

Firing high, that was fairly common in combat. Excitement while shooting at a fellow human being affected one's aim and trigger squeeze.

"Stop!" came a call from behind the Malibor hunters.

The fourth person.

Crip wanted to get a look, but rifles cracked again and again. Bullets tore past, dangerously close.

He hit heavier woods and accelerated on a perpendicular course, running flat out, trying to get the Malibor to separate. The trees were heavy. They wouldn't get a good shot. After he gained a measure of breathing room, he dove to the ground and crawled up behind a tree.

He didn't come all this way to die at the hands of recreational hunters. Crip didn't see the Malibor, so he moved where the tree cover thinned. He wanted a shot at the guide.

The hunters would be easier to manage once the one who knew the woods was out of the picture.

They didn't follow me, he thought, which meant they were going after Evelyn.

That wouldn't do. At least the rifle fire had stopped.

He crouched as he ran from tree to tree, in the direction from which he'd come.

The Malibor guide kept yelling for his patrons to stop. That told Crip where he was. Soon, he'd move across Crip's front.

Crip checked the power pack one more time and readied the weapon to fire. He aimed and waited.

"I said *stop,* you weasel-toed civilians!"

Crip would have liked the gruff man, except he was Malibor with information that wouldn't bode well for the Borwyn.

The two people were at war. And despite his calls for those in his charge to stop, they had figured shooting at Borwyn came without consequences. It was just another type of big-game hunting.

The guide jogged casually as if he didn't care about catching his hunters. Crip led him and the instant he stepped into a clear line of fire, Crip pulled the trigger. The pulse rifle had significantly greater power than the propellant-based rifles the Malibor were using. The obdurium projectile hit the guide in the chest with the force of a meteor.

He came off his feet. An instant later, his corpse hit the ground. Crip ran forward to a better vantage point.

Evelyn's scream froze his blood. A rifle fired a single time, and silence returned to the woods. The creek gurgled nearby.

CHAPTER 7

Become one with Septimus. Be one with Septiman.

Jaq didn't activate the magnetic clamps on her boots. She floated free to reduce the chance of making her head throb. She had reached an acceptable equilibrium. Jaq felt the sharpness of her mind return as the pain ebbed. Brad was on the bridge along with Amie and that was it. Every other member of the command team was occupied with damage control or directed repairs.

"Survival mode, Brad," Jaq said.

"What do you mean? If it's that bad, you should go back to bed."

"I'm talking the ship. You've been out there. Will *Chrysalis* fly like it used to?"

"I don't see why not," Brad replied. "The engines are operational using an experimental bio-pack instead of circuit boards."

"We'll be flying by Septiman's good graces and magic,"

Jaq said. She gripped the vertical rail by the captain's seat with one hand, relaxing as much as she could.

Brad stood beside her using his boots to hold him steady while keeping his hands free.

"The crew is doing a great job. I have no idea what it was like growing up in a ship that was in a constant state of being repaired. It was amazing that you made it spaceworthy back then, but now, we have a great deal more resources at our command, along with people. You've had an influx of technically capable hands, fresh minds and bodies, even the originals. You aren't relying solely on Bec's genius to carry the day."

Jaq closed her eyes and drifted away for a few moments. When she awoke, Brad's hand was holding hers to the vertical rail.

"Priority of work?" she asked.

"Life systems, so that means junction boxes, power conduits, routers, and juice, not the least of which is the power plants. Those are holding us back, but as many people as can be managed are working on them, including Teo. But..." He pointed at the dashboard filled with red lights, but one red light was the number four.

Energy storage was up to four percent.

Jaq looked at him quizzically. She had missed that number because it was red like the rest of the board.

"Teo is using the ion drive one hour on and one hour off to incrementally recharge the batteries, as it may be. We get one percent for an hour of the ion drive's time."

"A hundred and ninety-two hours until we're at one hundred percent, but we can't leave, not until the power plants can recharge the drives. In combat, we can burn a hundred percent in under an hour. If we can't recharge on the fly, we'll die flying fast."

"When we're charged up, the ship can protect itself. We'll have our eyes. We'll have the ability to provide a few creature comforts to help the crew recharge *their* batteries. This kind of work is grueling, and we need them to stay sharp. I suggest we run the crew six hours on, six off. Day and night shifts. We won't burn anyone out."

"Not eight and four? Gives us an extra four hours of work per individual per day. That adds up fast."

"But quality work and quality sleep. They need more than four and right now, we're running more like twelve on and four off. Six and six, Jaq. I'd like to implement that immediately. According to my math, it'll be eight days before we're at one hundred percent. It'll be nice to have the crew well rested to help us celebrate."

Jaq chuckled softly. "We need to celebrate the victories, even the little ones. I'm going deck to deck to thank everyone for what they're doing."

"You'll do no such thing." Brad released her hand. "I'll do it, again."

"You've already been around?"

"Every deck. Every member of the crew. Alby is personally feeding the team working on the power plants. I've never seen a group of people care more about each other than what I've seen on *Chrysalis*. That is because of you."

"It's them," Jaq countered.

"The people are a reflection of those in charge. It's a hard lesson learned the hard way." Brad patted her hand. "Stay here. Amie, make sure she stays here."

Brad kicked off and backstroked toward the hatch.

"Tackle her if you have to," he said as he disappeared into the corridor.

"Are you going to tackle me?" Jaq asked with a snort.

"Do you know how old I am?" Amie answered with a question. "My tackling days are a few decades behind me. Please don't embarrass me by making me use harsh language to stop you from overexerting yourself."

"Harsh language?"

Amie pointed at the headset. "I'm your communications officer. Words are my tools."

Jaq eased across the command deck to float next to Amie. She had joined the crew halfway into the renewal of hostilities with the Malibor. Jaq hadn't had any time to get to know the new crew members.

"Tell me about yourself, Amie. It appears that we have plenty of time."

Crip moved with determination, eyes dashing back and forth to look for any movement, any flash of color that wasn't as nature intended.

The sounds of birds slowly returned to the treetops. Crip stepped behind a tree and listened with all his being for a telltale footfall. The three hunters were amateurs. The only professional was dead on the forest floor.

There was a second professional, and he carried a pulse

rifle. Crip tried not to be angry, but he had gotten Evelyn killed. The Malibor would pay a high price for their actions.

Professional. Change the engagement zone. Crip draped his rifle over his head and shoulder. He faced the tree and climbed. He settled in two branches up. High enough that he would be out of the line of sight of the hunters, but not so high that he couldn't jump down without hurting himself.

His vantage point allowed him to see over the foliage occupying the dead space between trees. Two of the hunters hid behind a bush. Crip looked for the third, checking extreme right and left flanks, thinking the hunter might be sneaking up on him.

Crip watched while the two grew more anxious until they had a heated but whispered conversation. The third person never materialized. The two hunters made a decision and bumped fists. Their expressions suggested they were coming.

Crip decided to save them the trouble before they got their feet under them. He took aim and fired at the first one to stand. The other ducked behind the bush, but Crip could still see him. They were thinking two-dimensionally. He had no idea where the shot came from.

A pulse rifle accelerated the obdurium projectile to a high rate of speed using electricity and electromagnetic coils. It didn't have the smoke and flash of a propellant-based round.

The problem with concealment was that it only provided protection from being seen. It provided no physical protection. Crip aimed for the second shot barely two seconds after the first. He zeroed in on the top of the hunter's head and then lowered his aim to where he'd hit him center mass. He slowly squeezed the trigger. The report from the pulse rifle shook the trees when the round raced through the air at five times the speed of sound.

The Malibor hunter vaulted backward in a somersault and landed face-down amid a growing pool of blood running from his ruined chest.

That left one more hunter. Crip knew he had to go after him. The hunted had become the hunter.

Crip climbed to the ground and eased around the tree trunk. He was going to recover the two rifles with their ammunition and hide them, then he'd pick up the track of the third man.

Through the brush and into the small space where two bodies lay side by side. The rifles looked old but well cared for. Their wood stocks glistened from the polish. Their blued barrels were pit-free and smooth.

Crip searched them, looking up every couple seconds to listen before returning to the task at hand. The ammunition for the rifles came in two sizes. The two were not interchangeable. *Who does that?* Crip thought. *Civilians who didn't have to count on a single logistics source.*

Twenty-three rounds for one of the weapons and twenty-one for the other. It was better than nothing.

A nearby cry made him drop the two Malibor weapons and shoulder his pulse rifle. He looked into the trees at every gap.

"Come out, Borwyn. I have your girlfriend," a man's voice taunted. It was higher pitched than Crip expected, probably from fear. He'd heard three of his friends die.

"Come on out, Malibor, and talk to me. Do you know it's just me and you now? We can converse without the others interrupting us."

He thought of adding bravado about how he was going to kill him the instant he showed himself, but Crip thought better of it.

Was Evelyn alive?

The brush moved and the Malibor moved into the opening. A struggling Evelyn, hands tied using her sling, answered the question about her misplaced demise.

Crip breathed a sigh of relief. He looked down the sights of his rifle and stood so the Malibor could see her.

"Let her go," Crip said.

"Where'd you get that weapon, Borwyn?" The hunter ducked behind Evelyn and peered over her shoulder. It offered no shot. Crip kept the barrel raised. One mistake and the Malibor was finished.

"I want to reiterate that you should let her go." Crip's tone was firm, leaving no room for misinterpretation.

The Malibor held his position. "As soon as I let her go, you'll kill me. Maybe I should shoot her to let you know I'm serious. She's a Borwyn and means nothing to me."

Crip smiled. "She's a Borwyn and means a lot to me. If you kill her, then you'll have no one to hide behind." Crip slowly walked forward. He wasn't good with dragging out a negotiation. The Malibor knew very well that Crip meant to kill him. He was looking for a way out.

"She's coming with me. Sorry, Borwyn. That's how it has to be. I'm not going to harm her as long as you don't do anything stupid. If she gets hurt, it'll be your fault."

"Pretty sure it won't be. If she gets hurt, it'll be because you hurt her. You suck at negotiating, probably because your position is weak. Take yourself to the creek and throw yourself in. That's your only chance of getting out of this alive."

The man tried to aim his rifle around Evelyn's side, but it bounced all over the place. The safest place to be seemed to be where he was trying to aim.

Crip took more steps forward.

"That's far enough. She dies with one more step!"

Crip took one more step, staring down the barrel as he remained ready to fire at all times.

The Malibor panicked. He fired at Crip, but the round buried itself in the dirt between the two.

The hunter's rifle was a bolt action like the others. He didn't have a free hand to chamber a new round.

Crip ran at him. "Hit him!"

Evelyn leaned to the side and twisted, swinging an elbow wildly at the face behind her shoulder. She caught him on the cheekbone, staggering the Malibor.

Crip rushed in and hammered the butt of his rifle into the man's forehead. The Malibor hunter toppled backward, out cold. Crip freed Evelyn.

"I thought they had shot you."

"Right next to my head because I screamed." She spat on the man's face and made to kick him, but Crip stopped her.

"Although it would please me no end to see him get his head caved in, I think he'll be more value as a prisoner. We can always execute him later, if he proves to be too much trouble."

"You would let a Malibor live?"

"We already let the traders live and gave them your stuff as part of the trade deal. I don't hate the Malibor, but they have what is rightfully ours. We'll interrogate him to see what he knows. Maybe his knowledge will help us penetrate the city. We know nothing, and we need to know everything. He can help us with that. He wants to live. He'll give us the answers we need."

Crip tore the shirt from one of the others and used it to bind the Malibor hunter.

"I'll gather their stuff," Evelyn offered. She headed out to find the guide and then the other two to collect the rifles, ammunition, packs, and anything else that could be of use to the expanded combat team.

With four rifles, ammunition, and minimal rations, they were loaded down.

"Are we still going to hunt?" Evelyn asked, easily putting the carnage that Crip had wrought out of her mind.

CHAPTER 8

Fortune comes in different shapes and sizes.

Fantasia called for a halt. The group stopped and flopped to the ground. The youngest member of the combat team strolled toward the team leader. "Is anyone going to watch for Malibor or just me?"

"Why don't you take a seat, too?" Max suggested. "We'll sit facing outboard, quietly, so we can all watch and listen. Everyone is part of our defense."

"Then why don't we do it at other times?" Fantasia pressed.

"When our people aren't able to watch, like when they're eating or sleeping." Max patted the ground next to him. "Take a load off and relax. You have more energy than the rest of us, so you're going to have to dial it back a little."

"Die lit back? I don't know what that means."

"I guess you don't have equipment with dials. It just

means to slow down and take longer breaks because *we* need them, not that you need them."

She nodded. "I understand." Fantasia sat between Max and Tram. "Where'd you learn about Septimus?"

"It's our history. We recovered what we could from the computer core. We studied everything related to Septimus when we were growing up. And then when we were planning this audacious infiltration of our home world, we refreshed what we knew of geography, the city, and thanks to Deena, what we knew of the people who survived."

"You mean *us*. Is Deena one of us? She's a Malibor."

"Her mother was taken, and we think from your village. She could be a cousin to some of you. How she was born wasn't her fault, and it's not for anyone to condemn. She learned the truth about the Borwyn from us. We're the good guys," Max stated.

Tram chuckled while his eyes roved the surrounding trees and brush.

Fantasia took her cue and also looked outward. She removed a snack from her pouch without looking and started to eat.

"Make sure you drink water, too," Max advised. "We have a long way to go."

Fantasia smiled. "We're probably two hours away, at most."

"That's it?" Tram blurted.

"That's it. Did you pay attention to the geography lessons?"

"I'm the pilot. We had radar." He laughed at himself. "It's Septimus, our home, but I'm not a native. My parents were from here. I guess that doesn't make me an expert in all things of this planet. Dammit! I'm a spaceman."

"Is that a bad thing?" Fantasia asked. She stood, waved, and walked away, leaving Tram to his thoughts.

After the break was over, they moved out at a slower pace. Fantasia remained in the lead with Hammer and Anvil behind her to study how she moved through the brush. At some point, they wouldn't be able to use brute force to get through the undergrowth. A time was coming when stealth might save their lives. Learning the lesson then would be too late.

Max moved forward to catch up with the brothers.

"I'm just checking to see if you two could make any more noise? I wasn't sure, because I thought you were trying to be quiet, but I must have been mistaken."

"We are, boss man," Hammer, the older brother, said. "You have to admit that we're better than we were. This planet is crazy! Look at this stuff."

Hammer waved the barrel of his pulse rifle to take in the immensity of the flora, nearly muzzle-sweeping Max, who caught the barrel before the business end passed his face.

"Watch what you're doing!" Max growled.

"Sorry, but I've never seen anything like this before. It's a lot."

"Bushes, grass, weeds, and trees. Everything a family needs. Now quiet down. Do what she does." Max waved toward Fantasia, who slipped like a shadow between the plants and through the underbrush, using her hands to move branches out of the way with the least resistance and snapback.

"She's half our size."

"You're only as big or as small as you think you are. Become one with nature, by all that's holy. Now, shut your holes!"

Hammer looked at Anvil. "Septimus made him mean and grumpy. Maybe he should have traded in his woman for a new model. He'd be a lot happier."

"What?" Max almost came out of his boots.

"Who's being loud now?" Anvil whispered. "Septimus hasn't brought you any calm."

"You two are costing me any calm I might have otherwise enjoyed." Max smiled and shook his head. "Learn how to move like her, you knuckleheads. You're smarter than you look. Why can't you walk without making noise?"

"Because you keep talking to us," Hammer replied. He and Anvil shared a laugh at Max's expense and strolled away, making a visible effort to follow Fantasia's lead.

It was the best Max could ask for. He let the formation pass him until Tram and Kelvis appeared. "Are you two ready?"

"To take the gunship skyward? You bet."

"Not yet. We won't even fire the engines, but we'll need the ship ready to fly as soon as possible when we do want to go. And remember, we're here to find something we can use as arrow tips."

"That, too. We'll be ready. Any way you can get us more fuel? We could swing the war our way if we have use of the gunship."

Max looked over one shoulder and then the other as if there was someone behind him with whom Tram was talking.

"I have what you see me carrying. No fuel. We don't have the means to produce any fuel, either. Not out here. We have to get it from the Malibor."

"That would be best. Maybe we can fly in to the spaceport and just get some."

Max contemplated the audacity of it. "Maybe we'll do just that, Tram. And then shoot up the spaceport on the way out so no one else can use it. The first shots of the war for Septimus have already been fired—" He pointed overhead. "—out there by *Chrysalis*. We can fire the next shots using the Malibor gunship to deliver maximum damage. We'll have to keep the ship moving and keep it separate from the combat team. You'll be mostly on your own."

"I'm good with that. This walking is not for me. I prefer flying and if I must fight, it'll be with a big metal ship wrapped around me. Kelvis is good, too. Plus, we'll have Pistora with us. We'll train her in what she needs to know. It'll be good to have extra hands." He waggled his digits in the air.

Max nodded and walked away. He needed time to think. He joined rearguard to watch for threats coming up from behind.

A gunship. Eleven additional bodies, most of whom were with soldiers and would fill their own positions as soldiers. With bows and arrows.

Silent killers.

While the gunship would be a very loud and obvious killer. Local defenses wouldn't be geared toward a low-level insert. They would be focused on the sky and keeping an enemy from attacking from space. If their weapons were functional. It had been fifty years, but then again, the only ground defenses back then were the Borwyn's.

Five civil wars, though. The Malibor were surrounded by enemies, more of them Malibor than Borwyn.

Max needed intelligence about the situation inside the Malibor city of Malipride before they took any action. He needed Crip's strategic vision to integrate the vertical assault with a ground attack. It was more than Max could internalize. He needed time to see how best the parts fit together.

He needed Crip. It made him wonder how he was doing hunting deer, obviously getting the best job while Max was left babysitting the likes of Hammer and Anvil.

―――――

"I think we should cross the creek and go that way." Evelyn pointed northwest. "The deer will have run from here. The hunters said they were close when they ran across us, which they considered a better trophy."

"Of course they would. Hunting humans. Who would ever think that was okay? I don't have any latent desire to hunt Malibor. I only want them to stop shooting at me, whether from a spaceship or one of these rifles."

"I say we stash them on the other side of the creek, then return to the camp on that side. No sense leaving a trail leading any recovery party to us."

"We should bury the bodies. In space, we would have said a few kind words and flushed them out the airlock. Keeping dead bodies on the ship drags down the morale, you see."

"We should toss the bodies in the creek and let them float a long way from here. We should bury the blood puddles left behind from the damage done by your pulse rifle. We should probably kill that guy and toss him in the creek, too."

"We need information that he has. I'm not going to kill him unless he decides not to tell us. After he's told us, he won't be able to go back to the Malibor, so we'll probably just turn him loose."

"If he makes too much noise, we won't be able to find the deer. They'll keep running."

Crip had to be careful about giving the Malibor a chance to escape. The prisoner had seen the damage that could be done with a weapon the Borwyn shouldn't have had. "I say we string him up," Crip suggested.

"Kill him now? I'm good with that. These scum grabbed me. Let me, I'll kill him."

"I mean by his feet. He'll dangle like that until we come back." Crip waved the rope contraption for hanging game that he'd liberated from one of the hunter's bags. "They had such high hopes for their hunt."

"But then they went after game they shouldn't have, game that could shoot back." Evelyn smiled darkly.

Crip shivered. "That's a different side than what you've shown us before," Crip noted.

"I expect you put any of the people from my village in the same situation, you would get the same response. We've been taught to fear the power of the Malibor. I don't want to be afraid of those types of men. In fact, I refuse to be afraid. I was happy to see them blown apart. Too bad I missed the first one."

"It wasn't pretty," Crip replied. "Let's go hunt some deer. We have tendons and meat that we're responsible for bringing back to the camp."

"We can build a game-drag to put our prisoner in—and a deer, if we get one—but with the rope harness thing, it won't take long."

"I look forward to building my first drag, but first, we have bodies to chuck in the creek, blood pools to cover, and a prisoner to hang by his feet."

"We better get started, then. You can't finish something you never start."

Crip agreed with the sentiment. "I'll throw the bodies in the creek. You bury the blood stains, and then we're going hunting. Watch him while you work."

Evelyn kicked him in the chest before whistling as she walked away. Crip took the bodies, one by one, choosing to drag them rather than throw them over his shoulder because he didn't want to be covered in blood. Evelyn had told him that the deer would run from the smell of blood.

Three bodies floating downstream later, Crip has spotted a place to cross, shallows with rapids.

Crip draped the Malibor over his shoulder and lumbered into the water. Halfway across, the Malibor started to struggle, getting more vigorous with his attempts to dislodge himself from Crip's shoulder.

"Stop it!" Crip shook him.

"Hold still," Evelyn ordered. She wasn't talking to the Malibor. She pounded him in the head with the butt of the Malibor's own rifle. He jerked and then hung like dead weight.

"Thank you," Crip said.

When they got to the other side, Crip dumped the hunter to the ground. The damage to the side of his head was too great.

The fourth Malibor was dead.

"Sorry, but not really. He was going to be trouble. You would have gotten nothing from him except pain."

"You're probably right." Crip dragged the body to the creek and rolled him in. The current carried him away.

"What do you say we go hunting?" Crip offered. "Isn't that what we came here for?"

"We have four guns, too." Evelyn stacked the weapons behind a tree. She readied her sling and headed into the trees. Crip hurried after her.

CHAPTER 9

Better preparation leads to better execution.

Jaq hadn't left the bridge. She was starting to feel better after talking casually with Amie for a few hours. She was doing nothing, and it served her well.

"Thanks for the good conversation." She drifted across the bridge and pulled herself into the captain's seat. She checked the status board, happy to see that the energy gauge was up to six percent. The crawl was slow but inexorably forward. "Time to get a message from *Starbound*, isn't it?"

"*Starwalker* has assumed a position to relay."

"When did they do that?"

"After we were damaged. Brad shot a message to New Septimus."

"What about *Starstruck*? I thought that ship was the relay, leaving *Starwalker* in reserve."

"*Starstruck* has not been heard from. We have to presume it's been destroyed."

"How did I not know?"

Amie pointed to her own head.

"Right," Jaq conceded. "My condolences on the loss of one of your own. I dragged you all into this. Any news about missiles or other supplies out of New Septimus?"

"We only made a one-way broadcast to New Septimus. They don't transmit from there. There's never been an emergency so great that they'd risk revealing the location of our home." Amie nodded and tapped the comm. "I've sent a short note that we are ready to receive. A single bit has confirmed they are in position."

"Now, we wait. Once a week isn't very often."

"Not when you're doing absolutely nothing. It seems like forever. But the crew is working hard. The new work schedule seems to be well received."

"Already? How do you know?" Jaq wondered.

"I'm the comm officer. I hear *everything*." Amie waved her hands mysteriously.

"Of course you do."

Amie held up one finger and then turned back to her console. She tapped buttons, waited, then tapped more and finished with a flurry.

"Big message relayed from the ground team. You can read it on your terminal."

"They sent text?"

"Compresses better," Amie explained.

"I heard we got the message from the ground team," Brad said as a way of announcing his arrival on the bridge.

"We got it three seconds ago. You were waiting." Jaq pointed an accusing finger his way.

"I knew when we were supposed to get the message, and I wanted to be here for it. Then, I heard Amie from the corridor." Brad beamed a toothy grin.

Jaq waved him to her where he could read over her shoulder.

Made contact with Malibor traders from the city although they weren't immediately hostile, they were in no position to help us. They'll keep quiet about our conversation otherwise it would reveal their illicit trade.

Learned that the Borwyn west of the city are actively fighting the Malibor.

We've left the Eastern Borwyn as we've taken to calling them behind and are returning to the gunship.

We've also gained eleven hearty souls who have joined us. Seems like women are born at twice the rate of men in this village, so...

All our people now have girlfriends except for me, Danny Johns, and Danzig. All the single guys are no longer single, including Hammer and Anvil. Don't tell Brad his boys had an hour to find their lifelong mates, and they came through.

I digress. We are incorporating them into the combat team. Their skills in moving and living in the forest far exceeds ours. We'll train them to fight. It's nothing I planned, Jaq. It's the damnedest thing. I feel like I'm caught in the rapids with no control except to keep from drowning.

Septimus is beautiful. I'm not sure any of us besides Kelvis and Tram will return to space. We feel like we're home.

We had to kill four Malibor who were on a private hunt. Whenever they're missed, the Malibor may come out to look for them, and they'll be nowhere near us. We added four old-style propellant rifles to our inventory. We are fabricating bows and arrows for our local additions. We are increasing our team's punch. The rifles will help. When we meet up with the western Borwyn, maybe we'll be able to acquire more.

We have high hopes for a clean integration and a new plan of attack. We're going to take the gunship. Max, Tram, and the others have gone to check it out. They should return tomorrow. We'll need more time, at least two weeks, but it might be more like a month. I hope this doesn't cause any problems.

Keep killing those ships in space, and we'll take care of business down here. They won't know what hit them.

The battle is joined.
Crip, out.

"They've met Malibor smugglers. They've killed Malibor hunters. And they've doubled their number by taking wives from the local village. I wonder if they dragged them off by their hair, caveman style."

"My boys have girlfriends. Why wouldn't he want you to tell me?"

"It's Crip's way of guaranteeing that I would tell you. He didn't say that he'd taken their pulse rifles away. That's something. It's what he didn't say that you should listen to," Jaq said. "The western Borwyn are actively fighting the Malibor. That's good news, and that our people are going to join them, vastly increasing their combat power. I like it. They need a month? Oddly enough, so do we. Am I right, Brad?"

He nodded. "You are right in that it will be at least a month, Jaq. Did we send the ground team a note?"

"Of course. I drafted a short message that said we were severely damaged and making repairs. We need a month at least before we could return to Septimus. We listed the dead for them, too. They're all family to us. Which reminds me. I just heard about *Starstruck*. I'm sorry, Brad, that I dragged you into this and put your people at risk. Now, they're dying because of this accursed war."

"We fight to free Septimus." Brad stared at the main screen with unfocused eyes. "Didn't you read what they said? They love it down there, even though conditions are harsh, it seems. It's Septimus, and I'll do anything to get home. *We* will do anything," he corrected himself. He spoke quietly over his shoulder. "It's okay, Jaq. It's the cost we bear for going home. You've lost seven and I've lost one in that last attack. How many is too many?"

"All of them," Jaq replied. "If we lose all, then there's no one left to enjoy the spoils of our victory. And there will be spoils, Brad."

Jaq smiled, feeling unencumbered from the weight of her bruised brain. She was on the right side of getting better.

"I see pain between now and then, but it'll be worth it in the end."

"Is it worth having if it's easily gotten?" Jaq asked.

"The answer to that is obvious. That which is hard earned is most appreciated. Like Septimus. The air will smell that much sweeter, eh, Jaq?"

"For those who make it down, yes. For those who don't, their names will be delivered to the ground so they may be remembered. Promise me, Brad."

"Get a crack on the head and all of a sudden you see your mortality?" Brad asked. "I promise, but you're going down there with me. I'm not leaving my girlfriend behind."

Jaq chuckled softly. "I hear they have double the number of women as men down there, which is bizarre as to why, but that's beside the point. Maybe your girlfriend is down there and not up here."

"Pretty sure she's not," Brad replied. "We've got a ship to fix. I'll be back."

Brad flew across the bridge and into the corridor.

Jaq reviewed the message once more. Four Malibor dead. Eleven Borwyn added to the combat team.

"Crip, are you building an army? Good for you." Jaq relaxed into her chair and closed her eyes. The gel embraced her, and with fewer worries than before, she drifted off to sleep. *Septimus and its blue skies.*

"Dad," Teo said in an accusatory voice. She waited for him to say something.

"What do you need?" Brad asked pleasantly.

"A new freaking power plant!" she shot back.

Brad grimaced. "Well, besides that. How about a croissant?"

"They have croissants?"

"No..."

"You're not helping!" Teo sighed in exasperation.

"I'll take *Starstrider* to New Septimus. If we move enough people out of there, we could take one of those power plants."

Teo perked up. "One is fine except for the additional drain from the manufacturing process that I'm sure is up and running by now. Do we need anything they're going to produce? How long will it take to fabricate a few missiles, and are they effective enough to waste the time and resources?"

"Those are all good questions. We have a supply ship we can take to Sairvor, however, it's getting closer with each day. The longer we delay, the better we'll be for efficient flight to New Septimus. And we can fly in Armanor's shadow. The Malibor won't see us. The ground team asked for at least two weeks but more like a month for them to get into position and get their girlfriends trained up."

Teo frowned. She heard the words her father had said, but they seemed little more informative than a stream of consciousness.

"Girlfriends?"

"Seems like women are born at a rate of two for every male on Septimus. The combat team seems to have acquired the third wheel, as it may be. You know, you only need two and the third wheel starts to unbalance things?"

"A third point of contact inherently provides more stability. What do you mean third wheel? I thought they had the gunship."

"Just a saying, Teo, from the old days. I'm glad the combat team grew their numbers. I should have simply said, doubled the number of soldiers."

"Girlfriends to soldiers. I'd like to hear more, but I have an engine to rebuild from scratch, unless you can get me one of the plants from New Septimus. I like that idea. Because whatever we build here won't be as good as what we had or the big generator on New Septimus. It may not be super-efficient and it's a bit heavy, but it'll give us the power we need to get back into the fight. Still, it'll be best if we take *Chrysalis* to New Septimus and install the power plant directly. Does Jaq know about your idea?" Teo hesitated to call it a plan.

"Not yet. I just thought of it after hearing the frustration in your voice." He backed away. "I'll see if chef has anything special up for grabs. I'll bring you something."

"But no croissant. We used to get those back home."

"Because we had gravity and grains. They don't have either here, but maybe there's something in the Malibor rations. I'll check." Brad headed out.

"Don't forget to come back with food," she called after him.

CHAPTER 10

We fight together. We fight for each other. And we die together.

"What do you think?" Tram asked. "Can we go up there and check it out?"

Max studied the terrain. "That's a long climb to get to the ship. We ran down it in less than an hour, I think, but it's probably a four-hour climb." He checked the sky. "We don't have enough time to get up there and back today."

"We'll sleep in the ship. Nice racks." Hammer clapped his hands together and leaned his head into them in his best mimic of sleeping.

"Already that used to sleeping in gravity?" Max asked while he continued to study the slope. "I say we go tomorrow. Two groups. One that moves fast, and then you old people bringing up the rear."

Kelvis didn't take umbrage at being called old. Tram

wasn't that old, but he was out of shape. He accepted his lot in life.

"Tomorrow then," Tram said.

Fantasia inserted herself into the conversation. "I say we recce the site tonight. It's probably only two hours for younger legs. Just Max and I running up the cut."

Max looked to Tram and Kelvis. "I can do without a full night's sleep." He nodded to the youngest member of the team. "Our whole goal is to see if the Malibor have found the ship."

"That should be easy to discover." Fantasia started to walk away.

"Wait until it's a little darker." He twirled his arm in the air, signaling for the team to rally. "Set up, eat, and hunker down."

Tram, Kelvis, and Pistora nodded. "I'll watch over them," the woman said.

Kelvis shook his head. "We're not in the grave yet. We'll watch for bad guys. Don't abandon us. Make sure you come back, even if Malibor are up there."

"Of course. We're going low risk. Quick up, check the area, and return. We'll be gone for about three, maybe four hours."

The system's star was still above the trees. He held his hand out at arm's length with his fingers together and measured how many fingers between Armanor and the horizon. Two fingers.

"Thirty minutes to sundown. We leave in fifteen." Max moved into the trees to relieve himself. He listened and watched to make sure the small team hadn't been followed.

He drank deeply of his water. Max was splitting the party again.

Never split your party.

But the others added no punch. He was better off as the only one with a weapon.

Fifteen minutes later, he and Fantasia moved to the edge of the woods. They arrived with the last vestiges of daylight. The instant Armanor passed over the mountains before them, they hurried into the open.

"If they have IR, we're in big trouble," Max said.

"What's IR?" Fantasia asked.

She was mature for her age and as intelligent as anyone, but none of the Borwyn villagers knew anything about modern technology.

"Infrared. It sees a body's heat. In the cool of the night, we'd look like raging campfires."

"How?" Fantasia asked. She was much smaller than Max and seemed like she was barely touching the ground as she moved. Max felt like he was lumbering along compared to her.

"Technology. There are a lot of steps between here and understanding how it works. I don't have enough energy to explain it. I think I'll concentrate on simply breathing."

Fantasia laughed and increased her speed while there was still enough light to see. She ran as if on level ground.

Max wondered about the stamina of youth, but he accepted the challenge. Even though he was carrying his gear, not a pack, he was wearing his ballistic protection and vest with spare power packs. The pulse rifle wasn't too heavy, not even four kilograms. It worked him hard. Max had been honest when he said he couldn't talk.

He focused on the ground and his steps. He breathed fast but steady. Max established a rhythm. And they didn't stop until they were about five hundred meters from the gunship. They dropped behind a small bush and watched.

There were no lights of any sort radiating from the ship. It was cold. No one had fired it up. There was no movement around it. They waited five minutes that extended to thirty minutes.

Max was happy that he recovered his breath in the first five minutes.

"I don't see anything. Let's move. Stay behind me," Max told the young woman.

"You don't think I can handle myself?" she snapped back.

"I'm wearing body armor in case anyone shoots at us. You're not. Simple."

Fantasia nodded curtly and waited for Max to get out first. He walked slowly and deliberately, looking down the barrel of his rifle as he swung it back and forth in a figure eight.

It took a while to cover the last five hundred meters, but it was uneventful. Better to be ready.

They made a circuit around the ship before Max climbed the ladder and accessed the hand-pad. It read his print and powered the door open. "Wait there and listen for anything," Max called down the ladder.

Fantasia nodded and faced away from the ship. She drifted into the nearby darkness.

Max secured the hatch and turned on his portable light

rather than use any of the ship's power. The last thing they needed was to bring the combat team up the side of a mountain only to find the ship unusable.

It took Max less than a minute to find that nothing had been disturbed. If anyone had found the ship, they definitely hadn't gotten in. Max thought the answer was simpler. The Malibor hadn't tracked down the gunship. There was enough action in orbit to keep the sensors and systems busy. One gunship wasn't enough to attract attention.

Max eased through the hatch. He secured it with his palm print and descended the ladder to find Fantasia waiting for him.

"We're all alone up here, Max."

"Nobody's been in the ship. Everything is intact," he replied.

"No surprise. The Malibor don't come here."

"Now you tell me?" Max wondered why she hadn't shared that earlier. He was instantly angry with the youngster, still a child by anyone's standards, who was growing more confident and more than a little abrasive. "We're not your enemy, and we're not stupid, just ignorant. There's a difference."

She shrugged. "Ready to run back to the camp?"

"Hang on. What are you trying to prove and to whom?"

"What? Nothing."

Max took her head in his hands so he could look into her eyes. They misted and glistened. She tried to pull away, but he held her head firmly.

"Let me go."

"Not until you tell me what's going on inside that head of

yours. I can't have you growing more antagonistic with each step. You've already contributed the most of any of the volunteers who joined us. Be proud of that. Maybe I need to say 'thank you' more. I don't know. We're at war, and we only have one choice. We have to beat the Malibor into submission. It's the only thing they understand. I can't have someone who's toxic on the team. All it takes is one person at odds with the others. I'll send you back to your village first thing in the morning if you're going to be a festering cancer."

"Where did this come from? I'm doing the best I can, which isn't bad for a castoff, just like the others. We're not your best candidates. We're the dregs of the village. No one wanted us, not even our parents."

Max suspected the combat team hadn't gotten the best in the village, but they had kept up. They had kept watch. And the 'substandard' locals were far better at woodcraft than any of those raised on a ship.

"Keep your snips and sarcasm to yourself. You are the best on point that we have. By far, Fantasia. But only if you're a team player."

"I'm an adult," she stated.

Max hesitated. "And you've been drafted into the Borwyn army. Your time will come, and Fantasia will be the general of the forces that defend Septimus. Getting people to work together is a lesson we all need to learn and embrace."

Fantasia tilted her head. A crescent moon was rising, shining a dim light that cast no shadows. "General?"

"Peace is hard earned and easily lost. Talk with Danny Johns. He was born here, about seventy years ago. He was a soldier, right here on Septimus. His unit was driven away by the Malibor. There was nothing they could do because they weren't ready for the ferocity of the attack. After fifty years, the Malibor aren't ready for us. We've seen that in space. I expect to see it on the ground. And we'll retake Septimus, but it'll take an army and we have barely two squads. And back to my first point. We can't have any animosity. We fight together. We fight for each other. And we die together."

Fantasia dropped her chin to her chest and stared at the ground.

"I'm sorry. We competed for men. It wasn't healthy. And out of the eleven who came with you, I'm in last place. It makes me angry with the others, but I can take it out on the Malibor."

"Is that how you see it? I would have never guessed. You're too young. Any of our combat team tried to touch you, I would beat them senseless." He gripped her shoulder. "You're going to stay with Deena and me, and we'll find someone worthy of you together. We have a young man on the ship who saved us all. He's about your age, maybe a little younger. He's filled with the same drive as you. You need to meet him, so unleash your anger on the Malibor but stay alive. You have a date."

"A date?" She shook her head. "You're a strange man, Max. I see why Deena is so taken with you, and Crip, too."

Max looked down the hill. Now that his eyes adjusted, he could see the terrain. "Shall we? Forty-five minutes. I want to be in my bag and sound asleep before the hour is out."

"I'll go slow so you can keep up."

"Hang on," Max replied. He never, in his wildest dreams, thought being the leader of the combat team would mean he'd be counseling a teenager, but here they were. Some lessons were harder learned than others. He removed his harness and body armor and handed it to Fantasia. "I'll carry the pulse rifle and you wear the body armor, if you're going to run ahead."

She frowned but put it on out of sheer defiance of her limitations. She started jogging and was quickly breathing heavily.

Max loped along beside her.

"A little different when things are equal. You about killed me coming up the hill," Max said, talking in a casual voice.

Fantasia held up a hand. "Point. Taken," she gasped, but to her credit, she didn't try to return the armor.

CHAPTER 11

The stars are nothing more than a distraction from what's beneath your feet.

"Message coming in from *Starbound*," Amie reported.

Jaq gestured to put it on speaker.

"One cruiser has sortied away from the Malpace space station. It's moving slowly, estimate two weeks to arrival at Farslor."

Jaq took a deep breath. It was good news and bad news. The good news was that it was only one cruiser. The bad news was that it would get to them well before they could fight effectively.

"Acknowledge receipt of the message, please," Jaq said.

The communications officer confirmed with *Starbound*.

"Brad to the bridge," Jaq said over the intercom.

Amie sat in silence while watching the captain.

"It may not be optimal, but things are looking up. See?" Jaq pointed to an icon on her screen that had turned green. A subsystem of the electrical architecture was now online. A small section of the ship would have overhead lights active. It was a tiny victory.

Amie's weak smile wasn't enough encouragement, so she added a thumbs-up sign.

"Two weeks," Jaq muttered.

Brad clomped merrily onto the command deck. "We're going to Sairvor!" he announced.

"Are we?" Jaq asked sharply.

"You look unhappy. I thought you'd be happier when I told you that we're going to New Septimus to borrow their second power plant, load up whatever weapons they have available, and then return to Septimus to wreak havoc!" He gestured wildly as if caught in the midst of a heavy metal serenade.

"Malibor cruiser has sortied and is on the way here. Two weeks and we'll have company," Jaq explained.

Brad looked up at the screen. It showed him nothing he didn't already know. "I see why you're unhappy. I apologize for my ebullience. If we race to Sairvor ahead of the cruiser, we'll burn all our power and won't be able to defend ourselves. If we stay here, we'll conserve our power, but then we only get one shot at the fight. Any extended engagement would leave us out there as nothing more than target practice. Can we ask them to delay for a while?"

"That's not a bad idea, but how can we hold them up? Maybe flash *Starbound* as a decoy to draw them off course."

Brad shook his head. "The Malibor have already destroyed one of our scout ships. I don't want to lose another."

"Fair enough," Jaq replied. "We need Teo, Alby, Chief Ping, and yes, Bec if we want to talk through what we can do. We don't have a choice. How will we face the Malibor cruiser with our diminished capacity?"

"That is the big question," Brad replied. "A really big question. We can keep working on stuff right up until we engage, but stuff that's mostly fixed is going to get trashed quickly during combat. That'll set us back even farther, and right in the middle of a space battle, it could be a death knell."

"We have two choices, and both are bad," Jaq said.

"I'll rally the team." Brad climbed into his seat and made the notifications. He received an earful from Teo, but everyone else simply responded in the affirmative. "Give them ten minutes."

"Ten minutes to think of options." Jaq's mind wasn't the one hundred percent she needed. Was she sharp enough to defeat a Malibor cruiser? "Why isn't it accompanied by gunships? According to our information, they have two cruisers remaining and ten gunships. The cruiser should have two gunships with it."

"Do you have a death wish?" Brad asked. "It's better that we only have one ship to face."

"Is it better that we're not prepared to face what's coming?" Jaq got Amie's attention. "Confirm with *Starbound* regarding gunships."

Amie turned her attention to her terminal.

"One cruiser by itself or with two gunships, we barely have what we have."

"If they have gunships, then our only choice is to run,

out-system."

"Run for deep space. Buy time and fight them at Grabthor or Gellingen." The eighth pair of planets on the orbital plane.

"That's an option I hadn't considered. Offense wins battles."

"Defense wins wars?" Jaq shook her head. "In this war, offense has been the winning strategy. Defense is how we'll die. Our advantage is our ability to fire and maneuver. If we don't have our advantage, then we may have to retreat to regroup."

"What about *Cornucopia* and *Butterfly*?"

"We can't lose *Cornucopia*. They will have to fly ahead of us. We may lose *Butterfly*. We'll do our best to fly at an angle away from it. Maybe the Malibor won't see it."

"What're the chances of that?" Brad scoffed.

Alby arrived with Chief Ping. Teo and Bec were arguing on their way down the corridor.

"I'm not looking forward to this," Jaq whispered.

Brad knew exactly how she felt. Teo was getting snippy. The pressure of the job. And Bec was being his usual self, angering anyone with whom he talked.

Mary and Ferd showed up, too. "We heard you might need your flight crew." They took their seats only to find that most of their controls still didn't work.

"The Malibor have launched a cruiser from the space station. It's on a lazy flight path here. In two weeks, we'll have company. I need options."

"Just the cruiser?" Alby asked right away. "If there are no gunships with it, we can ambush it the second it comes around Farslor. We can hit it with enough that it'll never clear the shadow. We'll rip the nose right off it."

"We've asked for verification that it's alone," Jaq added. "Ambush using a lander?"

"It's a good way to use the asset. We don't have a lot of tools in the bag." Alby held his head in his hands until he clamped his boots to the deck. He struggled to pay attention.

"What's wrong?" Jaq asked.

"We're not ready for combat."

"We're not even close to ready for combat. We have a supply ship, and *Chrysalis* has a lot of damage that says the next impact might crack us wide open. Sucking for air isn't how I want to die, Jaq."

"Teo?" Jaq directed the conversation away from Alby, who was descending toward a dark place from which he would have a hard time escaping.

"We'll be at one hundred percent in stored power before then. That gives us a robust, if short term, capability," Teo said.

"We've fought full battles against multiple enemies with less than a hundred percent," Jaq suggested.

"That was with a power plant buffering. You'll find without the plant, the ship will burn through reserves at about twice the rate. If we fight, we better win quickly."

"*If* we fight," Jaq emphasized.

Teo nodded. "It would be best not to fight. Our repairs are tenuous, at best. It won't take much to shake the ship apart. If I can vote for anything other than fighting, then I'll vote for that."

"Brad?" Jaq looked to her deputy.

"Grabthor is looking pretty good right about now, Jaq. I say we run as soon as we have the power to do so, with *Cornucopia* running in front of us, in case they need to give us a tow."

"Is it that bad, Teo?" Jaq asked.

"I don't want to stress the bio-pack. I'd rather run it through its paces when we have circuit boards for backup." Teo dipped her chin to give her father a hard look, challenging him.

"I agree, Teo. No need to be willful." Brad waved her off as if chasing away a fly.

Alby brightened. "As your battle commander, I agree. We are in no condition to fight. We need to save the ship and the crew to fight another day, a day and place of our choosing. If we engage before then, we risk everything. The odds are against while the ship is in this shape." Alby looked with hope at the captain.

She couldn't fight the Malibor with her broken ship.

"Why are they flying so slowly?" Jaq asked. "They could be here in ten days if they wanted."

"I'll ask," Amie reported. With a burst transmission directed toward *Starbound* and away from Septimus, there was no risk of it getting intercepted. "Give it a minute."

Jaq glanced at the main screen, operating in a dark, low-power mode. The ship's status board was displayed in all its glory showing more red than yellow with only a couple green pinpoints. The energy gauge was at eight percent and continued to climb.

"Good job on that, Teo."

Bec cleared his throat.

"I meant you, Bec. I know it was your idea coupled with Teo's bio-pack. Engineering is a team effort in most cases."

Bec stared at the screen while tapping the side of his mouth.

Jaq closed her eyes. He was playing the same game he always played. He had an idea, but rather than saying it outright, he'd force her to ask a bunch of questions so he could make her look stupid.

Brad saw the exchange and intervened. "What's your idea, Bec?"

"Are you seeing what I'm seeing?" he asked cryptically.

"No games, Bec. We don't have time. What is your idea?" Jaq said, opening her eyes to look at the screen, knowing that she wouldn't see anything different.

"We have the moon on our side. We have *Cornucopia*. We have *Starstrider* and, what, *six* operational landers? I suggest we can mine this area, while hiding behind the moon. It served us before, and there were no survivors from that battle. The tactic remains sound."

Alby's eye twitched. "It still means engaging the enemy with a broken ship, or did you fix something and not tell us?" He didn't add that it was in Bec's nature to do just that so he could look more than a genius but a miracle worker.

"Nothing fixed beyond the ability to bring the ship to a hundred percent power. Teo is right that we'll reduce it twice as fast as you're used to. But a quick engagement shouldn't tax the ship if surprise is on our side. A cruiser without gunship escorts? They don't know we're here."

"That could be a deadly presumption, Bec," Jaq shot back, but his reasoning was sound.

"Untether *Cornucopia* and send it toward Grabthor. But first, unload what we need to fill four landers with explosives, extra rations, and if we ever find weapons on board on that ship, we'll take those, too."

"Still haven't found any. We've shifted a lot of boxes," Alby replied. "You're not going to fight, are you?"

"If we run and they chase us, we'll die when we run out of power. Whether they kill us or we simply lose life support, the end result is the same. The Borwyn lose the war. And then the Malibor will find New Septimus and our people on our home planet. We have to fight, as alluring as running is. I don't want to die tired. I'd rather punch them in the face until my fist bleeds."

The group nodded. Alby frowned but nodded. "I understand. Priority to E-mag repairs. If we're going to have power, then we'll have weapons to fire. No missiles, Jaq. Defensive chain guns and E-mags. It's all we have."

"Don't forget landers rigged to blow," Brad added. "I'll take that task if no one else wants it."

"And I'll keep working on the power plant. Maybe we'll get lucky and have a breakthrough on one of them to get some of our internal power generation restored," Teo said.

Brad gestured at Amie. "Inform New Septimus that we'll be coming for one of the power plants. Maybe in a month's time. Have our missiles ready and prepare to shut down the new fabrication facility."

"Bec. We need a weapon to take on this cruiser, something with a little more oomph than an explosives-laden lander. You have two weeks and unlimited access to *Cornucopia*."

"Probably nothing I can do," Bec replied.

His answer gave Jaq hope. She knew that he had something in mind but getting him to share what it was would be impossible.

"Ferd and Mary, prepare a flight path to take us to the far side of the moon where we stay in the planet's shadow. We cannot let the Malibor cruiser see us. Plot a course for *Cornucopia*, too, using the planet as a screen. Calculate how long they'll be able to travel at one-point-two gees acceleration before they'll be seen. Let us know when they have to leave to maximize their distance from Farslor so when the Malibor spot *them*, they think *we're* running away."

"Will they confuse a freighter for a cruiser?"

"When Alby is done with it, they will."

Alby grimaced but ended with a slow nod. "I see the wisdom in it. And a lot of work for a three-second spoof."

"Three seconds is all we need to send hundreds of obdurium projectiles through their hull. If you can give us three seconds, they won't get off a shot," Jaq replied. "All we need is three seconds. That's what we had with the Malibor's *Hornet*, and we destroyed it."

"We better be ready. Put Phillips on the E-mags. All other welding work is secondary. We need all our batteries operational," Brad said. "And Junior, too, even though he's only thirteen. Put him in a small suit and send him outside. He'll figure it out and do us proud."

Jaq closed her eyes once more. The pain in her head had returned. She wasn't sure if it was the concussion or the weight of their choices, none of which were good.

CHAPTER 12

The ground is hard, but a hard rain will soften it.

Danzig had a good laugh when he saw Fantasia wearing Max's body armor. She was dogged hard when she staggered past the observation post, barely able to raise her arm to wave. Danzig knew exactly what had happened—Max had taught her a lesson.

It was a good one, too. After Max took the body armor, she continued to stumble, still suffering under the burden. Her legs were little more than soft rubber.

Max strolled by after her. Danzig pointed at him and nodded.

"I figured you'd appreciate the turnabout." Max clapped him on the shoulder and continued to where Deena waited. He snuggled in close to her and they quickly fell asleep.

The rest of the ship recon team rolled into camp. It was early morning. They hadn't stayed out.

Max still rose before dawn. He was one of the last into his bedroll, but they hadn't burdened him with a shift on watch. He slept a solid four hours and considered it a bonus. No one had talked to him after he arrived besides Danzig on the forward outpost, where he watched for the ship team's return.

The small camp was already taking shape with a central fire and a slit trench for relief hidden between bushes. The creek ran nearby, where they collected fresh water for drinking and cooking.

Max took a knee while he scooped the fresh water into a dish. He let the water trickle over his lips and onto his tongue. The crisp, clear drink was like nothing he'd ever tasted. It was the joy of being on Septimus and the planet's purity soothing his soul.

When he stood, he discovered Crip walking toward him.

"Ship's untouched. No signs of Malibor," Max stated.

Crip nodded. "Unlike our excursion to get a deer. We ran into a Malibor hunting party. The Malibor go into the deep woods on extreme excursions. We sent four bodies downstream. The good news is they were carrying hunting rifles, so we have four bonus weapons and ammunition for each. Slug throwers, propellant cartridges. Old timer stuff. And we bagged one small buck."

"You and Evelyn?"

"She hates the Malibor in a way we can't contemplate," Crip said softly. "And I understand. They didn't consider the Borwyn anything other than prey, legal prey. They were easy to kill. Civilians. Not a clue what real war looks like."

"But they had weapons?"

"To kill deer, nothing more. They weren't good. We had one of them as a hostage, but he got himself killed before we could properly question him."

"*Got himself killed*. Sounds like being a hostage wasn't going to work out. It's okay, Crip. My only question is will they come out of the city to look for their people? If they do, will they find us?"

"Good questions, but like I said, we sent the bodies downstream. That'll give us separation. If they're found, it'll be a long way away. It's a risk, of course, but we lost our chance to avoid them when they saw us and started shooting. You know that I don't take kindly to getting shot at."

"Makes me mad, too," Max agreed. "There's no blame to be had, nothing to be sorry about."

Crip chuckled and shook his head. "We're not sorry. Evelyn is a fighter. She was nonplussed when I exploded two Malibor right next to her." Crip nodded toward their camp. "We'll finish making bows and arrows, then get to *Matador* to fly to the western forest."

Max and Crip found the others rising for the day. Everyone was in camp. A quick roll call had them all accounted for except for Fantasia.

Danzig waved and hurried away. He returned in under two minutes helping Fantasia, who walked with a significant limp.

Max's eyes shot wide. "What's wrong with you?"

"Blisters. My feet aren't used to running on hills," she said, shrugging and delivering an apologetic look.

"Bed rest for a day. Stay off your feet," Max told her. He spoke over his shoulder to Crip. "We ran up the hill to the gunship and back down. We were packed a little heavier than intended." He winked at Fantasia.

She didn't say anything about the body armor.

Crip spoke to the group. "We've encountered the Malibor and once again, they have lost a battle." He made a fist and shook it in front of his chest.

The group nodded in appreciation, tensing and wearing grim smiles.

"Where are we?" Crip asked. "Bows, arrows, strings?"

Harper raised her hand. "We found a stand of wood that will make for good bows, but we need to go back to cut more. The first batch wasn't as good as it needed to be. They broke under stress. We'll get more, cut them thinner, and then attach them using glue we can make from deer hide and tightened with its sinew. But we're going to need more than is in that little guy you brought back." Harper brushed her finger at Evelyn.

"I'm surprised we got anything, what with all the noise we made killing those four Malibor. Today will be better." She looked to Crip, but he shook his head and pointed at Max.

"Today *will be* better," Max declared with utmost certainty, eyeing Crip to see if he could get a rise.

He didn't. "I hope so. Seems like we need more materiel from the carcasses. And we could use some more meat. We've got hungry people. A lot of hungry people. We're going to need vegetables, tubers, stuff like that. Who knows that stuff?"

All the women except Deena raised their hands.

"You." Crip pointed. "I forgot your name, sorry."

"Mrs. Finley," the woman said proudly.

Crip looked at Finley, who smiled and shrugged. "New rule. First names except where you only have one name. What does Finley call you?"

She looked away.

"Out with it."

"Huggy bottom."

The others snorted and laughed. Crip closed his eyes. He was losing the cultural battle. "Okay. Hugs it is. You take Finley and four others to find and gather edibles that we can add to our diet. We can't live by venison alone."

Hammer raised his hand. "I'm willing to try."

"No." Crip motioned for him to put his arm down.

"Arrow team?" Crip pressed.

"Right here," the one called Sophia replied. "Along the creek, there are all the reeds we'll need to make hundreds of arrows. We only need fletching."

"Bird killers!" Crip blurted.

Mia raised her hand. "No luck yesterday. We never got close. But if we can use a little bait, like entrails, we might be able to bag a flock of scavengers."

"Max, make sure you and Evelyn are successful. Bird team, follow them out, then wait at a bivouac area until the hunt is successful. Build a trap area and put the entrails in. Then wait. Return to camp when you have enough feathers for a couple hundred arrows."

"Done," Mia stated. Each person selected their teams,

accounting for the men that would come with them and warning them to be quiet.

The loudest local was quieter than the quietest soldier.

"The rest of us will wait here, prep the work areas by building benches. We'll also rest and prepare to cover the watch tonight."

Deena took Max's arm. "I'm going with them."

Crip nodded. It didn't leave him with many people, but he wasn't the focus of main effort. They needed what they needed, and it took getting those materials. There was no *Cornucopia* carrying supplies for an army. They had to find it in nature and then create it.

Septiman provides for those willing to work, Crip thought. "Let's get to it."

It was the third day after killing the Malibor hunters when an aircraft flew low and slow over the area.

"Hunker down," Crip called. All voices passed the call, but the combat team members were already pressed up behind trees or huddled under overhanging bushes. They were all in camp, which made for a bigger footprint, but the camp was under the shade of heavy oak trees growing in a circle around a central open area. Large branches provided cover and concealment. Even with IR, unless the Malibor had a good angle, they wouldn't see the Borwyn.

That's what Crip hoped.

"It's not a military ship, is it?" Max asked. "Doesn't seem

to be armed. What's that red and white line down the side mean? Kind of ruins it for camouflage."

Crip replied, "I bet it's a rescue ship. Simply looking for the wayward souls. My guess is that it started at the headwaters and is following the creek. The easiest navigation for the hunters and those searching for them."

The ship rolled back and forth to cover both sides of the creek as it headed southwest toward where the hunters breathed their last. It was at least ten kilometers away plus however far they'd floated. All of it under cover of the great trees of the forest.

The forest that the Borwyn called home.

Crip snarled at the intrusion into their lives. "How dare they interrupt us while we're building the weapons we are going to use against them."

"Rude!" Max shouted and shook a fist at the receding sound of the small aircraft.

"Back to work, people," Crip called. "Weapons of war, coming right up!"

He pulled Max aside.

"If they come back, we're going to shoot them down, and then we'll run for the gunship."

"My thoughts exactly, Crip. Let them know they're not welcome here, but what about retaliation? They'll attack the village."

"Damn!" Crip looked around at the women working hard at making arrows, building bows, and teaching the soldiers all the steps. They also prepared vegetables, side by side with their team. "Maybe we should run now."

"That would probably be best, so we aren't faced with the

dilemma of retaliation. If they find the bodies, do you think they'll blame the local Borwyn?"

"I blew one guy's head off and hit two in the chest, leaving really big holes. The locals don't have any weapons that could do that, not even their shotguns at point-blank range."

"What about the fourth?"

"Evelyn caved in his skull with the butt of a hunting rifle."

"How'd that happen?"

Crip shook his head. "He didn't recognize the peril he was in and decided he wanted to give us grief. He lasted about two seconds."

"I'd like to feel bad for him, but he was raised to think the Borwyn were inferior. He paid the price for not having an open mind."

"He learned the hard way, but no one else got a chance to learn the lesson he sacrificed his life for," Crip replied. "But they'll learn soon enough. I can't wait to meet our fellow ground pounders on the far side."

"Rally the troops, pack our trash, and leave?"

"You go right. I'll go left. We'll let everyone know on the way. It's time to get out of here."

It was the middle of the night when they finally reached *Matador*. The locals were hesitant. They'd never flown before. Even Fantasia, who had seen the ship, but Max hadn't taken her aboard. He probably should have so at least one of them would be relaxed.

Deena pulled the women aside and talked to them while Tram and Kelvis brought the ship online.

"It's loud and you get tossed around if you're not belted in, which you won't be because we have more people than the ship is designed for. But you'll like it. Flying is incredible. Have you never envied the birds? Free to soar over it all. Moving at the speed of the wind and faster. You'll cover more ground in mere minutes than you can walk in several days. And if we see Malibor, this ship has weapons that can level a village in a flash! Like lightning from the worst storm you've ever seen. And this ship is ours, but we're low on fuel so we will fly straight to the area of the western Borwyn."

"I'm not sure they exist," Evelyn said. "We've never been that far. There are only rumors and the word of the Malibor. We've learned not to trust the Malibor."

Deena stepped closer and took the older woman's hand. "Then we'll be the foundation of our own army to challenge the Malibor. War is upon us, the war to end the war."

Evelyn nodded, tight-lipped. The other women kept glancing at the outline of the ship against the night sky. It was imposing sitting on its tail, pointed skyward. Internal lights came to life and bled through portholes and the starboard airlock, which they left open.

"You need to trust Crip and Max. They saved my life. Give them a chance, and they'll save yours, too."

"Crip saved me," Evelyn said. "Without batting an eye. I'd follow him anywhere. Kelvis, too, since he's my man." She laughed for some reason.

"Time to board," Deena said. "Follow your men into the ship and find a place to sit and something to hang on to."

"Ava!" Hammer called more loudly than he should have. The young woman jumped into his arms and they hugged. He guided her to the ladder and followed her up, half wrapped around her until she crawled into the airlock.

"See? Nothing to be afraid of," Deena said softly.

Two by two, they climbed the ladder and entered.

Crip and Danny Johns were the last ones up after making sure everyone else boarded. "Max, get a headcount. No stragglers. When we take off, we're not coming back."

Max gave him the thumbs-up and headed inside the ship.

"What do you think, Danny?"

"I'm back on Septimus, and it's a beautiful night. Do I need to think about anything?"

"I guess not. We have about everything we need, don't we? I would have never foreseen this mob. I'm not opposed to women as soldiers, but none of them on the ship wanted to join us. We trained hard. Maybe we did too much man-stuff and chased them away."

"Not anymore, my young friend," Danny laughed. "I see you struggle with them. You'll be just fine. Treat them the same as anyone else. They're up for it. They're good people, Crip. Hardened by a life in the wild. They will be great soldiers. You'll see when the time comes."

That will be sooner than we want, Crip thought. They needed to train on tactics and moving as a unit, a super-sized unit, twice the number of anything he'd deployed against an enemy before. Crip and Max were the most experienced soldiers, but that wasn't saying much. None of them had much experience. Crip had two fights that were just him—the takeover of *Hornet* and the hunters. He was a warrior.

He knew that he'd never return to *Chrysalis*, even though he wanted to see his friends and family again, especially Taurus. He'd build her the home she deserved and wanted.

But first, they had to win the war that had been going on for fifty years.

CHAPTER 13

Death from above—a vertical envelopment.

"Going airborne!" Tram shouted. "Grab your butts and hang on."

The engines roared, and the ship climbed slowly skyward.

"Throttle back!" Kelvis yelled from engineering. "You'll crash us halfway there."

Tram eased off on the throttle, slowing the climb before he nosed over to thirty percent. The ship flew crooked because the stubby wings weren't optimal for providing lift. The gunship needed the engines to keep it in the sky.

Tram maneuvered between the highest peaks and angled to the northwest, where another great forest spread to the distant horizon. Hills rose above the treetops at random intervals.

"If we land on a hilltop, we can kiss the ship good-bye," Crip said.

"Ground scans suggest those are the only viable landing spots."

"See if there's one that's lower than the others. If we hug the tree line, the ship may not stick out like a sore thumb."

"I've had a sore thumb, Crip, and it never stuck out at all." Tram slowed his approach, watching the fuel gauge carefully.

He rotated the ship and slowed. The radar showed clear skies in all directions, but Tram kept the angle high to avoid detection by ground-based systems.

They weren't to the middle of the woods. They were closer to the mountains as well as Malipride, the renamed main city on Septimus. It wasn't the best choice, but if the combat team wanted to use the ship again, they'd need the fuel.

The plateau wasn't as level as they would have liked, especially close to the trees. Tram had to move up the slope. He fired the engines with one final burst to slow the ship an instant before it hit the ground.

Tram shut down the engines. "We're here, boys and girls. I suggest you exit the ship as quickly as possible, in case we made ourselves a big, fat target."

"Arrow tips?" Sophia asked.

Crip called down to the small engineering section where Kelvis was running through his checklist to power all the systems down.

"I've got contact point replacements. Let me finish this and I'll pass them up." Evelyn waved through the hatch while she waited on Kelvis.

"I completely forgot about the tips," Crip said apologetically.

"It's okay. You don't have to think of everything," Sophia told him. "That's what you've got all of us for."

Crip had a hard time discounting her logic. "That makes the most sense out of anything I've heard. Go on now. Off the ship and join the others in the woods. We'll be down shortly.

"Bridge is secure," Tram announced. "You're the last one off, K."

Tram whisked through the airlock and waited for Pistora, who climbed down with him wrapped around her for 'safety.'

Crip knew the women could climb trees and ladders as he'd seen them in the village, but why miss an opportunity for physical contact? "Hurry up," Crip grumped at Tram. Crip ran a quick check through the ship to make sure everyone was off. He leaned into the hatch to the engineering section.

"Come on, Evelyn. Let's go. Lock the hatch after you leave, Kelvis."

"I'm finished down here. We're on our way."

Evelyn climbed up first, carrying a metal box that shook with the contact points, and Crip sent her out the hatch.

"How much fuel do we have left?" Crip asked when Kelvis appeared.

"Maybe not enough to get to a fueling station. We might crash trying to get there or have to ditch somewhere in between. I'd give it less than fifty-fifty."

"At least that means the Malibor won't be able to use it either." Crip moved out. He looked over the trees and toward the mountains before climbing down. Bathed in the light from Alarrees, the single moon over Septimus, the serenity of the Borwyn home warmed him.

No wonder the Malibor wanted it.

The tree cover was heavy, and once on the ground, Crip wouldn't have this good of a view again. It also meant the ship was visible to casual observers no matter where they might be.

It would get seen and Malibor would swarm the area.

"We need to get away from here," he mumbled to himself while climbing down the ladder.

Kelvis was right behind him. The airlock hatch thumped as it closed. The engineer accessed the panel and secured the hatch and ship. He powered the panel down to eliminate any power trickle. He had high hopes of returning to the ship and getting it back into the fight. He rested his hand on the hatch as if saying good-bye to a dying parent before descending the rest of the way to the ground.

He adjusted his pack straps and tottered down the hill and into the woods where the others waited.

"Danny Johns, you're on point with Barrington and Amelia. Hammer and Anvil, right flank with Ava and Mia. Left flank is Finley and Hugs, Binfall and Charlotte. Deena and I will take Tail-End Charlie. The rest of you ride the rocking chair. Stay where you can see the next person. Flanks, don't get too far out where you lose sight of the middle."

"We don't have a chair," Evelyn said.

"That means you stay in the middle of the formation. Take your cues from the point. Don't get too close or too far away. Danzig, help Fantasia. She's not walking too good."

"I'll be fine," the girl replied.

"You're not fine, but you will need to be, which means accept help now so you can help someone else later when they need it," Max snapped back. She withered under his midnight glare.

Deena stepped in. Danzig was too tall to let Fantasia drape an arm over his shoulder.

"Move into the middle," Max told her. "Crip and Danzig, with me at the rear of the column, diamond formation."

Danny Johns was already on the move.

Their weapons consisted of eleven pulse rifles, four hunting rifles, and ten bows with only a hundred arrows. As long as there weren't any extended engagements, they'd be fine.

Crip didn't count on that. When the fight began, it would be a slog. They'd lose people, and that would be the hardest thing to take. There would be no reinforcements. They were on their own until they met up with the western Borwyn, wherever they might be.

"Keep your eyes peeled. If our fellow Borwyn saw us arrive in a gunship, they may think we're Malibor."

"And try to kill us," Danny Johns finished by calling over his shoulder. "I'll do my best not to walk us into a trap."

The night below the trees was nearly as dark as space. The flanks were barely five meters from the mob of people walking in the middle. Danny Johns was less than five meters in front of Deena and Fantasia. The group was packed in so tightly that a single enemy with an explosive could destroy the combat team's efforts.

After an hour and maybe a kilometer traveled, Crip

called a halt. "Shelter in place. We'll move again once it's light enough to see. We're beating ourselves senseless trying to brute force our movements. At this pace, we can't get there from here. Get some sleep, people. Two on watch at a time for an hour then change out."

Max took care of the details. Danny Johns worked his way to the rear of the formation.

"There are trails out here. I don't know if they're game or people trails, but they are well worn. We're going to run across somebody or something. I'm glad you chose to wait for daylight. I'll be getting back to my post now."

Crip nodded. "I'll bring it up with Max. We better be vigilant. It would suck to get killed by people who are on our side."

Soon, the group was sleeping. They'd already learned to sleep when they could. The women and men were tangled in a pile of bodies that littered the open ground between the aged trees.

Crip strolled the perimeter, checking in with the watch to give them a small boost to help them through their hour. The men on watch were accompanied by their partners. Two on watch became four. They sat quietly and watched into the darkness of the forest.

At the front of the formation, Crip found Danny Johns. Crip wanted the original's experience.

"Did you have women in your units back in the old days?" Crip didn't mince words.

"No, but we should have. The survivors on *Chrysalis* rectified that. You're completely integrated."

"Completely? It's like you aren't a member of the combat

team. Everything we had on ground combat operations didn't have any consideration for female soldiers. It was all men."

"And that left us at half-strength. You know how that worked out for us. We ended up running for our lives. You're doing a good thing here, Crip. You and Max. Making everyone feel welcome, a part of the team without compromising any standards."

Although they were already whispering, Danny leaned close and spoke in a voice that Crip could barely hear. "Did you see what Max did to Fantasia? Made her wear the body armor for the run down the hill and then the movement the rest of the way to our camp."

"And now she's limping."

"You might want to double-check. The real damage could be to her pride." At Crip's look, Danny continued. "Whether you like it or not, you get to be a real leader, and that means you have to work with everyone. You can't just shout an order and expect it to be followed."

Crip tried to see the stars above the canopy, but it was just a pinpoint of light here or there. He couldn't get a good view of the starfield. "You're killing me, Danny. Of course I can *expect* the soldiers to follow orders. I shouldn't have to explain myself, because sometimes there isn't time."

"Just convince them what we're doing is the right thing," Danny pressed.

"How am I doing so far?" Crip wondered.

"Not bad at all. You seem to have equal disdain for the men and women alike. No favoritism." Danny pulled his helmet over his eyes. "If that'll be all, I need to get some shut-eye. I need my sleep because, well, I'm *old*."

"I don't have equal disdain…"

Danny waved off any explanation that Crip might make.

"Always a pleasure and usually enlightening, Danny Johns. Get your sleep."

Crip continued around the far side to run across another couple lounging casually while watching. Crip tapped their shoulders as he passed. He returned to the huddle with Deena and Max.

"I'll take the next stroll," Max mumbled.

"No need. Our people are on top of things." Crip settled, half-reclined, against his pack. "We have good people, Max. Soldiers all."

"I know."

"We'll see how the western Borwyn treat us. That will be the determinor."

Crip couldn't sleep. His idea of a worst case was getting into a firefight with his fellow Borwyn. He could see them racing toward that inevitable contact. An armed combat team moving en masse through Borwyn territory after arriving in a Malibor gunship.

Tread carefully, Borwyn soldiers, Crip reminded himself.

CHAPTER 14

The field of glory isn't a friendly place.

Jaq sulked. Her head ached, and she was supposed to be preparing to fight the Malibor. Everyone was occupied trying to fix the ship enough to survive the upcoming battle. It was madness to consider running as much as it was to think about fighting.

The better of two bad choices.

"Amie, can you ask Donal Fleming to join me on the bridge, please?"

The communications officer made the call and together, they waited. It wasn't long before Donal bounced down the corridor and rammed into the bridge's mid-rail.

"This zero-gee is really something, isn't it. I say, do you ever get used to it?"

"We were born and raised in zero-gee. We didn't have gravity until I was thirty years old, and then it was only snippets as we tested engines. Ours was a zero-gee existence. Needless to say, we're pretty good at working in it."

"I like gravity," Donal said. "The lack of it is disconcerting, but we'll make do. You wanted to talk with me?"

"You crafted the programming to better target the enemy when we were moving at high-speed."

Donal nodded. That's what he'd done, along with the thirteen-year-old Dolly Norton.

"We're going to use landers to see the Malibor cruiser coming around the planet. But then we're going to need to hit him with all batteries before he can see us."

"Easy," Donal replied. "We fire at the spot where he'll be. He flies into the stream of projectiles. You used that maneuver once when you hit the Malibor cruiser called *Hornet* as it came around Sairvor's moon."

"We're going to have to fire around the moon and off the edge of Sairvor's atmosphere. There will be a lot of bending going on. When we hit *Butterfly*, it was coming around the moon right in front of us. We have to double-skip our shots, which will affect his ability to return fire. He'll miss us if he doesn't have someone like Donal Fleming doing the math."

"Butter my muffin and call me yours," Donal blurted. "Can I select our position in space?"

"Of course. And the position of the lander, too. We can't get shot, Donal. This ship is barely holding it together. We need the best shots that can be made, Donal. We hit them or we die."

"No pressure at all, is what I hear you saying." He snorted and tried to slap his thigh, which sent him spinning until he grabbed the upper rail. "I need Dolly. We have something like thirteen days, right?"

"Thirteen days to be in position and ready to fire," Jaq replied.

"It'd be better with a month, but since we only have thirteen days, that'll have to do. I'll need fresh sensor data, so Chief Ping, too."

"Sensors aren't online."

"You'll have to get them online and then I'll need the newest information," Donal replied matter-of-factly.

"We'll work it. The good news is that your computers are operational. Not much else, but you'll have that."

"I'll take it. A double-skip shot from all batteries. It's not as hard as it sounds."

"It sounds nearly impossible," Jaq said.

"Okay, maybe it is that hard. But it's math and physics, baby!" Donal backflipped toward his station at the back of the command deck. He missed it and kicked off the wall to fly past it once more. He caught the mid-rail and pulled himself into his seat. "I meant to do that."

Donal was an original, older than any member of the first-generation *Chrysalis* crew, a volunteer from New Septimus.

Thirty of them had come on board in their time of need after losses from the first battles and the departure of personnel allocated to the expeditionary resupply station. With *Cornucopia* and the ERS now attached to *Chrysalis*, they were back to a single crew.

The equalizer was the combat losses. Eight in the last battle. They nearly lost another four in the area behind the sealed bulkhead. Once it was resolved, there was no time to lament what could have been. They got back to work as if nothing had happened.

They had no other choice.

"Alby," Jaq called over the intercom. "Respond on a direct line."

Almost immediately, Alby replied, "I wondered how long it would be before priorities changed."

"Never at a loss for words, are you, Alby? E-mags are top priority, but we need the lateral spatial distortion sensor brought online. You've got a week."

"Holy Septiman's hairy balls, I thought you were going to ask for something hard. There's nothing wrong with the lateral array. We simply cut power to it to save what little energy we have available. I can turn it on with the flip of a switch but recommend we wait until we're at fifty percent reserves before we do, just in case it turns out to be a big drain."

"Stop goofing off, Alby, and get back to work."

"Yes, ma'am. Never a dull moment when you're elbow-deep in a bank of wires."

Jaq closed the channel. She called over her shoulder to the original, "You'll get your data, Donal, and then you need to do great things with it. Like you said, no pressure. Get your team in place and get to work."

The early morning came with a pre-dawn chill. Max roused the sleepers while those keeping watch stayed alert. He implored them to keep quiet as they awoke and ran through their morning ablutions.

They had made it through the first night, which gave Max both hope and despair.

He hoped that would give them time to find the western Borwyn and keep from getting into a firefight with friendlies. His despair was that the Borwyn had not yet contacted them. It was unrealistic for the good guys, flying in to save the planet, to expect those being rescued to welcome them with open arms.

They were going to be skeptical and wary. Max worried that the first meeting would start with someone getting hurt.

"Crip, what do you think about sending two-person teams out to find our fellow Borwyn? A soldier and his partner. The women look like they're local with their deer hide clothing. They could be what we need to get the western Borwyn to hesitate. Otherwise, it's going to be real hard to start a conversation. Walking with this mob, they'll think they're under attack."

"I was worried about the same thing, Max. This is a critical step in the evolution of the war to reclaim Septimus. We don't need it to be stillborn. They *have to* listen to us," Crip replied.

"They don't have to, unless we appear less threatening. I suggest we move another kilometer or two and then set up camp. Then we send out our teams to find our fellows."

"We couldn't be more aligned, Max. Your plan is my plan is our plan. I'll take point."

Crip moved to the front. He slung his pulse rifle so it hung tightly to his pack. He wanted to appear non-threatening. He counted on his body armor to protect him in case of friendly fire.

He hatcheted his arm down in the direction of travel and stepped off. The formation spread out, separating like they hadn't been able to the night before. Crip gave himself a good twenty meters in front of the others, looking back to gauge the distance, then added another ten. The others wouldn't be visible if he were to contact the Borwyn first.

He tensed, expecting to get hit by an arrow—like he'd seen his people get shot on Farslor. It made the steps difficult. He knew his boots were hammering the ground instead of stepping lightly, but he couldn't help it. His legs felt like tree trunks. His body was stiff, like he was dragging an extra body's worth of weight.

After an hour and a half, Crip raised his hand over his head and held it there. He had covered what he thought was two kilometers. If they were to continue, someone else would have to take point. He was exhausted.

He panted and gasped for air, finally dropping to a knee and twisting the pack off his back to let it land roughly on the ground. He stared at the ground while collecting his wits. When he looked up, it was straight into the barrel of a modern weapon, similar to his pulse rifle. The bearded figure was wearing a camouflaged material with colors of the woods.

Crip raised his hands. He studied the features of the newcomer.

"You're Borwyn, just like me," Crip said, still breathing heavily.

"You're not like me," the man replied in a hushed voice. "You and your people are surrounded. You know that you make a great deal of noise when you travel. We heard you from the mountains."

Crip laughed. "That's what the ladies keep telling us. We were born and raised in space. The women are from the eastern forest. Do your women outnumber your men?"

"What a stupid question. Maybe you should stop talking. You sound dumber with each word."

Crip stood, with his hands raised, so he could face the man properly.

"We're from *Chrysalis*, a ship that survived from the last space battle fifty years ago. Our parents saved the ship, but it came at a cost, their lives, and ours spent rebuilding the ship from the inside out. We've returned and engaged the Malibor fleet. We've destroyed nearly all their cruisers and most of their gunships. We are winning this war. The last phase is distracting the ground-based leadership for a final attack on the ships at the space station in orbit over Allarees."

"You use the old name. Malpace is what it's called now."

"And the city, Pridal. This is how we know it. Not the abomination of Malipride."

"Crip," Max called, walking up with his hands over his head. "We have company. It looks like you already know."

"Thank you for not shooting us," Crip told the man in front of him. "I'm Commander Crip Castle, deputy of the Borwyn cruiser *Chrysalis*. This is Sergeant Max Tremayne, leader of our combat team. We have a small army of people because our pilot and engineer are with us. They flew the stolen Malibor gunship on a plateau a few klicks behind us. But you already knew about our ship."

"How could we miss it? You people have been making

noise from the second you came over the mountains. And you haven't stopped!"

"Help us to understand," Crip pleaded. "We heard you're making war on the Malibor. We're here to help you. We want to take the fight into the city itself. We have a plan. We just need to be sure no one is shooting us in the back."

"How about you climb back into that ship of yours and leave." The Borwyn seemed less than amused by anything Crip had to say.

"Do you speak for all of your people?" Crip finally dropped his hands. "We're soldiers and we're going to fight the Malibor. It would be better if we coordinated our efforts. And once again, thank you for recognizing that we weren't your enemy."

"To me, it looks like you kidnapped a bunch of Borwyn females for your sordid pleasures."

Crip threw his head back and laughed. "Max, ask Deena to come up here, and Evelyn. They'll provide a good perspective."

Max nodded and walked slowly backward, keeping his hands over his head.

Evelyn appeared shortly but not Deena. It made Crip wonder if she looked Malibor enough that they had already separated her from the others.

"Tell the nice Borwyn soldier why you and the others from your village are with us, please." Crip kept his hands in front of him. His rifle remained slung over his shoulder. The Borwyn hadn't made him put it down.

Crip felt good about the meeting. They'd passed the first and hardest test—meeting them without it being a firefight.

"They were men and single," Evelyn said.

Crip and the Borwyn soldier waited for more, but Evelyn didn't expound. Crip laughed once more. "See? Clear as mud, eh?"

"Yes, we also birth more women than men," the Borwyn admitted.

"What's your name, soldier?" Crip asked and took a knee. He was still dogged from the hike, despite the rush of meeting the Borwyn. His body went from feeling heavy to extreme fatigue. "Don't mind me. I'm not used to Septimus standard gravity."

"Corporal Teneris. Gather your people. We need to go to a more secure area where you can meet Commander Owain, but that will be a day or two before he's free."

"We have our own food but could use water. We're mostly self-sufficient."

"I have a hard time believing that. Have I told you how much noise you idiots make?"

"The women move like a light breeze. They do the hunting and all the hard stuff. We just sit back and look at their butts."

Finally, the corporal cracked a smile. "They put up with that?"

"No. They'd punch us in the face if they caught us and figured out our sordid ways."

Evelyn snorted. "We killed four Malibor on the other side of the mountains," she said with more than a hint of pride. "Crip did. Blew them away with his pulse rifle. Three shots. Three dead Malibor."

"You said there were four."

"I crushed the skull of the fourth with the butt of my rifle." She made to pull it off her shoulder, but it wasn't there. "Your soldier took it from me."

Crip offered his hand. "Corporal, the battle is joined."

Tenaris smiled and took Crip's hand in a firm grip. "Victory is ours. Not sure about you guys, yet, but we'll let the commander determine your fate. Keep your ship warm, you're probably going home."

"We *are* home, Corporal."

CHAPTER 15

A war that never ends.

Borwyn Commander Glen Owain surveyed the land before his position. The Malibor infiltration team had not appeared.

That worried him.

Owain's company was the lead for the assault battalion. One battalion of five companies. That's all there was. Some militia worked haphazardly on the frontier, but they were little more than an annoyance to the Malibor infiltration teams.

"What did we hear from last night's patrols?"

"Three of four have returned," Deputy Commander Eleanor Todd replied.

The commander was instantly on alert. "Where was the missing patrol's route?"

"The farthest away. That's why we're not alarmed. Give them another hour to get back. But that begs the question, Commander, why are you concerned?" She sounded tired and almost pleading. The nights were long as winter approached, and the days were filled with activity. It was the time of the long year where little sleep happened.

It was her third passing as a soldier, and she was already too old for it. Halfway to the end. The passes where Septimus was closer to Farslor lasted a year, and three years where they were farther away. This was the end of the current pass, even though that no longer mattered since the Malibor were firmly entrenched on Septimus. They no longer had to cross space to get to the planet.

They were already there. The Borwyn were no longer defenders of the planet, but the insurrection force. Only the western Borwyn. They had great disdain for the Borwyn who lived east of the city and east of the mountains. They were no help in the war that had gone on for three generations.

Eleanor knew this would be her last. It was a job for the young. Commander Owain was the same age but seemed perpetually youthful. He was blessed with tight skin on his hands and arms. Smile wrinkles teased the corners of his eyes, while dark brown eyes missed nothing going on around him. He kept his hair short for convenience's sake. But most of all, he was possessed of a keen mind and magnetic charisma. Even if he were new, he'd be in charge, no matter his rank.

It was better that he had years of experience behind him to handle the rigors of this pass.

"Establish a recon in force, two platoons, same route as the patrol. Hurry," Glen said, concern creasing his forehead but only slightly.

"What do you know that I don't?" Eleanor wondered

while simultaneously gesturing at the officers waiting for the day's orders.

"A Malibor gunship was spotted coming over the mountains. Anything different has to be treated like it's the vanguard of an all-out attack."

"We have no information that they have an assault force deployed. Well, not beside one gunship."

"That's what you and I don't know. Send out the platoons. Recce the area and let's get an answer as to what happened to our patrol, and if they can't be found, then we have to assume the enemy is bringing a major force to bear, the first time in a long time. The battle is not yet joined, but it could be soon. Our troops are as ready as they'll ever be. The only thing left is that we choose the battlefield."

"To do that, we need to know where they are and with how many. I understand." The deputy commander nodded and closed with the officers to give them their orders. It took less than a minute before the chosen lieutenants in charge of third and fifth platoons hurried away.

Glen returned to watching the ground ahead of the headquarters shelter. It had been occupied the day prior. They'd stay there for a random number of days before moving on unless they knew their location had been compromised, and then they'd move right away.

The shelters littered the landscape, ready for occupation but without supplies. Those had to be hauled fresh each time because the Borwyn couldn't risk them falling into enemy hands. They moved into the forest with little and were forced to live off the land because the trees were too big. The massive forest wasn't a place for a major force to be resupplied. Living off the land was part of their standard procedure. It was also their major weakness and why the Malibor were hesitant to consolidate their forces.

A land army made them an easier target. They operated in no bigger than platoon-sized units. They were ready to consolidate if the enemy arrived in force. It was the Borwyn's greatest threat, but the Malibor didn't embrace completely eradicating the Borwyn from the forest. At least, they didn't have the military will to see it through.

The Borwyn would make it costly.

Because there was no way off Septimus for either side in this perpetual war. There were no ships to send the Malibor or the Borwyn home and no diplomatic vehicle to negotiate their return. With both sides claiming Septimus as their home, it was a fragile peace of limited aggression. Each did just enough to keep the other on their toes.

The two sides remained at loggerheads. All communication had been cut off three passes earlier when the Borwyn realized the Malibor weren't interested and had only used the negotiations for subterfuge. The western Borwyn refused to orchestrate their own demise.

"What do you expect the platoons to find?" the deputy commander asked.

"Nothing, as in, no sign of our patrol and no sign of the enemy, either."

The deputy shook her head. She would have come to neither conclusion. "I expect the patrol to appear and that they will have information on where the enemy is located."

The commander returned once again to looking through the opening in the field bunker. "Patience, Eleanor. We will know soon enough. What do you recommend for our course of action if your premise is true, and then, if my premise is true?"

"If we find the enemy, we close with and destroy them. If they have killed our patrol, then we revise our patrol plan to find them. Move the company forward to deny them access to this area."

He nodded slowly. "Have Second and Fourth Platoons move out. First Platoon will check in when they return. They've intercepted the crew of the gunship."

"But we don't know if anything happened to the recon patrol yet." Eleanor joined him at the window. "We should wait for First Platoon to return.'

"In either case, we can't stay here." The commander dropped his eyes to the ground beneath his feet. He pointed out the window without looking. "Because the enemy isn't here but out there."

"Search and destroy?" The deputy commander didn't see the value. "We've never had good luck with such missions. They melt into the background until they disappear in entirety."

"Makes you wonder if locals are helping them," Glen suggested.

"Are they? You know something, don't you?"

Commander Owain smiled sadly. He didn't reply. He clasped his hands behind his back but only for a few moments. "Pack up and move, that means us, too."

The logistics train was cumbersome. Keeping the company fed was no small feat. There were carts pulled by horses, but they were unloaded each time to limit the targets an enemy could strike. They didn't put their eggs in one basket except when they repositioned, and the platoons provided extended security for the movements.

They moved a lot. It was a well-practiced maneuver.

It didn't mean they liked it.

The deputy headed outside. Her hooch was on the other side of the encampment. The commander and deputy commander spent most of their time physically separated for increased survivability.

It was a hard-learned lesson from previous engagements.

The commander never unpacked completely. His was a two-minute effort to collect his gear, stuff it into his pack, and return to the headquarters shelter where he resumed watching the field before him and listening to the rustle of the troops preparing to leave. They snatched furtive glances at him.

In this, he always stood alone. Moving was a hassle for the troops and it always came without warning.

The only way to keep a secret was to tell no one.

Glen Owain never worried about information leaks because he kept key information to himself. He was the only commander who carried that concern. No one else believed a Borwyn could collaborate with a Malibor. Glen didn't believe it either, but he knew the Malibor had ears to hear and eyes to see. They would use that information against the Borwyn.

"Kava for the road?" a young recruit asked while holding out a tin cup.

The commander nodded and smiled close-lipped. He took the cup and sipped from it. The recruit hurried away to finish her part in the shelter pack-up. The kava jug needed cleaning out. He got the last of the liquid before the dregs were dumped into a hole in the ground. A quick rinse and the jug was stowed.

The radio crackled. "Contact."

Glen tipped his head to push his earbud against his shoulder. It helped drown out the background noise.

"Third Platoon contact. Five enemy infantry. Cornered at grid seven-four-one, three-six-nine. Small arms only."

"Roger," the commander replied. "Capture if possible, collect the intel."

The speaker repeated the order and signed off. The message had been delivered.

Third Platoon had found what they were looking for and joined the battle.

"Break, break," Glen transmitted. "Fifth Platoon in support. Reinforce Third Platoon's position while providing security."

In case Third Platoon had been drawn into a trap, Fifth Platoon would be ready to counterattack the ambush.

Deputy Commander Todd hurried into the nearly empty shelter, weaving through the troops carrying gear to the waiting carts. "Do you know where that grid is?" she asked.

"Yes." The location was well inside the route of the lost patrol and too close to the shelter. The enemy infiltration team had almost been on top of the headquarters. "They ambushed the patrol and backtracked them to find us, but they didn't escape our lines."

"If there's anything good that comes from this," the deputy replied. She looked into the distance in the direction of the grid reference. "But nothing good ever comes from losing troops. Six soldiers gone, just like that."

"The war has peaks and valleys. Our peak is a Malibor valley, but our valley..." He let the thought trail off. He pointed at the nearest cart. "Take the headquarters team to the next shelter. I want to go out there."

"By yourself? Are you high?" Eleanor moved to block the exit.

The commander raised his eyebrows. "I am quite possessed of all my faculties. This enemy recon team has been caught. If we can capture one or more of them, maybe we can learn a thing or two. I have to know why they are more active now. An infiltration force and a force on a gunship? What else is coming?"

"We'll capture them. You don't need to walk into an active combat zone by yourself."

"Sometimes, leaders need to do just that. Now is the time."

Eleanor put her hand out to stop him. "Glen, now is not that time."

He smiled and gently moved her hand. "I'm going, and then I'll come back in the company of Third and Fifth Platoons. I'll let them know I'm inbound when I get close, so I don't get offed by my own people."

"And that," Eleanor said. "You shouldn't go. They can meet up with you at the next shelter. It's barely a thirty-minute hike away."

The commander eased around his deputy. "Then I am barely thirty minutes away. Two grids only."

"Glen, please don't go."

"The decision is made."

"It's your decision. Unmake it," she argued. "The decision is *made*. You sound like a meathead."

Glen chuckled. He took a moment before turning serious. "There's only a certain amount of insubordination I'm willing to tolerate, Eleanor."

"I'd like to say I'm sorry, but it's my job to offer alternatives while advising you." She stepped back even though the commander was nearly out the door.

"And the decision is *made*. I'll stay in contact." He pointed to the radio clipped to his belt. "See? Full charge. Good for a week."

"You better reappear before the week's out." She jammed her fists into her hips and lifted her chin as she looked upon the commander. He glanced at her over his shoulder.

"As you were, Deputy." He strode away, heading for the nearest brush. In an instant, he disappeared. Barely a leaf moved as he passed through.

Glen Owain found the shadows from tree to tree, stepping toe to heel to keep from making a sound. He carried a pulse pistol, a weapon that fired a stunning charge. Two in rapid succession, the double-tap, would deliver death.

He knew the terrain well. He had no need to refer to a map. His life had been spent studying the ground outside the former Borwyn capital city. He was convinced the final battle for primacy would take place there.

Glen followed an elevation line along a hill rather than stay going straight, climbing and descending. He knew after he reached a steep decline, he'd cross the next saddle and follow the ravine downward. At the bottom was a narrow creek. He'd cross that, turn right, and keep going until he ran into his soldiers.

He keyed his microphone. "Third Platoon, Owain," he said using the brief comms procedure adopted by the battalion to limit the radio signature, keep the enemy from triangulating their positions.

"Third Platoon, go."

"I'm inbound, fifteen mikes. Don't shoot me." The commander's intent was crystal clear. "Status, question mark."

"The five are contained. We are closing in."

"Roger. Minimal casualties. I say again, minimal casualties."

"Message received. Third Platoon, out."

Glen transitioned into a distance-eating lope, casual, soundless, head on a swivel, and eyes constantly scanning the shadows.

He ran faster as he approached. Time was the enemy if he wanted any of the Malibor recon patrol to survive. Glen's soldiers would avenge their brothers. The enemy would be shown no mercy, despite their commander's orders. The only way for Owain to forestall the enemy's demise would be to personally oversee their capture.

The teams weren't undisciplined, only that they'd been conditioned to fight the enemy to the death. The Malibor could not be allowed a foothold in the forest.

"Commander Owain inbound," he shouted while running toward Third Platoon's position.

"Halt!" a voice boomed from the brush.

Owain pulled up short, raised his hands, and squinted into the shadows.

"Identify yourself."

"Commander Owain. You know who I am." Glen realized he still had his pistol in his hand.

"The commander is recognized. You are clear to enter Third Platoon lines."

A private stepped out from behind the bush and waved the commander through.

"Private Krasen will escort you to the front line," the guard stated.

The commander nodded. An even younger soldier appeared and gestured for the commander to follow.

He maneuvered through the undergrowth like an old pro. Movement to contact was something the commander trained his troops on extensively. Not being seen was an advantage his company had.

Why had the patrol been seen? He could only speculate that they had walked into an ambush or lost their focus because they were still close to the shelter. In either case, he'd lost six of his people to five of the enemy. The Borwyn could not trade casualties with the Malibor.

The private moved quickly with the commander right on his heels.

A single pulse shot caught Glen's breath in his chest. He didn't know why he had become obsessed with the potential of a Malibor captive.

"Cease fire," Owain ordered using his command voice. His escort slowed to dodge behind a tree, then another, before dropping to the ground and low-crawling to a rapidly dug fighting position.

The commander squeezed into the hole with the three soldiers already packed into it. "Thanks, Private," he told his escort before giving one hundred percent of his attention to the scene before them.

Another hole opposite, less than fifty paces away. A head popped up to look and was already going down before it was high enough to expose the Malibor's dark eyes and bearded face.

The commander angled his mouth over the small berm in front of the fighting position. "I am Commander Owain. Surrender and you won't be harmed. You have my word."

A haughty laugh answered him. "Believe a Bore-hog? I don't think so. We'll fight you, and we'll probably win because you lack the hanging eggs to get the job done."

The lieutenant next to Owain snarled. Glen chuckled before whispering, "Don't let them get to you, son. They're scared. They don't want to die, just like you and I don't want to die." Glen leaned toward the berm and shouted. "You make it easy not to like you."

"Why would I give a hoarfrost goat snuggle about whether you like me or not?"

Glen replied, "Although entertaining, I feel our chat is drawing to a close. Here's what we're going to do, and there isn't anything you can do to stop us. We're going to cover the area in smoke. If you try to shoot your way out, you'll be cut down. The survivors will be patched up enough to talk with us and then you'll be sent to the prison camp. If you stay in position, we'll fill your hole with grenades but special low-yield ones that shred flesh but don't dig deeply enough to kill. I never envisioned a use for such a terror weapon, but here we are, and you leave me no choice. Smoke will commence in five minutes. No need to respond. We'll hear your cries of pain soon enough. And you *will* cry out. No one dies in silence."

The lieutenant looked terrified. "Sir, I wasn't issued any of those grenades. We don't have them to deploy."

"No one has them. I was bluffing. Get your smoke ready. That part was real. We're going to cover the area and then we'll toss grenades in their direction. We'll move closer and toss some more. Don't come in straight. And tell your platoon not to fire unless the target is clear and right in front of them since we're in a circle. Friendly fire isn't friendly at all, Lieutenant."

The young officer looked confused. "They're in a bowl. We trapped them before they could gain the high ground. We have superior firing positions all around, but not clear lines of sight since they're within heavy brush."

"We can still see them when they raise their heads, at least from this side. Brush is their egress. Have your people send smoke grenades into the brush. That'll probably start a fire. We'll drop smoke on this side, just one can. It's important that we see them, and no one fires from this side unless I give the order."

"But if we're not going to fire while we maneuver, then how will we secure them?"

"Grenades. They'll cave as we get closer to blowing them up from within their own position."

"If a grenade goes into the hole with them, they'll probably all die," the lieutenant posited.

"Possibly, but they're fifty paces away. Have you ever seen anyone toss a grenade that far?"

The lieutenant furrowed his brow as he thought. "Not without a running start," he suggested.

"We'll shake the ground around them and give them pause. And then we'll maneuver along the left flank where the trees have heavier trunks. They are armed, and since they have nothing to lose, they are extremely dangerous."

"Roger." The lieutenant used his earbud and lapel microphone to issue the order to pop smoke in one minute and counting.

"You three, with me when I head out. Over there." He pointed to the left of their position. "Run like the wind across the open until you set up behind a tree. First grenade gets dropped once we're in position."

The commander took in the faces of the small team he'd taken over, including the lieutenant. They carried a determination borne of defending their planet from invaders but behind their set jaws was a fear of the unknowns of combat. Owain's company had fought a number of battles, but he'd been hit with mortar and missile strikes and bore the brunt of the battalion's recent casualties. Half his people were new.

Maybe that's why the patrol was lost. Inexperience had cost them. Nothing more. The Malibor face Glen had seen wasn't that of a young man. The enemy was a grizzled veteran. Where did the Malibor get such men? They usually sent younger troops into the woods on the penetration missions. They collected information at the cost of their lives, if they were spotted. Younger men ran faster.

It was something Owain would ponder at a later date or ask directly if he was able to wear this group down.

"Have your medics stand by," the commander urged the lieutenant. "I want them alive, and if they get wounded, we're going to treat them." He corrected himself. "They'll probably be wounded."

"Roger." The lieutenant made the call while the commander checked his watch. He popped out of the hole and immediately ducked back in. A Malibor pulse pistol barked and splattered dirt from the berm over the four soldiers behind it.

Clicks and pops signaled the arrival of the first five canisters. Two white and three black mixed to form a heavy gray cloud that drifted forward from the brush. The commander nodded and two soldiers with him sent their cans forward. They trailed a thin stream of smoke as they sailed through the air, no more than twenty paces in front of their position. The cans clanked on impact with the rocky ground, skipping and bouncing until they came to a rest.

The commander checked the area once more to verify if he could see through the screen before him.

No view at all after twenty-five paces.

He clambered to his feet and ran. The others followed him. He didn't bother to zigzag. The enemy couldn't see him. His greatest survival tool was speed. Glen slid to a stop behind the third tree, giving the first two to those behind him.

He estimated he was a solid thirty paces from the enemy position. "Hose 'em down. Let 'em know we're coming!" the commander shouted as much for the Malibor as for his soldiers. The enemy would know they moved but still couldn't see their targets. The Borwyn couldn't either, but that was to their benefit and part of their plan.

The lieutenant fired the first shot at where he thought the Malibor fighting position was. The other two sent pulse rounds in that direction.

It gave the commander time to back up and run, get a few extra paces on the range of his grenade. He let go with all he had, feeling a slight twinge in his throwing arm from having not warmed it up first.

The grenade sailed in the direction where the soldiers were firing. "Cease fire," he told them in a conversational tone.

They stopped hammering away with their pistols and ducked behind the tree, waiting for the grenade to explode.

"Get ready." The commander pointed in the direction he intended to move. The lieutenant nodded.

The grenade exploded but the sound was muffled, as if it had been contained.

He ran. The enemy's first howl of pain came after he had only managed two steps. They weren't far away, maybe twenty paces. Glen bounced from tree to tree as he worked toward the enemy's flank. They had to know that was where he was coming from. Glen made a finger gun and gestured toward the Malibor position. The lieutenant and other two soldiers took the order and began firing.

The commander moved another ten meters. He could hear moans and groans directly in front of him.

He drew a line across his throat and gestured as if he were keying a mic. He held his finger over his lips.

The lieutenant ducked behind a tree and faced away from the enemy. He nearly whispered, "Cease fire, cease fire. Friendlies heading in."

Glen counted down on his fingers. When he made a fist, he punched it in the direction they would go. Four abreast, they charged, pistols raised and ready to return fire.

The commander dove to the ground before stumbling into the hole that seemingly appeared out of nowhere. The lieutenant tried to stop but went headfirst into the Malibor's fighting position.

The lieutenant's pulse pistol barked rapidly.

"Cease fire!" the commander shouted and leaned over the pit with his pistol hovering, looking for a target.

The lieutenant held his hands up. Two soldiers eased over the edge of the hole, providing additional weapons cover.

"This battle is over," the commander declared. "Get the Malibor out of there. Injured first. Medic!"

Together, the four Borwyn moved the Malibor to the level ground above. The smoke continued to drift in and out with the lack of a breeze.

Five enemy. Three dead, but two very much alive. Glen Owain couldn't wait to talk with them.

CHAPTER 16

Beware the wrath of a patient soldier.

Crip followed Tenaris. They carried their pulse rifles, but the western Borwyn had relieved them of their power packs. They took the rifles and the arrows. That slowed down the combat team's captors as they were encumbered every bit as much as the combat team.

But there was no doubt the western Borwyn were in charge. They encircled the team from *Chrysalis* along with the women from the eastern forest. The mob moved with more noise than the captors were comfortable with, yielding many calls for quiet until Tenaris demanded they stop.

"What is wrong with your people?" the corporal whispered furiously.

"Zero-gee, makes you clumsy in gravity. We're doing our best. For what it's worth, we get enough grief from the women. We don't need it from you, too."

"Your women are right. We also see that they are fanatically loyal to you. How long have you been here?"

"We've known them for less than two weeks, and you're wondering how we've developed our relationships. We don't give them a hard time. Wives, girlfriends, sisters, and daughters. We treat them as family because they are."

"Family? You've known them for two weeks. You can lie to yourselves but not to me. I don't trust you, spacer, but I don't believe you're a Malibor, either, as opposed to the Malibor you have with you. She doesn't give us a great deal of confidence that you're not traitors to the blood. You showed up in a Malibor gunship."

"Don't hate me because I'm beautiful," Crip replied. "We'll earn your trust."

"The battle is joined, Commander. We only need to see which side you're on."

"Victory is ours. It'll be a Borwyn victory."

The group returned to hiking, maintaining a good pace. With each step, the combat team grew quieter. Crip had been right in that they were trying. Even Hammer and Anvil were getting better, but they received instant feedback from Ava and Mia, who rode them hard, excoriating them because they wanted them to live. The Yelchin boys had made a good impression with the two they referred to as their queens.

"We treat them well." Crip settled on the simplest answer. Not that their village had treated them poorly, but they wouldn't have the opportunity to save their planet from the Malibor if they'd stayed. Neither would they receive all the rewards that would come from the inevitable sacrifices.

Give them liberty or give them death.

It was the decision they'd made. All they had to do was keep their men and themselves alive.

"Maybe you have some redeeming features. I haven't seen them, though. I do believe in the love of a good woman." Tenaris looked around. "If you ever repeat that, I'll deny it. Now shut up and focus on moving without sounding like a mad horse trying to escape its nightmares."

"You have horses? I look forward to seeing one and finding a creature that's louder than us. That'll be something."

Tenaris shook his head.

They continued for another three hours without a break before moving into an area with a series of log-and-dirt bunkers that blended into the terrain.

"Damn. Something must have happened," Tenaris muttered. He pointed to narrow wheel tracks in the ground that disappeared the second they entered the heavy growth. "Moved to an alternate site."

Corporal Tenaris produced a radio with earbud and spoke softly. "First Platoon to Command. Check status."

"First Platoon. Alternate site Exterminor Seventeen."

They used nonsense words over the radio. Upon establishment of a site, they would immediately designate an alternate site—no name, only a vector and distance from the current site. "Thirty minutes to the alternate site," Tenaris stated. He led the way into the forest with Crip by his side.

They moved quickly along the path pioneered by the cart, even with the weeds and bushes hurrying to grow over the route.

"Our stuff grows quite well. That's why there won't be

any roads," Tenaris said, relaxed about making noise as he spoke openly.

"Are we safe now?" Crip asked.

"Safer, yes. We're in Borwyn territory. We move headquarters often to foil missile attacks."

"How often are there missile attacks?"

"Hasn't been one in years. So our movements work."

"You haven't tried spoofing the Malibor to get them to waste their missiles? Never mind. Did you know that in the past fifty years, the Malibor have fought five civil wars and now they're fighting the return of *Chrysalis*? We've killed six Malibor cruisers and something like twenty gunships. They have very little left that can fly. We're close, Tenaris, very close to them not being able to fight back. That's when we destroy the rest of their ability to make war. We finish them, and then put their people into the woods."

"We like the woods," Tenaris said. "Maybe we don't want to leave."

"Shouldn't that be your choice and not the Malibor's?" Crip pressed.

"I guess so. Like your choice not to stay on your ship?"

Crip nodded and smiled. It was a valid point. "*Chrysalis* is the only home I've ever known, all the while longing for something more. It was Septimus that my soul needed. We aren't real religious on board the ship, but we do have our shepherd and we thank Septiman. The eastern Borwyn seemed to eschew Septiman. I don't care either way. Maybe I'm a heathen, but a happy one. I wish Taurus could see this place."

"We never gave up on Septiman, and he didn't give up on

us. He gave us the means to fight back." Tenaris waved his pulse pistol. "I like yours better. Where'd you get it?"

"We built them ourselves, but with limited resources, we only have eleven of them. We used to have twelve, but I traded one to buy us time. Without the power pack, it's useless." Crip handed the weapon to Tenaris.

"You traded a pulse rifle with a Malibor?" He caressed the clean lines of the weapon while checking its weight and balance.

"On Farslor. The Malibor there were abandoned and are little more than cavemen. They've lost all their technology. They use bows and arrows, wear hides, and live in dirt huts."

"Farslor? You've been to the sixth planetary orbit?"

"Checking out a power source that remains hidden beneath the ruins of a once-major city. It's a wasteland. The Malibor bombed their own city," Crip explained.

It didn't take long to reach the first outpost.

"Halt!" a voiced called.

"Corporal Tenaris, First Platoon!"

"Advance and be recognized. Hold your weapons over your head," the voice ordered.

Tenaris put his arms up with the pistol in one hand and Crip's rifle in the other. He walked slowly forward until directed to stop.

"You are recognized. Welcome to the headquarters. Do you have Malibor prisoners?"

"No. They're Borwyn. We need to talk with the commander."

"He's not here. You'll have to speak with Deputy Commander Todd."

Tenaris nodded. "No sudden moves, people. Follow me and don't stray," he barked as if the group hadn't already traveled tightly together for hours.

"Put on a show for your people," Crip whispered. "I get it. We're not the big bad Malibor, but until you can guarantee that, you have to make it look good. We're not going to attack our fellow Borwyn. We're not Malibor who think civil war is an answer."

Tenaris nodded but remained tight-lipped.

Eleanor Todd met the group outside the main bunker. "Our guests who flew in a Malibor gunship?" she asked.

"Commander Crip Castle." Crip thrust his hand forward.

She looked at it for a moment before taking it and shaking with a firm grip. "What were you doing in a Malibor ship?"

"Using it to infiltrate Malibor defenses. If your people check it, you'll find that it has a Borwyn power source. We recovered the ship out of cold storage in orbit around Farslor."

"Why should I believe you?"

Crip pointed to himself and the rest of the large party. "Because we're Borwyn. You can see that."

"They have one Malibor with them," Tenaris offered.

"Half-Malibor. Her mother was captured in the east some twenty years ago. We captured her when we boarded the wreckage of a destroyed Malibor cruiser." Crip didn't go into the lengthy explanation about the ship being a captured Borwyn cruiser.

"Deena, Max, Danny Johns, Tram, Kelvis, and Evelyn,

could you join us, please?" Crip called over his shoulder, never taking his eyes from Eleanor. "Kelvis and Danny Johns are both originals, born here before the war. Danny Johns fought on Septimus against the Malibor before getting evacuated."

"That would make him over seventy years old. No one lives that long," Eleanor countered.

"New Septimus, a place they escaped to, helped prolong their lives. The survivors who saved *Chrysalis*, the Borwyn flagship, have all passed. We are their children. Although it's taken fifty years, we've come home."

Eleanor stepped back at the revelation that she had not been prepared for.

"There were survivors, and you continue to fight back, just like us?"

"Wait until you hear about what we've done to their fleet," Crip offered. "We almost have space supremacy. Every time they've sortied against us, they've lost their ships. They hide now, last I saw before landing on Septimus. We've killed more than half their cruisers and gunships. They're learning what it's like to be afraid."

"I'd say they're afraid to come out here, but they aren't. They send infiltration teams to test us. We have to be ready. We can never let our guard down, and that's why we secured you."

"You had to suspect since you sent one platoon to deal with a unit the same size as you," Crip countered. The ones he called joined him, fanning out to face the lieutenant commander.

"If they couldn't have handled you, they would have

called for reinforcements. We have five companies out here ready to fight."

"Should you be telling me that, since we're not on the good guys list yet?" Crip gestured to Deena. "Tell her your story."

When Deena finished, Danny Johns stepped up.

"I was here before you were a gleam in your daddy's eye. I was born here, and I plan to die here. Stop doofing around and get us something to eat. Then we're going to need five pulse rifles, but pistols will do. We will need water and as much explosives as you can spare."

"Is that all you need, Mr. Johns?"

"Private Danny Johns, Alpha Company, Fourth Rifle Battalion, Borwyn Defense Legion." He stood ramrod straight, military style, with his hands at his sides.

"Private Johns, you're correct. We are remiss. You can help us set up the mess bunker. We haven't been here long enough to get everything squared away."

"My name is Evelyn," the middle-aged woman interrupted. "We came with these men because we believe in their mission to free all of us from Malibor oppression, reclaim our planet."

"That's it?" Tenaris asked. "It's not because they were the only available men?"

"That is offensive," Evelyn scolded. "I'm not saying it's not true, but it's still offensive."

Crip covered his mouth and coughed.

"I was born on the station, like Brad Yelchin, but I was alive when the Malibor attacked. It's time to deliver our vengeance," Kelvis added.

Eleanor clapped Crip on the shoulder but looked at Tenaris. "What do you think?"

"I think these guys need a lot of help before they can be considered a Borwyn combat unit, but I bet the commander would love hearing he's been plussed up by a whole platoon." Tenaris winked at Crip. "We knew you weren't Malibor from the first second we saw you. We wanted to see you squirm, but you didn't."

"Thanks for that. Can I have my pulse rifle back? I feel naked without it, and the power packs too, please."

"In due time, Commander," Tenaris replied. "That's Commander Owain's call. I'll take you to the mess bunker. I could use something to eat, too."

"Thanks, you guys," Crip told the small group that said their piece. "Rally everyone and dump our gear outside the mess bunker."

"I want my arrows," Evelyn demanded. "You know what we went through to make those?"

Eleanor Todd nodded. "Give them their arrows, but keep the power packs. For now. Crip Castle, how about you tell me your story?"

"We have comm gear to talk with our spaceship, via an intermediary. What do you want me to tell them about the situation here on the ground?"

"That is a completely different story," Eleanor replied.

CHAPTER 17

When it's time to fight, fight like your life depends on it.

Jaq left the bridge as soon as the others were gone. She went to Medical first, where she found Doc Teller.

He checked her pupils, flashing his penlight across her eyeballs. He checked the glands under her jaw.

"Are you stalling?" Jaq wondered.

"How can you tell?" He stopped his unnecessary prodding. "It would be best if you took another day, but if you have to get back to work, I don't think your relapse would be today or tomorrow. It might bite you ten years from now. Is one day worth the cost to your life?"

"Seeing as we're twelve days from a fight we are ill-prepared for, the answer is a resounding 'yes.' The cost is worth it. I don't have to tell you what happens if we lose this fight."

Teller shook his head. "I know. You're cleared for full duty, Captain. Give 'em hell."

"I'm grabbing my tools and getting to work," she promised. Jaq spun out of the medical lab and raced down the corridor. The next stop was the mess deck.

She found Chef clipped to an upper rail and hovering over the kitchen while a small group of crew members enjoyed Malibor rations.

"If I didn't know better, I'd say you were smoking cigarettes like we see in those old-time vids. The down-and-out chef making her way through the tangled morass of life." Jaq helped herself to a Malibor entrée and hydroponics microgreens.

"With all the Malibor rations, I don't have much to do. I'm happy that you reinstated the rotation through the mess deck so we get the bags recycled, but again, with the Malibor stuff, we have far more bags than we can use, so we've been cleaning them and sending them to *Cornucopia* for long-term storage."

"Good idea, Chef. We might as well enjoy the Malibor rations now. I assume you're stockpiling our stuff."

"Filling every nook and cranny with them. We'll be set for a long, long time."

Jaq smiled. "That is the best news I've received. Even though we could use the hydroponics team elsewhere, because we have to live for today, but we also have to plan for tomorrow. Once *Cornucopia* is detached, how long before it comes back?"

"Two days," Chef declared.

"I like your confidence." Jaq held a bag with her fingers while popping a thumb out to show her approval.

"Two days is how long it'll take your body to process

those Malibor rations if you don't drink enough water. Make sure you hydrate."

Jaq shook her head. "Thanks for slapping me back to the reality of right now." The captain hurried through eating, taking a seat by herself so she could think. She strapped herself down and plowed through her lunch in less than three minutes. Jaq returned the bags to the scullery and snagged a water pouch on her way out. She saluted Chef with it as she left.

Her third stop of the day was engineering. Jaq's mind was clear, and her body was free of aches. It was the best she'd felt in a long time. She wondered if she ever got as much rest as she needed. Maybe her brain was bruised, but her body was well rested for the first time in as long as she could remember.

Jaq flew down the central shaft, waving at others when she passed. She said a few kind words, too. Everyone had been working tirelessly, and she appreciated their efforts.

She made it to the engineering section without fanfare and flew inside. She activated her boots and thumped to the deck. The engines were currently idling, not producing the miniscule power they were building. Heavy cabling trailed from the housing, through the space, and into the power generation space.

Jaq took three slow steps, staying clear of the floating cable on her way to look at the damaged power plants, not that they'd changed since the last time she saw them.

A scream froze her in her tracks. The woman's voice rose until it cut off with a gurgle.

Jaq released her boots as she pushed off, racing to where the scream had come from.

Inside, Jaq found a scene from her worst nightmare. Blood floated in small spheres. A male crew member drifted toward the overhead, his face a mess and streaming blood.

Teo clutched at her stomach, where more blood forced its way past her fingers and into the air.

A crew member with wild eyes held a spanner in one hand and a fire axe in the other.

"Explain yourself!" Jaq roared, reattaching her boots to the deck.

He menaced her by shaking his spanner. "They're Malibor!" he shouted. "And I'm not sure about you, either." He waved the spanner at Jaq, tightening his grip on the axe while holding it over his head, ready to bring down on his next target.

"Then you might as well kill me, because if I'm Malibor, we're doomed. Let go of the axe, Milford. We need to tend to Teo and, who is that, DaRenn?" Jaq took a small step forward, then another.

The man shook, whether in frustration or anger, Jaq couldn't tell. He threw the spanner, but it was from his off-hand and flew wide of Jaq. He pulled a small knife from his coveralls.

"Don't take another step," he warned.

"We need to tend to our people, and you. We're all Borwyn, but even if we weren't, we still wouldn't treat our people like this. Hand over the knife and the axe, please." Jaq took one more step.

"NO!" he shrieked. In a motion too quick to follow, he drew the knife across his own throat.

Blood shot from the wound in a stream that arrowed off

the far bulkhead. With each rapid beat of his heart, more blood shot across the space. Jaq vaulted toward Milford, hoping to stem the wound, but he was already drifting after quickly losing consciousness.

"Get Doc Teller down here," Jaq called over her shoulder while pressing on Milford's throat. The heartbeat was already gone. "What happened to you?" Jaq pleaded with the corpse.

She pushed him away and turned to survey the space. DaRenn looked to be in worse shape. At least Teo was conscious.

Jaq swam for the top of the power plant to kick off toward the crew member floating overhead. When she reached him, he was already growing cold. The axe damage to his skull had been lethal.

She pushed him toward Milford. She was both furious and crushed. The enemy wasn't inside their ship. They were coming, twelve days away. Fighting themselves accomplished nothing, but then again, he hadn't been fighting *them*.

He'd been fighting demons inside his own mind, and he'd lost.

Jaq joined the two helping Teo. She was pale and sweating but awake.

"Not your fault, Teo. Doc Teller will fix you up. We'll take it from here. Your job is to get better. Get that beautiful mind of yours back up to full speed."

"That's gonna leave a scar," Teo muttered.

"No more naked shower pictures, then?" Jaq quipped.

"More? I thought I put that part of my life behind me," Teo managed. "Thanks, Jaq."

Jaq shook her head so hard that Teo winced from the vibrations. "Nothing to thank me for. Ship's beat up and so is the crew. All we can do is our best. Some days, that's better than others. The rest of the time, it might not be so good, but it's still the best we can do."

Doc Teller bounced off the hatch frame on his way in. He caught the mid-rail and stopped. "Get everyone out of there." He waved the survivors toward the engine room.

The two crew and Jaq brought Teo out. Once in the engine room, Doc Teller tried to close the hatch behind them, but the cables prevented it.

"Why?" Jaq asked.

"Being in a bloodbath like that isn't good for anyone's mental health. I'll find someone to clean up the area because I know you need to get back to work on the power plants."

Jaq blew out a breath while staring at the deck. "Thanks, Doc. That was hard to see." She looked up. "What are you seeing of the crew's mental health? Milford just snapped, but no one goes that quickly. There had to be signs that we missed." She hung her head and looked at the deck. "Signs that I missed."

"Hang on," the doc replied while cutting Teo's jumpsuit open. He checked the wound. "Deep, but nothing inside is hurt. Skin, abdominal muscles, but the organs are intact. Hold pressure here." He showed the crew where to press and turned his attention back to the captain. "You weren't released to duty until thirty minutes ago. You absolutely and positively are in no way responsible for this man's breakdown."

"I'm responsible for everything that happens on this

ship," Jaq replied. "You take care of Teo. I'll take care of the power plants. They are my personal number-one priority."

"Maybe they shouldn't be," Brad offered from the hatchway as he hurried across the engine room to check on his daughter. He'd only been one deck down, working on the landers. He might have heard Teo's scream from that close.

"Get her to Medical. I'll stitch her up there and give fluids," Doc Teller told Brad.

With the help of the two crew who continued to apply pressure to the wound, the four left Jaq by herself in the engineering space, where she was left with the vivid memory of what had just happened as well as the mountain of work that they couldn't possibly finish before the Malibor cruiser arrived.

Was that what Brad had meant? Since there was no way to get the power plants online before the battle, they needed to concentrate on other items they could finish. Bulkheads and structure that would help them survive more Malibor railgun impacts.

Her mood darkened with the revelation.

She tapped the call button on the comm unit on the bulkhead. "Amie, give me ship-wide, please." Two clicks confirmed that the intercom was open. "This is the captain. All primary engineering personnel are to secure what they're doing and report to engineering. Thank you."

She didn't care if they were on or off shift. She needed to adjust priorities. With a simple question, Brad had shined the light on a problem that was manifesting through too much work that wouldn't bear fruit.

It took two minutes before the first engineer filtered in.

Jaq greeted him and the others as they arrived. There were a dozen members of the primary engineering team. Jaq was happy to see Vantraub arrive.

Once they were all accounted for, Jaq talked with them.

"I need your help, and I'm not talking about doing the impossible of getting the power plants operational in less than two weeks." Jaq collected her thoughts.

Vantraub interrupted. "What happened to Teo? Most of us passed her in the shaft."

"Milford snapped and attacked her and DaRenn with an axe."

"I didn't see..." Vantraub groaned instead of finishing her statement.

"The bodies are in there." Jaq waved toward the power plant space. "There's also a lot of blood that needs to be cleaned up. I'll take care of that myself, but what I need your help with is priorities. If we stopped working on the power plants and committed our resources to other issues around the ship, what could we finish that best prepares us for the upcoming battle with the Malibor cruiser?"

Vantraub couldn't take her eyes from the hatch, jammed open because of the cabling. "I'll help you, Captain. I'm not afraid of the sight of blood."

"Thank you. We'll get to it when we get to it. Until then, priorities. We need to make sure we have the best chance to survive the battle. Every time we survive, we get to fight another day. And if we survive, that means another Malibor has joined the stardust in an ever-expanding universe. May Septiman grant us the strength to win this fight and survive once again."

"Emergency bulkheads and power distribution panels. So many systems are fried," an older engineer offered.

"Priority. Emergency bulkheads or power distribution. What is number one?"

"Power distribution. Need that before we can fix the problems with the emergency bulkheads. If you want ship survivability, then it's the process of isolating sections of the ship that will keep us alive."

"E-mag targeting," Alby offered. Jaq hadn't seen him enter the engineering section. She thought he was still outside the ship. "We're repairing the systems, but the port side is shot without major work. Starboard, ventral, and dorsal systems will be one hundred percent in a day or two, but the targeting is questionable. If we're to hit what we aim at, we need to take the time to align the systems. That means test firing."

"How many people do you have helping you?" Jaq wasn't sure if Alby was suggesting a different priority.

"Enough that I can move four to power distribution," Alby offered. "We were going after everything, with DC teams fixing whatever they could in their areas. It was so much that it was overwhelming, but we've knocked down a lot of little issues. Your focus is right. Now is the time to pick an entire system and bring it back online, then the next, until we're ready to fight. Twelve days, Jaq." He nodded brusquely. "We'll be ready."

CHAPTER 18

If we're the good guys, we need to act like it, even when we don't feel it.

"Patient is stabilized." The medic wiped his hands on the Malibor's uniform before stepping back.

Commander Glen Owain scowled. "Take it easy."

"They killed six of our people." The medic busied himself with putting his equipment away.

"They did, but they are in our care now, even as prisoners. Don't descend to their level. If we're the good guys, we need to act like it, even when we don't feel it."

The medic nodded tersely before walking away.

Two of the Malibor insertion team had died when the grenade exploded inside their fighting position, the place they chose for their last stand. One more died shortly thereafter, leaving two survivors. Both were badly injured but would survive.

Glen wanted to interrogate the two Malibor before turning them over to battalion.

"Can you speak?"

The prisoner groaned before grumbling, "Do you think I'm an illiterate Borwyn?"

Glen chuckled. "You make it easy not to like you. Illiteracy is related to the written word, but I'm being pedantic. What were your orders?"

"Nothing. We were on vacation and then you came along."

"This is a dangerous place to take a vacation. Pridal not have enough distractions for you?"

"Malipride is what the city is called, Borwyn. Maybe there's fun to be had in hunting the subhumans known as Borwyn," the Malibor replied.

Glen chuckled again. The enemy's attempt to get under his skin was falling flat. "That's a distorted view of fun, but I expect no less from the likes of you. Are you broken somewhere we didn't treat, beside your brain, that is?"

"Why did you save me?"

"I have questions," the commander replied.

"I'm not going to answer them."

"If your answers can help us arrive at peace, why wouldn't you?" Glen took the man's face into his hands. "We didn't let you die because we aren't that way. I don't feel compelled to kill every Malibor I run across."

"But three of my people are dead, if I heard correctly." He winced before exhaling with a ragged gasp.

"And six of mine are. This isn't a contest. I want to know what you were looking for."

The Malibor closed his eyes. "The enemy. You, so we could better determine how to kill you and your people. It seems that you have spaceships and are attacking our fleet. We are going to make you pay. I make no apology."

"I need no apology." Glen stood and stepped away from the Malibor soldier. "I've spent my adult life in military service. Thanks to people like you, I've had a job. Turns out, I'm pretty good at it, too. Still, I think we can do better, our two peoples. Malibor came to Septimus and took our city away from us, but why? The forest is pretty nice, so we kept you from here, but then again, here you are. I'm glad Borwyn are attacking your fleet. Still not sure why. Septimus is a big planet without a lot of people. I bet we could both live here if we wanted. By the way, who determined that we needed to fight?"

"You," came the snotty reply. The soldier grimaced with spasms of pain that flowed through his body. "Let me sleep."

"It wasn't me. You're not giving me a good impression of the Malibor. Despite your ability to travel in space, you come across as less than intelligent. You'd think with as much pain as you're in, you'd be more forthcoming."

"Torture!" the soldier gasped. "That's all you Borwyn know."

"Medic," Glen called. The man didn't want to come back until the commander stood and straightened his uniform. The look on Glen's face quashed the rebellious attitude. "Give this man pain medication. A mid-level dose. I want him to be able to talk."

The medic was ill at ease helping the Malibor soldier, but Commander Owain had given him no choice. He stood with his arms crossed and loomed until the soldier complied. It made the commander angry but then again, maybe he could use the friction to his advantage.

With a flood of chemicals pumped into his arm, the Malibor soldier's relief was visibly instantaneous.

The commander fixed the medic with a cold, hard gaze before stabbing his thumb over his shoulder. The medic was more than happy to hurry away.

"Not everyone likes my decision to keep you alive."

"Who cares if a Borwyn is happy?" The acerbic edge was gone from his voice, but his confrontational side remained.

"What makes you happy?" the commander pressed, leaning close to catch slurred words.

"Killing Borwyn." He chuckled faintly while his eyes rolled back in his head.

Glen gently shook him until he reopened his eyes. "But why?"

"Because they're the enemy. Stole our home world. It's warm here. Have you ever been to Fristen? So cold."

The man's beard seemed to make it obvious that he came from the extreme cold, like those who lived in the polar regions of Septimus. That accounted for his age. He was new to Septimus. They'd brought soldiers from the Malibor's original home world of Fristen. Glen had been under the impression they'd abandoned that planet long ago.

"We didn't steal your home world. I don't know that a Borwyn has ever stepped foot on Fristen. From what I understand, we've always been here on Septimus. This is the Borwyn home, and Fristen is the Malibor home. I think you might just be angry people embracing a lie so you can be angry."

"You make it hard to like you," the prisoner said, repeating Glen's words as his eyes fluttered.

"We'll talk again and soon." Glen patted his arm. The man's breathing slowed and became steady. "Stretcher, please."

The medic was nowhere to be seen, but the deployable stretcher was in the platoon's kit. A private rolled it out, happy to be free from carrying it on his back.

"Where's the lieutenant?" Commander Owain expected the private to know the answer, but the young man looked frantically about as if the officer would magically appear. "It's okay to say, 'I don't know.'"

The private looked relieved but then saw the disappointment in Owain's face. "Sorry, sir," he mumbled.

"You carry the front end. I'll take the back, as soon as I return from talking with the L.T." Glen motioned for the private to stay with the prisoner.

The enemy who stole their planet, Glen thought. How could they be so angry over a lie? Was it a lie? How many eons had passed if it were true?

None of it made any sense. If someone told Glen that he was living on a stolen planet, he wouldn't take it personally enough to go on a suicide mission to kill Malibor. What was the prisoner not saying? There had to be something else.

"Where's the lieutenant?" the commander asked the first corporal he came across. The young woman pointed toward a small gaggle of soldiers.

They all looked young to him. Most were new, including the lieutenant. This was their first pass.

The commander eased up to the confab and listened while the lieutenant explained his plan to move the platoon to the new headquarters location. He pointed repeatedly at a map in his hand. At the end, he asked if there were any questions.

The grizzled platoon sergeant, a three-pass veteran like Commander Owain, pointed to a valley that led to a series of hills. "What I hear you saying, L.T., is that we head up that valley until we reach the new headquarters?"

The group looked over the lieutenant's shoulder toward the route and nodded. They broke up and headed for their squads.

"Sergeant," Glen said, motioning for him to stay. "I'll need you to take charge of our two prisoners and make sure they get to the head shed alive. Keep the medic with you."

The sergeant nodded to confirm receipt of his new orders and left.

"Next time, Lieutenant Maple, just have the sergeant manage the tactical move. Don't get quagmired in the details when you have bigger things to worry about, like my prisoners."

"Sorry, sir." The lieutenant looked more put out than apologetic. "I'll do better next time."

"Are you saying that because you think I want to hear it?" The commander raised a hand to forestall what would have been a nonsensical answer. "Listen to the sergeant. He knows things you don't, and he has to worry about things you shouldn't be worrying about. You need to trust him and then build your own credibility."

The lieutenant lifted his chin before he deflated. "I don't think heading up that valley is the best way to go. Opens us up to ambush from two sides."

The commander smiled. "Ask the sergeant what his recommendation is for moving the platoon. If you disagree, then tell him why. This isn't hard when you look at it as a group effort where you have all the responsibility and will shoulder the blame if anyone in your platoon gets it wrong."

"That sounds like I need to keep a tight hold on it."

"That's exactly how it's supposed to feel, but that's exactly why you shouldn't. I know that doesn't make any sense, but I'm the one you have to answer to. I'm not going to flay you alive for trusting your platoon sergeant. Work with him, and you'll find carrying the burden isn't so bad."

The lights blinked but didn't completely light up behind the lieutenant's eyes. The seed had been planted. The commander didn't have time for more.

He strode away before the lieutenant could extend the conversation. It was a learning moment. There would be many. No need to belabor it. Glen returned to the prisoners to find the medic hovering. He pulled a rag over one of their faces and shook his head.

"Don't lose my last prisoner, Doc."

"He was hurt too bad. Nothing I could do with that one."

The commander stared at the medic until he looked away. "I said, don't lose my last prisoner. I don't care if you have to give him your blood or you have to do a naked rain dance. He has answers to my questions but only if he's alive. Do you get me?"

"Sir, he's the..." The medic didn't finish his statement.

"And we're the good guys, Doc. Keep him alive so we can get some information out of him. We can make a world of difference from him, if you get what I mean." The commander exaggerated his nod.

The medic smiled. "I'll keep him alive for you, sir."

The commander had nothing in mind with his statement, but sometimes the best explanation was ambiguity. Let the listener fill in the void with their preconceptions.

He made to pick up the back of the stretcher. "What are you doing?" the medic asked. The private watched indifferently. He was on the front of the stretcher regardless of who was on the back.

"My patient. My job. You make sure we don't get shot." The medic put his kit by the patient's head. He took the handles and nodded to the private. Together, they lifted the prisoner.

"Thanks, Doc. You, too, Private." Commander Glen Owain took a moment to smell the air while the squad tossed the freshly deceased into the Malibor fighting hole. Half the squad was filling it in. A field grave. They'd mark it and add an electronic tag to it.

Glen closed his eyes and listened. Soldiers going about their duties. Entrenching tools tearing at the dirt tamped down as a berm. Hushed voices airing grievances.

If they aren't complaining, they aren't happy. Owain took it as a good sign. When he opened his eyes, he found the lieutenant standing by himself holding his map.

The commander suggested he put it away by motioning toward his cargo pocket. Maples tucked the map away, pumped his fist in the air, and headed into the brush.

The platoon sergeant rolled by. "Moving out," he said before maneuvering next to the commander. "What do you think, sir?"

"I think Third Platoon fought the good fight and didn't lose anyone."

"Every day we don't lose a soldier is a good day."

"First Platoon lost six last night, but we caught and eliminated the enemy patrol. We celebrate the lives of those lost by winning the fight in their honor."

The platoon sergeant walked in silence, head always moving as he watched the soldiers fill the lanes, weapons faced outboard, eyes roaming.

"Did he have anything good to say?" the sergeant asked.

"Said we stole their planet. You ever hear that the Malibor were native to Septimus?"

"That's crazy talk. Brainwashed morons. Who else would let themselves get dumped into the forest with no hope of recovery or survival? We didn't find a long-range radio on them."

"I can't believe anyone would hate that strongly to come here in the first place. We'd talk with them if they offered, wouldn't we?" the commander wondered.

"Above my paygrade, Commander."

"Thanks, Smitty. We've been at this a while, haven't we?"

"Not sure I could do anything else," the sergeant replied. "This is a pretty sweet deal. Hiking and camping, shooting guns, and getting paid for it."

The sergeant tipped his hat before moving off to correct a pair of soldiers on the left flank.

Pay. They were able to eat without having to do any of the growing, hunting, or gathering. The Borwyn stopped using money fifty years earlier, but the adage remained.

The enemy. Glen Owain had fought them his whole adult life, and his only justification had been that they tried to kill him first. He would keep fighting them as long as they remained his enemy, but he wanted to know why.

CHAPTER 19

Not prisoners, but not free. Not an enviable balance.

Crip woke refreshed. The combat team hadn't had to put out a watch the previous night. They were under the protection of First Company, Borwyn Assault Battalion. He strolled out of the bunker they'd declared as the barracks for the newcomers.

The local women were curled up against their soldiers. Fantasia looked like a child sleeping between Danzig and Danny Johns, her adopted grandfathers.

Max stirred, instantly alert. He noticed Crip standing. He started to get up, which roused Deena. They both stood and joined Crip heading outside.

A guard stood at their doorway.

Crip greeted him. "A fine morning to be a soldier. Are you keeping people out or in?"

"Do I need to keep your people in?" the private replied.

"I don't think so."

"The lieutenant commander didn't want you bothered since your group looked tired, but if you're awake now, I'll be on my way."

"We've got it from here on out. Thank you. Commander Todd was correct. We needed the sleep. We've been running on fumes for a little too long."

The private saluted and hurried into the next bunker over. The mess bunker was the other way. The slit trenches were the first order of business, followed by something to drink.

When they reached the mess bunker, they found a robust serving line with a dark liquid they called coffee. It resembled chernore, which was produced to resemble coffee, but they'd never had the pleasure of the real thing. Even with the Malibor rations, no coffee had been discovered. It was like they refused to export it off-planet.

But there it was, in all its glory in a bunker made of dirt and logs.

"Smells funny, kind of nasty," Max said.

"I don't like it," Deena said.

"You've had real coffee?"

"Of course. How backward do you think I am?"

"My wife! Keeping secrets from me that could affect the very core of our relationship."

Deena gave him the side-eye and bumped him with her shoulder. Both Max and Crip took a cup.

"Are we supposed to like coffee?"

Crip looked at it and sniffed it. They got out of line after getting dirty looks from those behind them for holding up progress.

Max took the first sip. "It's like drinking dirt with reactor coolant added for flavoring." He took a second, bigger drink. "I like it."

Crip sipped it, making a face afterward. "I'd like to rinse my mouth out now."

"It's an acquired taste," Eleanor suggested, sidling up next to them. "I trust you slept well."

"Under your kind security, we did. Thank you for that. Is the commander back yet?"

"Inbound. We'll meet with him this afternoon. They've eliminated the infiltration team and have taken one of the enemy prisoner, but he's injured. We'll assess him when he gets here and refer him for advanced medical care if warranted."

Crip scanned the area. "What does your advanced care consist of? I haven't seen anything that's not the most rudimentary, which also begs the question of where you get your weapons."

"There's a secret bunker in the mountains where we have it all—power, resources, equipment, and more importantly, people."

Crip grinned. "Borwyn are survivors. We've found pockets of survivors across the Armanor system. It's refreshing. I don't want to know where the bunker is, only that we can get what we need to draw the Malibor into a battle they can't win."

"We haven't been that bold. We're only doing our best to keep the Malibor out of the forest and away from the mountains. If we do that, the Borwyn survive."

"I look forward to mapping our way ahead. We have the

gunship and enough fuel for a quick trip to the spaceport. If we can refuel, we can destroy the Malibor's ability to make big moves against us, whether in space or on the ground. We keep hitting them when they're down. I bet their people will be open to negotiation once we remove their ability to make war."

"I'm sure the commander will be happy to discuss this with you." She took a sip of her coffee, smiling as it flowed over her tongue. "You sound like him. Most of us are happy killing Malibor who come into the forest, but he wants to talk with them, as you'll see with the survivor that he's bringing back. A survivor who will see our defenses and our people."

"Do you have a prisoner of war camp?"

"No. We don't keep prisoners. Our engagements are usually lethal."

Crip looked to Max and Deena. "Our engagements are in space and usually end with one of the ships losing power and venting atmosphere, if they weren't blown away completely."

"That's what I like to hear." Eleanor gestured toward the coffee jug. "More?"

She helped herself without waiting. Crip and Max took another cup while Deena settled for plain water. Eleanor led them through the food line to get pancakes, vegetables, and fried ground meat.

Deena drew skeptical looks from the Borwyn soldiers. She didn't shrink from their withering gazes. "I'm just like you," she told one of them.

Eleanor climbed onto a chair and yelled for attention. The bunker quieted almost instantly. "These are Borwyn who have been killing our enemies in space as well as on

Septimus. Welcome them as long-lost friends. Yes, Deena is half-Malibor, but she's not responsible for how she was born, only how she acts. She's on our side and if anyone has a problem with her, you'll answer to me personally."

She sat on the chair where she'd just been standing. "Sometimes, they're faster getting the word. That'll help calm the masses, but keep in mind, we're on edge because we lost six of our own yesterday in an ambush by a Malibor infiltration team."

"We'll tread lightly, but we're here to take the fight to the Malibor. I hope your people can get behind that. We'll fly our gunship right down their throats and serve up a nice serving of Septiman's fury."

"Are you believers?"

"I used to be indifferent until we met the Malibor the first time in orbit around Farslor. After a few close calls and a lot of death, belief helped me keep moving forward."

Eleanor replied, "You don't strike me as someone who lacks confidence." She leaned sideways to glance behind Crip. "Where's your *partner*?"

Emphasis on the word partner because the combat team had partnered with the women from the eastern Borwyn village. "Mine is on *Chrysalis*. Her name is Taurus, and I miss her, but I have high hopes that she'll join me on Septimus to enjoy what is paradise to us."

Eleanor looked around the mess bunker. "Paradise. Being on a clean starship and dancing among the stars is what I'd call paradise."

"The grass is always greener," Max said. "We like it here.

We'd like it a lot more if we could walk around without fear of being shot."

"Everyone wants that, but it's not to be had." Eleanor took a big bite and chewed quickly.

"Not yet," Crip promised.

The vanguard of Third Platoon moved into the area and spread out, creating a cordon through which the medic brought the prisoner on a stretcher. Commander Glen Owain and Lieutenant Maples walked in behind them.

The prisoner was unconscious, and Glen was worried that he would lose him.

"Get him into surgery. He's got internal bleeding somewhere and we have to find it," the medic stated. The small group rushed to a smaller bunker next to the main headquarters.

Glen watched them go. "Save his life, please," he urged one last time.

Eleanor Todd approached him with Crip, Max, and Deena in tow. "They didn't want to die, they shouldn't have killed our people."

Glen gave her a quick glance but no more attention than that. His eyes fell on Crip first, then Max, but they spent the longest studying Deena. She held Max's hand tightly and leaned against him.

"When do Borwyn take Malibor wives?" Glen asked, but it wasn't accusatory. The tone was curious.

"When they are half-Malibor and we find them freezing to death in space," Max replied.

"Max and Crip saved my life, and they gave me a new and better one," Deena claimed.

"Commander Crip Castle." Crip held out his hand.

The two men shook warmly.

"Glen Owain, at your service. We have a lot to talk about."

Eleanor led the way to the headquarters bunker where the communications equipment was set up and operating. A field-expedient radar system scanned the skies looking for inbound aircraft or missiles.

"Talking about at your service, we have our combat team with their partners plus a flight crew for our Malibor gunship. We pack a lot of punch."

"It seems so." Glen studied the slung weapons over Max's and Crip's shoulders. "Pulse rifles?"

"Borwyn design. Manufactured on board *Chrysalis*, former flagship of the Borwyn fleet."

Glen turned to Eleanor. "Do you think our people could reverse engineer these? I bet they hit a lot harder than our pistols."

"We'd love to show you how they work. We have obdurium projectiles for them and power packs that we can recharge using a solar collector."

Glen nodded. "We have those, too. Call it Borwyn ingenuity."

Crip leaned his elbows on the table, clasped his hands, and focused one hundred percent of his attention on Commander

Owain. "We're here to create a distraction for *Chrysalis* to exploit, a two-pronged attack, you might say. We defeat their forces in the sky and we defeat them on the ground."

"You were going to do that with a dozen people?"

"That was our initial plan, and we've doubled our numbers. We're not facing them head-to-head. Deena's been in the city. We'll infiltrate and sabotage their warmaking industry. And we'll also do it through brute force with the gunship. We're here to hurt the Malibor and create the conditions where they have to sue for peace. The time of Malibor rule on Septimus has come to an end."

"I like how you think. Let's put our heads together and see if there's a way we can help each other. Minimize our losses and maximize theirs. But infiltrate Pridal? That's a big ask, Crip."

CHAPTER 20

If they don't expect it, it's an ambush. If they expect it but can do nothing about it? That's when they run screaming.

Training. Training. Training.

It went both ways. The women taught the battalion personnel how to fabricate and use bows. All of them were subjected to hours upon hours of fire and maneuver, hand and arm signals, and moving silently.

The women, wearing their deer hide clothing and not looking military in the least, moved even more quietly than the western Borwyn. The bows created a silent and lethal distance weapon.

The soldiers were intrigued by the possibilities.

The combat team got better with each movement—even Hammer and Anvil, who were arguably the least dexterous of the bunch.

Crip and Max could have had their egos bruised at how the western Borwyn treated them, but they'd never been exposed to any training that they didn't have to devise themselves and never on a planet in a forest with experienced professionals guiding and watching their movements.

Danny Johns was quickest to adapt, but his age limited his abilities. Even though he wore his age well, the physical demands were for those more youthful.

"Maybe we can move Danny into an administrative role. He's the oldest soldier here, by a wide margin," Glen told Crip. The two commanders worked side by side in each of the training evolutions.

Crip saw that as a positive. Respect for the rank and experience, even if it wasn't experience in ground combat operations.

"Let's ask him." Crip waved Danny Johns over.

The old soldier jogged up, saluted, and tried to stand at ease, but he was huffing and puffing hard enough that he ended up putting his hands on his knees.

Crip waited for him to straighten before talking. "Would you like a more administrative role?"

"What do you mean by that?" Danny's eyebrows scrunched downward in a rare expression of anger.

"I don't want you to die while we're moving to an objective. You've fought the good fight, Danny Johns. This training is kicking *my* butt and I'm half your age."

"Sir," Danny started formally, "there's nowhere I'd rather be than giving it back to the Malibor on the front lines of this fight. I won't hold anyone up. If my body gives out, you have my permission to leave me behind. Let my carcass rot while you win the war. I'd rather die of a heart attack on a free

Septimus than watch the battle from afar *hoping* that we win the fight."

"That's what I expected you to say. You're on the combat team and not going anywhere else." Crip knew what the answer would be but wanted Glen to hear it for himself. "He won't hold us up. If he gets a crack at the Malibor, I don't think you'll see a soldier who's more composed."

"I don't doubt that. Make him your logistics liaison to make sure your team is supplied. Our people can be a little bit stodgy, but no one will deny an old man his flask of water. I'd like to give your women pulse pistols to supplement their bows. If we close with the enemy, volume of fire comes in handy."

Crip faced him. "What happened to one shot, one kill?"

"Even on the best days, the pistols aren't accurate past fifty meters. We don't have pulse rifles."

"Maybe you should. Eleanor said you might be able to reverse engineer and build them. I might be able to get you the plans. I think we still use the same base software, so you should be able to read the drawings."

"There's a limit to how much we can ratchet up production, depending on the base metals and higher level of technology. It takes a full day to produce one pulse pistol."

"Then we better start. We contact the ship in a couple hours. We have a lot to tell them."

"I'm curious to see how your equipment works. Burst transmission to Farslor?"

"To a scout ship, using stealth technology well outside orbit of Septimus. They transfer to a second ship in the dead space between the fifth and sixth orbits, who then relays the transmission to the far side of Farslor where *Chrysalis* is located. They'll send a burst transmission in reply."

"We've never thought about long-range communication because we never knew there was someone to talk to. Why are you telling me the location of *Chrysalis*? If one of us is captured, we'll end up telling the Malibor."

"I haven't told you key details, and I don't expect you to get captured. All our people know the details because we came here together. The women, not so much. They don't get the astrogation references since that wasn't part of their education."

"Ours either, but we do know the planets in the Armanor system and the orbits and the fact that our system was constructed and not natural."

Crip had heard the same suppositions because of the two planets in a single orbit with twenty-four planets in the orbital plane. It wasn't a naturally occurring arrangement. "I don't think about it too much. We'll credit Septiman and call it good."

There was no reason to waste time talking about something that didn't affect anything they were doing.

"I agree. I look forward to hearing good news from *Chrysalis*."

———

"Nine days, Brad," Jaq said softly. "We haven't completed what we needed to move forward. They're still working on the power distribution systems. Even with cleaning out *Cornucopia's* supplies, we don't have enough new parts to replace the damaged and blown circuitry."

"We can probably find more on *Butterfly*," Brad offered. The remnants of *Chrysalis's* twin ship floated two days' worth of easy travel away from Farslor.

Jaq activated the intercom. "Alby, are you available to talk?"

After a couple minutes and a second call, the light showed an inbound direct communication. "Jaq."

"Alby here. What do you need?"

"Are there any power relays, transformers, or junctions left on *Butterfly* that we could scavenge?"

"I've been thinking the same thing, but last I saw, we'd taken most of the good stuff. If there are parts remaining, they will be hard to get to and will need to be rebuilt or reworked in some way to make them usable."

"That's what I was worried about. We don't have enough time to get there, pull parts, get back, fix them, and then install them." Jaq dropped her head. She was tired again, but her head didn't hurt. She kept her wits about her, which wasn't the best since she was acutely aware of everything that needed to be done but wouldn't be completed before the Malibor arrived.

"Is that all you needed?" Alby asked.

"That's it. Break's over, back on your head."

"That joke has never been funny, Jaq, but I appreciate the consideration. Back into the flames of my existence."

A gentle scrape sounded the arrival of a crew member to the command deck. Brad beamed when he saw who it was.

Teo pulled herself toward him using the mid-rail.

"Should you be up?" Brad asked.

"Doc says I'm okay as long as I don't do anything too physical. I thought I'd go for a walk."

"And you came here to see your old man. I'm honored."

Teo smiled. "I came to talk with Jaq, but it was a bonus to see you. I thought you'd be elbow-deep in a crawlspace trying to will the ship back together."

"I'm taking a break," Brad replied. "It's good to see you up and about."

"Milford! I'm still in shock. We were working together, and I never knew that he was standing on the precipice ready to dive headlong into the abyss. I'm mortified thinking about who else is on the edge."

"We're working our way through them, talking with those who were there, getting them time off, and by time off, I mean working on the mess deck. Nothing makes people happier than getting something to eat. Even with all the work to do, we've installed a screen in there so people can watch videos. It's low power consumption, so the cost is minimal and well worth it. We want people to leave refreshed."

"I wondered why so many people were in there." Teo looked at the captain. She didn't believe Jaq would have approved the screen because it took people away from work.

Jaq read Teo's expression. "It was a good idea. Morale is something I pushed back into the recess of my mind. We were focused on the singular goal of engaging the Malibor and destroying them. Once it turned into a series of running gunfights, damage, loss, repair, and then fight again, it has worn us down. Even though the end should be in sight, we're not seeing it. All we see is that we're hiding behind a planet waiting for the Malibor to take their next shot at us."

"The people will rise to the occasion," Teo said. "They aren't ready to curl up and die, not yet. Milford was angry. His eyes burned with his fury toward the Malibor. He wanted to lash out and was being prevented by mundane tasks. We need to beat the Malibor. In this next battle, we need that ship to be an expanding cloud of fragments, and we need to show that on all screens throughout the ship, no matter what else is happening. Give the crew their vengeance."

"Vengeance gets you killed." Jaq slowly shook her head.

"Not your vengeance, theirs. You'll fight the battle with a cool, calculated mind, as will all of your department chiefs. Perception can become reality for the crew. We will fight our best, but we want to give the finger to the Malibor for forcing us into this lifestyle."

Jaq chewed on the inside of her cheek while looking at Brad.

"Chip off the old block," he offered.

"And with each victory, we get one step closer to our goal of returning to Septimus. The combat team is loving the planet, and I doubt we'll ever get them back on board the ship."

"I don't blame them. Ship life is hard." Teo waved. "Thanks for listening."

Jaq gestured for her to return. "We should hear from the combat team at any moment. You might as well listen to what they have to say. Did you hear that Hammer and Anvil have girlfriends?" Jaq was killing time while watching the clock. Gossip about family relationships held no interest for her, but

Teo needed to not worry about the ship. A distraction would help.

"Larson, are we ready?" Crip asked for the third time.

Larson rolled his eyes for the third time. "I'll tell you when it's ready. Please stop asking." He fiddled with the controls, double-checked the wiring, and then turned it on, but it didn't power up.

"You wouldn't have to have a spare power supply, would you?" Larson asked.

"We might." Glen waved a private over and directed him to pick up a piece of equipment designated BA-5590. "We lost the Malibor prisoner. He was hurt worse than I thought."

The silence was heavy and abrasive while they waited. They collectively held their breaths as Larson tried to adapt the new battery for the connectors on the long-range communication unit.

"Patience, people," Larson said and started humming. It didn't take long.

He hit the switch and the unit came to life.

Crip wanted to grumble, but they were on Septimus. It was a beautiful day, and they were going to speak with their ship that was some seventy-five million kilometers away, accounting for the orbital differences since Farslor was heading toward the lull.

Crip recorded his message. "*Chrysalis*, this is the ground combat team. We have made contact with the western Borwyn and are integrating with their assault battalion. They have modern weapons and we're developing a plan for infiltration and exploitation. Gunship has enough fuel to get to the resupply site at the spaceport. We will attempt to refuel, then destroy the spaceport along with any weapon systems we can find. Unit intact. No losses, no injuries. Request current enemy fleet OOB and design drawings for pulse rifles. Best to my lovely Taurus. Danzig passes his greetings to Camilla."

"Compressing and sending," Larson confirmed. "Now, we wait."

"Let me tell you a story about Larson," Crip said.

"How about no?" Larson blurted.

"We were stuck on Farslor because the oxygen recharge sealed itself from the heat and didn't open. We thought we were refilling the tank, but we weren't. We almost stranded ourselves, but we fixed it in time, in the blowing cold of Farslor. Don't go there on leave, if you have half a brain. Anyway, Larson produces a full memory chip of videos and rigs the screen inside the lander to play them. So, we watched vids while we waited. Unlike now."

"The story was going so well, too." Larson shook his head.

Glen replied, "Soldiers have an ingenuity that is second to none. They can take a terrible situation and make it tolerable, maybe even enjoyable, in ways that civilians can't relate. Good job, Larson. Thanks for getting the comm unit online."

They nodded to each other, ending with all of them staring at the radio unit.

"It could take a while," Larson told them.

CHAPTER 21

Without the dark, we'd never see the stars.

"Message coming through," Amie reported. She decompressed it and hit 'play.'

After listening to Crip's message, *Starbound* added their own message. *Cruiser is accompanied by one gunship.*

Jaq formulated her answer. "For delivery to combat team: Two cruisers and ten gunships remaining, as far as we know. The space station is hollow, and they have hidden ships inside the spindle. One cruiser and one gunship are inbound to our position in nine days. We have minimal engine power, limited E-mags, but have options to engage. Next comm: ten days. Keep fighting the good fight. The battle is joined. Pulse rifle plans pending. Standby." Jaq signaled for Amie to send the message.

"Transmitted," she confirmed.

"Can you dig out the plans for the pulse rifles?"

"I don't know where to even start looking. I haven't been on board very long and don't understand your filing system."

Jaq nodded and dove into her seat to bring up her computer screen. She dug through the files and found what she was looking for. The file was larger than she liked, but Crip had asked for it. He was on the ground ready to strike at the heart of the Malibor's government. She wanted him to have what he needed.

"He's with the western Borwyn. What kind of numbers do they have? What is their capability? He didn't tell us much besides they have modern weapons. I do like the gunship idea, although it's beyond bold. High risk, but high reward."

Jaq sighed. "There's a gunship with the cruiser."

"I heard that. I'm not ignoring it, just thinking through our options. We have to hit the cruiser with less than a full barrage because we'll need to allocate a battery to the gunship. At least one battery."

"If the cruiser survives the first barrage, we're going to have real problems, Brad."

Brad faced the main screen. Too many red lights. Too little time to change it. "Disconnect *Cornucopia* in five days?"

"And send them away. We can't let that ship fall into Malibor hands. It's still chocked full of stuff we can use. We've never had anything like it, and I'm growing used to it. Uncomfortably so."

"We're taking advantage of it to the fullest, Jaq. We'll onload as much of the rations as will fit on *Chrysalis* before *Cornucopia* bails."

The two watched the screen knowing that nothing was

going to change. The only good news on the board was the energy gauge. It was green with sixty-eight percent. They could maneuver and they could fire, but they'd lose energy quickly and wouldn't be able to recover it.

"We better get Donal and Dolly up here working on the calculations for our E-mag skip shots."

"I think we can do better than burning off the projectile momentum by shooting them through two different gravity wells. I think we can go a different route, but we'll still need Donal and Dolly. I think a more aggressive approach is called for."

"We're going to have to take risks. Are they worth it? They will be as long as we survive."

Jaq listened raptly as Brad settled in to describe a different plan.

The combat team sat in a tight circle inside the mess bunker, which doubled as a meeting space. Tram, Kelvis, Ava, and Mia hung about the outside row. Crip raised his hands for silence and stepped aside.

Glen Owain moved into the open space and surveyed the crowd. Eleanor stood by the door. "We like what we see from you. You are the most motivated new additions we've ever had. But then again, you know what this war is about and the cost of failure. We can say that we've been fighting it longer, but no one is fighting it like you. I salute you, spacers."

He backed up his words with a crisp salute. Crip returned it on behalf of the entire combat team.

"Thanks for the kind words, Glen. We can't take action until after *Chrysalis* has engaged the Malibor cruiser. We'll learn about that engagement in ten days."

"What if something happens to *Chrysalis*?" Glen asked in a low voice.

"Then we won't hear anything, and we'll be on our own, where we'll continue to fight the Malibor with every tool at our disposal." Crip's reply was quick without waffling or lamentations. "This is a war and people die."

Max clapped. "It's the hard truth, people. We'll fight whether *Chrysalis* is with us or not. It won't be easy, but what about our lives has been?"

Faces hardened by challenges looked back at him.

"Crip Castle and Max Tremayne, the dark clouds of a bright day," Glen quipped. "Have a little faith in your people. From what you said, the Malibor have already sortied their best ships against *Chrysalis*. What makes you think this cruiser is anything other than a tub barely able to maintain course and speed, let alone deliver withering fire?"

"You have a point," Crip conceded. "Sometimes, we're left alone with our own thoughts for too long. I miss Taurus. I miss Jaq Hunter's wisdom and insight. I miss zero-gee. Gravity, day in, day out? I think I've lost quite a few centimeters in height."

"We all have," Max said.

"I haven't," Danny Johns said with a laugh. He had spent the last fifty years on New Septimus. It was only recently that he and the other originals were re-introduced to zero-gee.

"Except you old people." Crip pointed at Danny and Kelvis.

Tram raised his hand. "I'd like to go back and check out the gunship. See if the Malibor have violated it."

"Although it is in our plan, I don't think we can go there, not yet anyway," Glen said. "We don't want to tip our hand or expose a small force to an unnecessary ambush. Can you bring it closer to the mountains?"

"Only enough fuel to get it to the spaceport, unless you can get us more, but it is highly toxic and corrosive. I doubt you manufacture it at an indoor facility," Tram explained. "No. If we fly it, it's a one-way trip. The only way to fly back is if we refuel wherever we take it."

"The answer is *not yet*. We'll dispatch the team when we're sure we have a plan. As of right now, I'm not sure what that plan looks like. We talked about infiltration, but how? We look different from Malibor."

Deena stood. "Not all of us, and only one has been in the city before. I'll go alone."

"Hang on," Max blurted. "We never talked about you going alone."

"You knew it was inevitable. I'll find a way to get a small team through the gates or under the wall or something. There has to be other ways into the city. I'll find one and let you know. If I can't, then let the sabotage fall to me. I can do what needs to be done."

Max's hand started to shake. He looked at the offending appendage as if it, too, had abandoned him. "But you're my wife."

She raised an eyebrow at him. "So? We have a job to do and I'm the only one with a reasonable chance of success. It's for all Borwyn. It's for the peace that has eluded us for fifty years."

The group watched the two look lovingly at each other, which made Crip miss Taurus even more.

"Deena's right," Crip said. "One person won't be noticed. One person will be able to get in where a group can't. Deena will be able to do what our entire team couldn't. But she needs a radio that they won't be able to find."

Glen replied, "That's something we'll have to work on. It'll probably require a trip to the mountain. We can't take everyone, because our people in the mountain would lose their minds, but we can take a couple of you. Have any of you ever ridden a horse?"

Crip took Glen by the shoulders and shook him. "Space, the final frontier... We'd never even seen a horse before you showed up, let alone ride one. Then again, Danny?"

"Fifty years ago, we had powered vehicles. I never saw a horse before we met the good people of the western Borwyn." Danny Johns tossed his hands up in surrender.

Kelvis shrugged and shook his head.

"There it is, unanimous. We don't have a clue."

"I'll try it," Hammer offered. "Me and Ava can ride together."

"I need someone with more of an engineering mind," Crip said.

"I'm not doing it," Kelvis replied.

"You're ship's crew. You and Tram aren't in the running. What about you, Larson? You should love seeing an advanced society."

Sophia gripped his arm hard in a way that wasn't obvious if she was for or against the trip.

Larson shook his head. "I'll go if there is no one else."

Sophia let go of his arm and inched away from him.

"No need," Crip said, hoping to calm things on the home front. "I'll go and I'll take Fantasia. If anyone can learn to ride a horse quickly, it'll be her. Max, you hold down the fort while I'm gone. Keep training and think kind thoughts about my backside. I've heard stories."

Max recoiled. "I'll do no such thing. I refuse to think about your backside in any context."

"You're thinking now, aren't you?" Crip joked. He clapped his hands. "In the interim, think about ways to disrupt the Malibor on Septimus. How can we impact their command and control, keep them from getting information to their troops in the field? As we've seen, the Borwyn native to Septimus are better operating in the woods than the Malibor from the city. Whether they've imported more warriors from Fristen remains to be seen, but I expect we've seen all we're going to see from that effort. We will remove the forest as a viable Malibor operating area."

"Area denial is a sound military strategy. One might never know you people grew up on a spaceship." Glen gave Crip a thumbs-up. "You might as well leave right now. Eleanor will take you. Just do what she says. She's supremely competent in woodcraft. She'll keep you out of trouble."

"We'll do our best to not be trouble." Crip crooked a finger at Fantasia. "Grab your trash. We're leaving."

Max and Crip gripped each other's forearms and slapped shoulders. "Stay safe, my friend."

"Always," Crip replied. Eleanor gestured for them to join her. "Were you ready for a trip to the mountain?"

"It was inevitable. Yes. We planned for two of your group to travel to the mountain today. We have three horses ready. Thank you for not picking the big man. He's too shmoopy with his woman."

"What does that mean? Affectionate? Loving? Happy?"

"It means distracted." Eleanor looked down her nose at Crip, who only chuckled.

"That won't be us. No distractions here. Eyes on the forest. Butt in the saddle."

"You'll pay for that last part if you haven't ridden before. You'll get bumped a lot. Grab an extra blanket from stores." She leaned around to look at Crip's backside. "Better make it two."

CHAPTER 22

End each day thankful for the day you had.

"This is the most horrific torture in the entirety of the Armanor system. I've not seen anything worse, or even heard of anything more calamitous."

The horse continued trotting and with each bump, Crip winced and whimpered.

Fantasia giggled while Eleanor shook her head. "Spacers are babies," she said over her shoulder.

Eleanor urged her mare to greater speed.

"Oh, Septiman grant my aching body peace!"

"Would you stop crying? We'll be there in a few more hours."

"Hours are like days. Pain shows that we are still alive, so I get to feel alive for another week, maybe two." Crip looked to Fantasia. "Why aren't you feeling it?"

"Because I'm not sitting. My thighs hurt a little, but that's it. Also, I'm not a hundred kilos."

Crip winced anew.

He sucked air in through his teeth and it whistled when he forced it back out. He gritted his teeth, puffing out his cheeks with each breath.

"How long before we make the return trip?" Crip asked.

"Maybe a day, maybe three," Eleanor replied. "You shouldn't worry about it. Everyone's first time is a bad experience."

"You don't learn to ride growing up?" Crip wondered.

"No. We only learn after we join the military, and then only if we need to ride. Most never get the pleasure."

"*Pleasure*, she says." Crip stood in the stirrups to lessen the impacts. He wasn't sure if he could do it for a few more hours, but he was going to try.

"What do you do growing up inside a mountain?"

"Probably the same as growing up inside a spaceship. Not much of anything fun. Once outside, I never wanted to go back in except to get some Freneche stew every now and then. Otherwise, I like it out here."

Crip did, too. He thanked Septiman every day for being allowed to stand on the planet named in His honor. In the big scheme of life, his saddle sores were a minor inconvenience. He'd get over it.

But there was a certain manliness about complaining about it to his female companions. He felt liberated and started to laugh.

"You didn't eat any of those mushrooms around our camp last night, did you?"

"No." Crip continued to chuckle. "It's facing my own mortality through the seat of the saddle. Nothing more. Help me look less overwhelmed when we get inside, if you would be so kind. What am I going to see?"

"The entire world inside a massive cavern and then numerous levels down. It's probably very much like a spaceship once you get out of the main cavern. We grow food, raise livestock, mine, and more. It's the entire world in a microcosm, out of sight of the Malibor."

"We do the same thing, except for the mining, but that's on asteroids and planetoids. The rest of it happens aboard *Chrysalis*. I'm sure the city under the mountain will look enormous in comparison."

"Probably. We have some fifty thousand people in New Pridal. That's right, we named it that after we heard the Malibor renamed our lovely city to Malipride."

"I don't blame you. I'll think of it as your version of *Chrysalis* but on a grander scale. You said fifty thousand? We thought we were doing okay by reaching two hundred and fifty survivors. Our lives were pretty hard."

"We can't say that. We worked hard, but I can't imagine what you did, living in such close proximity to every other person."

"We believed we were the only Borwyn who survived the Malibor attack fifty years ago. Imagine our surprise finding survivors on New Septimus, and then here. So many Borwyn survived. It's refreshing."

"You mean you undertook a war against the Malibor with your ship thinking that you were the only survivors? Talk about an all-or-nothing gamble. You put it all on the line. That took a huge amount of confidence."

"Jaq Hunter is hard to deny, and you know what? She

was right. We've whittled the enemy fleet down to a fraction of what it was. We're winning. All except that last battle, but we'll recover and be ready for the next. Jaq will make it so. She'll beat them."

Eleanor nodded subtly. "That's a lot of confidence in your captain."

Crip shrugged. He didn't have anything else to say. He trusted the captain to win the fight. He'd seen her win when she had no right to, against overwhelming odds.

"Sometimes, you just have to trust people," Crip finally admitted. "Like when we met Tenaris and he brought us to your company."

"The battle is joined, eh, Crip?"

"Victory is ours, Eleanor. I can feel it in my soul."

Crip was ecstatic to climb down from the horse and hand its reins to a waiting Borwyn. They walked past guards hidden in the underbrush. Eleanor waved to them, and they saluted back.

They continued to a massive door set into a cave mouth with two guards out front and two more inside, watching through a narrow window.

Upon command, they opened the door.

The security was impressive, exactly like how *Chrysalis* kept the enemy at arm's reach or beyond. There were three more heavily armored doors before they crossed the threshold into the cavern.

A fantastic city greeted them, with more people than

Crip had ever seen in one place before, and this was the Borwyn going about their everyday duties.

This day was nothing special to them.

"Why are you walking funny?" Fantasia whispered.

"If anyone asks, I'm telling them you're my daughter and not allowed out of my sight because you're such a troublemaker."

"Who would believe that?"

"You ever seen a grown man lie his way out of a problem? That. It'll be that. How about we take in the sights and you not give me grief over that damn horse."

"He had a name," Fantasia pressed. "Gildenhaal. If you showed him how much you loved him, he would have treated you better."

"But I didn't love him," Crip replied.

"I know, and so did he." Some of the locals waved. Fantasia and Eleanor waved back while Crip nodded to them.

"Follow me." Eleanor led them through a growing group of people who lined a walkway to watch the newcomers. Most didn't wave, choosing to watch in silence. Fantasia waved at them all the same. She remained nonplussed by the attention.

"Have you ever seen so many?"

"Not even close," Crip admitted.

They flowed into a building with a door made of wood. Crip stared at it until he caressed it. It was shaped, yet the grain said it was natural. "How did you make this?"

"Woodworkers made that. We can only use deadfall,

though, since cutting down trees might highlight us in a way we don't want," Eleanor replied.

Three elderly people were waiting for them in a room arranged for such meetings. The three sat on a short dais behind a table above an open area where visitors were to stand. Eleanor led the group front and center of the ancient individuals hunched above them.

Their hair was white and faces cracked with advanced age.

"Originals," Crip said softly.

"You know that we still exist," one of them croaked. "That is good."

"We have a couple with us. Danny Johns served in the Borwyn military before being evacuated fifty years ago. Kelvis was on the space station during the Malibor attack." He had the good sense not to say that the originals he knew looked half the age of those at the table.

"We bring the plans for pulse rifles, like Commander Crip Castle is carrying," Eleanor said by way of introduction. "And this is Fantasia of the eastern Borwyn, having joined the star soldiers."

In the conversations at the camp, no one had ever referred to them as the star soldiers, only spacers. Maybe one was derogatory. Crip didn't worry about it. They designated them as foreigners, outsiders even. Crip and the combat team did not know the ways of the western Borwyn, but they were learning.

"Call me Crip." He would have approached and shaken their hands, but they made no effort to welcome such a move. Eleanor stayed where she was. Crip decided it was best to follow her lead. He only had one chance to make a good first impression. "I bring news from the stars."

"Which is?"

"The Malibor fleet has almost been annihilated. They have two cruisers and ten gunships remaining. *Chrysalis*, flagship of the Borwyn fleet, will engage one of the last two cruisers in a week's time. We almost have complete space dominance. The Borwyn have returned to reclaim the space above Septimus."

"Where were you these past fifty years while we fought the enemy by ourselves?" an old woman demanded, shaking a skeletal fist in Crip's direction.

"Rebuilding a ship nearly destroyed. Our parents died young from the exposure, but not before passing their knowledge and determination to their children."

"Then where did the elders come from?"

"We discovered them conducting reconnaissance from New Septimus, a colony they established inside the moon orbiting Sairvor. That information is not to be shared, by the way. You deserve to know as we're asking for your help."

"How so?" a third ancient voice asked.

"We need to distract the Malibor fleet headquarters to allow *Chrysalis* to deliver a decisive blow. We're going to infiltrate one of our members into the city to identify targets and give us the information we need to exploit them. A member of our team is half-Malibor. She grew up in the city and then joined the Malibor fleet. We rescued her from an enemy ship that we defeated. She has been an integral member of our crew ever since."

The originals looked at each other. The one in the center banged a gavel. They rose and tottered away.

Once they were gone, Crip turned to Eleanor. "We accomplished nothing."

"That's not true. Those three are the council of elders. The real work happens out here. But they've been made aware of what's going on. It makes them feel included, especially as they age beyond reason."

"I've never seen a really old person who looked that old."

"I won't pass on your observations," Eleanor promised with a smile and light laugh. "I should have warned you. Let's talk with the city managers."

Crip made eye contact with Fantasia.

She shrugged. She never understood political machinations or their purpose.

Eleanor strolled down a hallway with a polished stone floor and walls made from a pressed particle board that gave it a sandy beach appearance. They turned into the first office, where they found a much younger crowd.

Crip breathed a sigh of relief. He wanted to take care of business with people who were aware and ready to work with the combat team. Crip wanted pulse rifles for the new members of his team and a commitment that if western Borwyn wouldn't help, they could at least stay out of the way.

"Magnus Fredricksson, at your service," a voice boomed. The oversized individual it belonged to walked forward to lean on a counter. "You're the star soldiers, come home to make war on the Malibor. We've been doing it, but we're stale. I think we're losing our edge. It'll be nice to have fresh blood."

"You have a problem with Glen Owain's company?"

"Relax, Eleanor. We know who you are." The man laughed heartily, his voice like thunder within the confined space.

"We have plans. We need an asset commitment order to start building pulse rifles."

"Hold your horses, hot stuff." Magnus held out his hand for the information. Eleanor dropped a chip card into the big palm. He returned to a computer and loaded the files. "Simple but effective. What kind of dart velocity do you get?"

"Eleventy billion kilometers per microsecond. If we don't dial things back, we create black holes that suck in the entirety of existence," Crip deadpanned.

"Do that, not the other stuff," Magnus replied. "Let me talk this over with the fabrication engineers. We'll see what we can do, Easy E. You rest that pretty head of yours and we'll do the hard work."

"You can pack that big head of yours right up your ass." Eleanor showed him the back of her hand, which he found vastly amusing. "We're done here."

Crip wasn't finished. He had questions. "When will you have the pulse rifles manufactured? We could make do with nine but an even dozen would work better. Tomorrow good? We need to get going."

The man roared, doubling over. He straightened to wipe the tears from his eyes. "Did you hear that? Tomorrow! Oh, stop it, you're killing me." He slapped his thighs until he finally calmed.

"When will they be ready?" Crip pressed, seeing no amusement at all.

"Two months for the first prototype. Another month for manufacture, probably longer."

"Three months?" Crip nearly came out of his boots. "We're fighting a war out there and we're at the crux of winning or dying. We need those weapons."

The big man shrugged. He glanced at Eleanor. "You might want to educate him on how the work is done here. We can't shift any production because we have such limited capacity. War comes second to the survival of the Borwyn people."

He lost his smile and glared at Crip.

"There are good people out there—" Crip pointed straight up. "—who are risking it all to force the Malibor to return to the Borwyn people what is rightfully ours. We're close, and if we have to do it without those pulse rifles, so be it. We'll do it without you, but you know what? We'll not prevent you from enjoying the spoils of victory. When we win, all Borwyn win, whether you helped us or not."

Crip stormed out.

Fantasia waved at the big man. "Nice meeting you," she said with a smile and nearly skipped out of the room.

CHAPTER 23

Passion can be one's undoing or the catalyst for change. The wise know when to dial it up or dial it back.

Crip leaned against the wall in the corridor. Eleanor leaned her shoulder against the wall and faced him. "Now you see why people join the military. We refuse to be satisfied inside the stone prison. You'd be surprised how many people have never been outside."

"You have people who can go outside but don't?" Crip dropped his head back against the wall and stared at the ceiling.

"It's not that easy to go outside because we have to avoid being seen. The Malibor have no idea how many of us there are."

"Join the military and see the stars!" Crip said softly. "Or simply be born to the survivors on *Chrysalis*. You'll see the stars every day while longing to plant your feet in the dirt of our ancestral home. As long as one of us makes it, we all win."

Fantasia leaned against Crip's other side.

He wrapped his arm around her shoulders. "Sorry you had to see me get angry."

"I understand," she replied. "Not all battles are fought on the front lines."

"Damn! You're starting to sound like me."

"Maybe I've been paying attention."

Crip looked at his companions, who were there for him and sharing in his minor angst.

An older woman walked down the hallway. She smiled and waved at Fantasia before looking at Crip and Eleanor. "Your daughter is so cute."

Crip tried not to snort. "Takes after her mother. They both make my life hell."

Eleanor slugged Crip's shoulder. "Thank you for your kind words," she told the older woman.

She poked a finger into Crip's chest. "Good job, ladies. Don't let him get the upper hand." She trundled away with one last wave at Fantasia.

"I guess I deserved that, in some bizarre way, as Septiman punishes me for my violent thoughts."

"You should be proud of being mistaken for my father. He's a good hunter, good provider," Fantasia said, puffing her chest out and raising her chin.

The door to the office opened, and the big man stepped into the corridor.

Crip instantly bristled. "Give me a real example of a pulse rifle—" He pointed at the one over Crip's shoulder. "—and I can cut a month off, I bet. Say, two months."

"Sorry, but I need this. Two months is just as bad as

three. If it would cut it back to two weeks, then we could make it work. I think I'm going to need my weapon in a month or less. We'll need all our pulse rifles. Thanks for looking for another way."

"You seemed a little put out. Three months. We'll do what we can to deliver early. These look fairly simple, but the power source will take some work."

"I can share an extra power supply. Each of us carry three, just in case." He pulled one of the packs from his vest and handed it over.

"You may have bought yourself a month, star soldier." He saluted with a wave and returned to his office.

"Your family's hungry. You should feed us," Fantasia said.

"Are your kids as big of upstarts?"

"I don't have any kids, but if I did, I'd want them to be just like her," Eleanor replied and winked at Fantasia. "Follow me."

Eleanor knew the city even though she spent her time in the field. She knew where they could get something to eat. Crip hoped it wasn't like the food they were offered on New Septimus. That was not a pleasant surprise.

The spread in New Pridal wasn't for overeating, but it was fresh, and the sausage made from their own livestock was like nothing Crip had ever tasted before.

"I see why people aren't in a hurry to leave the city. It's dirty outside, and food doesn't get delivered to your table."

Eleanor gestured for Crip to lean closer. "It's still better outside," she whispered.

"I agree. When are we going back? I'm not in a rush,

mind you, as I may have bruises that will preclude sitting comfortably until they're healed."

"We have to see the military council first. We need approval for Deena's infiltration because she knows too much about us. That's also the reason why she didn't come with us. We can't send someone into the city who knows that much."

"She won't tell them anything," Crip replied. "She won't."

"The Malibor don't play by our rules. They'll do whatever they have to to get her to talk."

"Then she better not get caught. She'll go down fighting. We'll make sure she has a knife. I didn't see any stunners on the Malibor, so every fight will be a fight to the death."

"Is the information she can get worth the risk? You don't have to answer me, but you will have to answer the military leadership. You're here so they'll consider you as part of their command. They may even want to give orders to *Chrysalis*. How do you think those will be received?"

"If the orders are what Jaq is going to do anyway, then she'll agree. If they're not, then she won't. She gives the orders, and that is non-negotiable, but I'll tiptoe my way around their questions or statements, depending on what they expect. Am I at risk? I'm not sure I'll take their orders, either. I respect you and Glen so will give great consideration to any of your requests, but in mind, they are requests. We work together. I'm Jaq Hunter's deputy on a mission that she approved. I will continue to carry it out to the best of my ability. I won't take kindly to anyone trying to cancel that order."

"Keep your cool. They may try to test you."

Crip finished his meal. He was getting better using a fork

and knife, which had been foreign to him before the team landed on Septimus. New Septimus food was inedible bordering on repulsive, so he hadn't practiced with what they called utensils.

The mess bunker was the first real test. Before that, he used his field knife and fingers, sipping soups directly from the bowl.

He studied the fork as if it was a piece of alien technology.

"You'll be fine. I painted the worst case. They'll probably ask a few questions and leave it at that."

Crip saw the humor in it. "With a wife like you—" He turned from Eleanor to Fantasia. "—and a miscreant daughter like you, it's a wonder I'm still sane."

"There's only one miscreant here," Fantasia shot back.

"I'm ready," Crip said.

"Let's see if they're available. We may have to wait." They followed Eleanor through a labyrinth of corridors and alleyways to get to the far side of the mountain. It took more than thirty minutes at a brisk pace.

"Are they on the far side of Septimus?" Crip wondered.

"There's a way out of the underground on this side to a sheltered valley where the new recruits train. There are also more advanced courses they conduct here. We take the best out of the field when they age and put them here as trainers," Eleanor explained.

They entered a larger office carved out of the living rock. Beyond, there was a well-lit tunnel leading outside.

"They don't have the big doors on this side," Crip observed.

"This is away from anything Malibor, but there are doors. They tend to leave them open when training is ongoing."

"Can we see?" Fantasia asked.

"Let's see the council first." Eleanor gestured with her head, and they walked across the space to an area in the back where they found an elder individual in a dress-style uniform, not a field outfit. It looked out of place, in Crip's mind. He saw every individual as a combatant, but that's how they had to view them on board *Chrysalis*. There was no retirement, only death, where your body was sent out the airlock after the appropriate honors were paid.

Life was simpler on board the ship. Fight, make repairs, and fight again.

"Lieutenant Commander Todd. I heard you had returned with a couple of the star soldiers. My compliments to you."

"General Ochobi, it's good to be back, but we won't be here for long. We needed to deliver the plans for pulse rifles that Commander Castle was kind enough to share with us. He also has a request for a new operation that the star soldiers will undertake."

"Let me hear it," the general said. He had deep blue eyes that focused with an intensity Crip found unnerving.

"General, one of our members is half-Malibor. She grew up in the city and is willing to go back inside to identify key targets as part of a plan to create a diversion that will allow *Chrysalis* to attack Malibor fleet assets in orbit. We want to impact their command and control. Once we achieve dominance over the space surrounding Septimus, that'll effectively end the war. After that, it's handed over to the negotiators to seal the deal. The Malibor are on the cusp of losing this war. We're going to push them over the edge."

"I've heard some things about this. What assets are you using to prosecute your war?"

Crip bristled, but Eleanor squeezed his arm. He looked down at her and smiled. "I'd like to think it is the war started by our ancestors and we're bringing it to its natural and better conclusion. The Malibor have enjoyed a fifty-year respite, where they saw fit to fight themselves in five different civil wars. This has greatly weakened them. The Malibor do not belong on Septimus, although they have a whole generation who knows nothing other than Septimus as their home. That makes it difficult, but once we've achieved military supremacy, it'll be easier to negotiate. Our asset is the *Chrysalis*, a Borwyn cruiser of unrivaled power and speed. We've also gained a loaded Malibor cargo ship destined for Sairvor and a gunship. We also have four stealthy scout ships that the Borwyn from New Septimus had."

The general studied Crip as if assessing the value of a work of art. Crip stood his ground.

"I agree that the Malibor are greatly weakened. *Chrysalis*? That was the Borwyn fleet flagship, was it not?"

"Still is," Crip said. "Under command of Captain Jaqueline Hunter. She was the nominal leader of all surviving Borwyn, until we found that there were more survivors. Now, she's simply in charge of all fleet assets."

Crip steeled himself, ready for the general to lay claim to *Chrysalis* and everything the crew did.

"I see," was all he said. He sat back and laced his fingers

on top of his head. "Star soldiers. What do you think of that name?"

Crip did a doubletake. He glanced at Eleanor, who nodded toward the general. "I like it. We are all soldiers in the war to liberate the Borwyn from the Malibor's vile embrace. We were born and raised among the stars. We are determined fighters, committed to our cause."

"I'm old enough and smart enough to know about command and control. I can read people. Your defensive posture suggests you expect me to give orders to your captain and take over your ship. I don't even have a radio that will reach space. It would be beyond arrogant to think that I can give the *Chrysalis* orders. I only ask that you work with our people, Eleanor and Glen, to make sure what we do is worth the risk, and under no circumstances can you reveal the location of the mountain. The Malibor still retain enough firepower to destroy our home and everyone who lives here."

"We will protect New Pridal with our lives, like we have with New Septimus. Revealing the whereabouts of Borwyn survivors doesn't help our goal of liberation. And thank you for understanding."

"Freedom for our people has an allure that is undeniable. We continue to fight to keep what we have. The Malibor throw troops at us every now and again to keep us honest. Maybe they just like to fight. Five civil wars suggest violence is the only thing they understand. When they've lost their ability to fight, will they come to the negotiating table? I would love to see the day we slap that smug, self-righteous expression off their faces. I thought I would not live to see the day. Septiman knows that I have been conservative in my military deployments. Low risk, low reward."

The general hung his head while Crip, Eleanor, and Fantasia watched.

He straightened and continued in a strong voice, "Take the fight to them, Crip. Infiltrate the city with your spy. Infiltrate the city with small teams. Destroy their ability to attack us. Destroy their fleet. Destroy the Malibor!"

Crip recoiled from the sudden fury, but it waned as quickly as it had waxed.

He raised a cup with the acidic coffee they favored on Septimus. "Here's to the next generation. May they relish the freedom paid for with the efforts of those such as yourself and this mystical Jaqueline Hunter. I hope I get to meet her. Carry on, Commander."

The general didn't have to add to keep him apprised. They would tell them what they were doing and any support they needed.

"Thank you, General." Crip didn't have anything he could say. The general returned to the computer screen on his desk. It had an aging yellow case. Ancient computers from a bygone era kept alive, just like the people, for 'some day.' That nebulous point in the future when their fortunes would change.

But nothing was going to change unless the Borwyn grabbed it by the horns and slammed its face in the dirt.

Crip returned to the corridor. "We better get back to the company. Our work here is done."

CHAPTER 24

We face our enemy with one hand tied behind our back, yet we remain confident.

"We should have cut *Cornucopia* loose yesterday," Brad groused.

"I agree, but we weren't ready. Offload continued, especially since we discovered more spare parts. Going through them was painful and time-consuming, but the end result will save us time. Are there any crates left to move?"

"No crates to move, but everything has to be strapped down. We have a double-shift locking things in place. They're going as fast as they can, and they understand that close counts. If a load shifts, that's fine. Just can't have them break free. *Cornucopia* will accelerate as quickly as possible, without stressing the engines. Contingency in case of loss is to continue to Sairvor. They'll move what they can to New Septimus, but without landers and only one scout ship, it'll take a while to send the supplies down the tunnel."

"Contingency. In case we lose this fight. Three days. The cruiser and gunship are getting close. Cut *Cornucopia* free. They can firm up the loads while accelerating. We have no choice if they're going to get a head of steam before the cruiser comes around Farslor."

"I'll see to it." Brad pulled himself off the bridge.

Jaq leaned against her seat. Only three days, and the repairs were nowhere near completed. The power distribution systems had been brought online two days prior. That led to downstream projects which were made easier with power.

Emergency bulkheads were getting the treatment now. Those went to ship survivability.

The E-mags had been manually aligned but not tested. The sensor systems were operating, but only the passive. Active systems needed to be calibrated. The energy gauge was at one hundred percent. Their greatest success was restoring the power, but it was ephemeral. It would take a week to recharge once the cells were drained. Their power plants were out of service. They'd stopped all work on them a week earlier.

The ship was marginally operational.

"We can see there's something out there, but we won't know exactly where it is. We can shoot at it, but we're not sure we can hit what we're aiming at. We can run, but our power will fade quickly. Most of our emergency bulkheads will work, but what if they hit us where they're out of order?" Jaq was talking to herself. Amie was on the bridge, but she was collecting verbal reports that she transcribed into the computer system. It saved the workers time.

Jaq scanned the empty positions around her. Soon, the crew would be back in their chairs, but would they be functional?

"I'll be in the engine room," Jaq said, waved indiscriminately, and swam toward the corridor.

She continued to the central shaft and down.

She passed only one crew member on her way. They waved to each other, but both were in a hurry to their particular destinations.

In engineering, Jaq found Bec piddling around at a newly installed workbench. No one else was there. She found the power plant space empty, too.

"Is no one working down here?" she asked Bec.

"What's fixed is fixed and what isn't fixable isn't, so no. They're elsewhere working on stuff that has a chance of getting fixed."

"Thanks for that." Jaq could feel her blood pressure rising. "What are you working on?"

"Power. We put a small plant in the gunship to help run it. Could we get the power generation needed from a smaller plant on board Chrysalis? I contend that size doesn't matter. We use radioactive sources for our plants, but I don't think we're being efficient about it."

"Do we have time for this?" Jaq wondered, throwing her hands up in quick frustration.

"This could be as impactful as the ion drive, Jaq. Do we have any more lead? I need it for shielding."

"I have no doubt you'll find it. We have three days until the cruiser gets here, Bec. Do you know where Teo is?"

"I don't. They tend to simply leave without checking out

because they don't have to notify me of their foibles, and I'm happier for it. Thank you for letting me explore the boundaries of what's possible."

"Any idea when you'll have something functional?" Jaq pressed.

"How long have you known me?" Bec answered without looking up from his work.

"My whole damned life, Bec, and I continue my struggle of turning you into a decent human being."

"If only you understood me. Now, go away. I have work to do."

Jaq didn't need a second invitation to depart.

She decided that she didn't need to interrupt Teo wherever she was working. She'd head to the lander bays and then to the port roller airlock to check on *Cornucopia*. She wasn't sure how many of the crew were leaving on the freighter. She'd have to get everyone to their battle stations an hour before the cruiser cleared Farslor's horizon.

When they hit the engines, Jaq expected her crew would hear clunks and bangs as unsecured tools and loose parts found their footing under acceleration and the apparent gravity it delivered. Like water would always find its lowest level, anything loose would get trapped by intervening fixtures, like decks and bodies that hadn't thoroughly checked what was over their heads.

One deck down, Jaq strolled the corridor that provided access to where the landers were stored. The hatches were open on the four that were being refitted as remote sensor stations and bombs.

Jaq wasn't fond of the idea, but they had little else to use against the Malibor. Sending the landers out and blowing them up in proximity to a Malibor ship was an act of desperation. Without missiles, the only weapon at their command was the E-mag batteries, which required a direct line of sight. The golden rule in combat was that if you could see them, they could see you.

Brad's plan was more audacious with more moving parts than firing a double-skip barrage. It had a higher chance of succeeding, but the risk was greater.

Jaq agreed with Brad that the risk was acceptable. They'd use *Chrysalis's* speed to their advantage.

She found Brad's feet first. They were sticking out of the loading hatch on Lander Three.

"Whatcha doin'?" she asked, squeezing into the hatch with him.

"What are you doing?" Brad asked. He was elbow-deep in his homemade explosives, attaching the final wiring and detonator.

"Is this going to work?"

"Look at that penetrator!" He pointed at the overhead of the passenger compartment. "Well, you can't actually see it from here. You have to go into the storage area."

She tried to squirm past him and into the overhead, but Brad caught her leg and pulled her back to him. He held her close.

"What are you doing?" Jaq casually asked.

"I was hoping maybe we could christen the lander, you know, knock off a piece before we all die."

Jaq furrowed her brow while she stabbed him in the chest

with forefinger. "Is that how you think? Knock off a piece? Who said romance was dead?"

"Probably you." Brad let go and grinned. "A man can always keep his hopes up."

"We're not going to die, but I appreciate the consideration. Was I your first solicitation?"

"First and only, Jaq." Brad turned serious. "We're doing the best we can, but this one is different than all the other battles where we had plenty of punch available." He looked past Jaq into the access tube to make sure no one was near. "I'm worried. One lucky shot from the Malibor and we're done."

Jaq pulled his face to hers. Their lips connected without sparks or fanfare but with the warmth of promise. "That's your down payment. We'll take some downtime *when* we win this fight."

She scooched past him. He pinched her butt.

"Don't let the crew catch you doing that," she warned while continuing to the hatch leading to the nosecone. "What the hell am I looking at?"

"They're titanium spikes. It's a big slug thrower. The explosives down here act as propellant. See how it's a shaped charge? The full power drives forward, sending the projectiles into whatever is in front of the lander. Range is probably fifty to a hundred meters. Point-blank will be better. I've rigged a proximity fuse along with a remote detonator. I'd prefer to use the prox fuse because once these are gone, they're gone. At a hundred meters, it might be a complete waste of an asset. If we don't use it, then we can recover it.

It'll pickle itself if it receives no additional instructions for two hours."

"You've thought of the contingencies. I expected no less. We're going to use them, but I hope we don't need to explode them. If we have no landers on this ship, then we're dependent upon the charity of others to shuttle us to the best vacation spots."

"The last lander is on *Cornucopia*. Even if we use these three, we'll have one in reserve."

Jaq nodded. She glanced one last time at the madness that was titanium spiked with cups at their base to pick up as much of the blast as possible to drive them forward. In the main cabin, the shape of the charges made sense.

She kissed Brad once more before corkscrewing her way past his outreached hand to escape the lander.

"What's next on the repair schedule?" Jaq called into the lander.

"We're going to align the E-mags and the sensors. We're going to hit what we aim at, Jaq. That's the only way we'll survive this."

"Keep at it and stop distracting yourself with your lurid thoughts."

"Man thoughts. It's what men think about when they're racing toward their doom. No one wants to die not having gotten some. It's upsetting."

"It is? I find dying more upsetting than not getting some, as you say." She waved and continued up the tube. She turned at the top and shouted, "Focus!"

"Yes, my captain!" Brad called.

In the corridor, Jaq stopped to straighten her uniform.

There wasn't much for her to fix as her uniform was a coverall. She tucked the short hair on one side of her head behind her ear, even though it wouldn't stay. Zero-gee was unforgiving for any hairstyle that didn't involve being too short to flow away from one's head or tied down in some way.

She smiled to herself. Jaq didn't need any complications, but she was starting to think that Brad wasn't wrong. *Knock off a piece,* she thought. *Men.*

Jaq took the central shaft up and pulled herself down the corridor to the port roller airlock. The cabling had been tucked up inside the corridor as it was no longer connected to *Cornucopia's* systems. Alby and Godbolt stood inside the airlock, but the hatches on each side were open.

They were in a clinch, faces millimeters apart.

Godbolt was first to notice Jaq, waiting and watching.

"Commander, the ship is ready to depart," she said stiffly to Alby.

"Take it on the designated course, slingshot around the moon to pick up speed quickly."

"It's okay," Jaq said. "Our relationships give us all a reason to survive. Carry on, Godbolt, Alby. Take a few moments and then get underway."

Jaq had more questions for *Cornucopia,* but the only thing she could do was create doubt. They were as ready as they would be. There was no time to fix anything that wasn't ready.

She moved down the corridor and turned her back to the airlock. She locked her boots to the deck and waited.

The airlock hatch thumped shut and started to cycle. Alby waved at the small window. Jaq expected Godbolt was waving from the far window.

When Alby turned, his eyes glistened.

Jaq's breath caught. The whole crew was feeling it. She closed with Alby and took his hand to hold it in both of hers. "The better we focus on the here and now, the better chance we'll have of seeing our loved ones. I want to see every member of this crew alive and happy. We can't win if we don't survive. We don't deserve to win if we get our loved ones killed."

"I didn't mean to fall in love..." Alby started, but Jaq stopped him.

"You've got nothing to apologize for or even explain. I wish you all the best, but right now, we have less than three days to be as ready to fight as we can be. And we need to be ready to win. I can't have people saying their final good-byes. Don't let this be that. Don't you want to see her again?"

"Yeah, I do," Alby replied. "I know what the priorities are. Next up is targeting and sensors. We have power restored throughout the ship, but it's fleeting. Once used, we don't get it back unless we perform unnatural acts, cutting off water for a half-hour at a time. But we'll get there. Excuse me, Captain. I need to get going."

"The battle is joined, Alby."

"Victory is ours, Jaq." Alby flew down the corridor, pulling himself quickly to the central shaft.

Jaq had a pair of hands and a keen mind. She would help align the targeting systems. That meant the outer hull. She went up to Deck Two, where she found a team of three people working on one of the E-mag batteries.

"Mind if I join you?" she asked.

"I've only done this one time before and it wasn't me doing it."

Jaq smiled. "I'll teach you how to do it, but we only need two to do it right. Is there anything else that needs to be done?"

"Next battery around the bend," the one who had done a calibration before replied.

"You take it. If you have any questions, yell." Jaq pointed to the youngest of the group. "You're with me."

The four split into two groups of two.

Jaq dug into the status panel. "First thing you do is a system diagnostic, let it tell you that the components are energized and the handshake with control systems is complete..."

CHAPTER 25

Release that which resides deep within.

"I'm not sure riding a horse made anything better," Crip complained.

"You look like you've gained weight." Max studied Crip's contour. "While we've been out here working our butts off, you're living the pampered life."

Crip laughed. He took a few shaky steps. "I may never walk normally again." He returned to his bemused friend. "Pulse rifles in maybe two or three months. Otherwise, they didn't have anything else for us besides a radio set that Deena can use. The only news that matters is they won't stand in our way. We're a go for whatever we need to do. The star soldiers are unleashed upon the Malibor."

"Star soldiers. I still can't get used to that because when we're deployed as soldiers, we're on the ground." Max shrugged one shoulder.

"Your intellect is truly mindboggling." Crip pushed his

friend. "I wish Taurus had come with us. We're making a difference down here. You should have seen the general's face when he started to believe that the Borwyn would be free. I don't see how we can accept anything less."

Deena checked over the radio with Eleanor's help.

Fantasia strolled up. "Hey, Dad, Glen wants to talk with you about Deena's infil plan."

"Yes, my dear husband, let him know that Deena is ready," Eleanor added without looking up.

Max stared unblinking at Crip.

Crip stared back. "Things happened that were important to sell the locals of New Pridal. It deflected questions requiring long explanations."

"I'm not buying that," Max replied. He smiled. "Will you be my daddy, too?"

"I'll be right back." Crip continued to glance over his shoulder, giving his best glares while Max blew kisses.

"Evelyn told me what you did when you went hunting with her, how you killed the Malibor. You said it wasn't your first time?"

"No." Two days to New Pridal and two days back, but they had talked very little. They made little noise while traveling and were too tired and in too much pain to chat at the end of each day. "Deena's rescue, maybe we should call it liberation. They tried to kill me when I only wanted to talk with them."

"I'd say we never talk with Malibor..." Fantasia's young voice grew fainter. "But that isn't true. We've been trading with them my whole life. We've traded away what little freedom we have. That's why I wanted to come with you, not because I couldn't find a husband."

"You're a little young for that." Crip spotted Glen coming toward him.

"Is Deena ready?" Glen asked.

"As much as can be. She has the radio. The two soldiers that are going to take her to the border are geared up."

"I didn't mean that. Is she *ready*? She's not Malibor, not anymore."

"That's the big question. Will she show her disdain for them and give herself away? I don't think so. Maybe she'll find that most of them go about their lives without any consideration of the Borwyn. Most of them have probably not seen one of us."

"We're not that different," Glen said. "Maybe the Borwyn who remained in the city mixed genes more than we suspected. She might find a whole population ready to rise up against the true blood Malibor."

"I was under the impression that Deena was a rarity?" Crip hadn't heard anything suggesting Borwyn had remained in the city.

"She has a rare look about her. That much is true. It's like the best of both races, and I think that's why they treated her poorly."

"That makes no sense," Crip replied.

"I've been fighting the Malibor for a long, long time. Much of what they do defies logic, but one thing I do know is that they punish what they see as different. They aren't tolerant. What you and your people aboard *Chrysalis* showed was the opposite. You not only tolerate differences, you embrace them. And if you're Max, that's literal."

Crip smiled. "Hard to argue with that logic. Deena knows only too well. She hasn't told us her plan once she's in the city. Only that she will find the headquarters, communications facility, and troop counts. I'm sure it'll take a while. Any aggressive reconnaissance would highlight her in a way that we don't want. We have time to do it right."

Glen agreed with a nod and tight-lipped smile. He was the commander and wanted to know more, but information came with the risk of sharing it. If you wanted to keep a secret, you told no one. Deena's movements within the city needed to be private knowledge.

The second she was gone from the camp, they'd move, leapfrogging the next prepared bunkers to a new site that even her escorts didn't know. They'd find directions written in a secret code when they reached the alternate site after the drop off.

Limiting exposure of the company.

Eleanor joined them.

"She's ready to go." Eleanor gripped Crip's upper arm.

Crip nodded curtly, lips a tight line.

Glen watched the exchange. "What happened on the trip to the mountain?"

"You make friends when you get to know people. I wish we could do that with the Malibor, like we did with Deena. We need to keep being the good guys. In the end, every human, no matter where they came from, will have to appreciate that. War isn't natural. Fighting is not what Septiman intended for us. For hundreds of years, we were peaceful, then along came the Malibor. We fight like our lives depend on it, even though there are those who are perfectly happy in hiding."

"I see," Glen replied. "There are those in the mountain who will never come outside, but we're still fighting for them. They should have the freedom to. Whether they want it or not, that should be up to them. Send Deena on her way. Let's start the next phase of this war."

Crip and Eleanor returned to find Deena with a small pack on her back and her three escorts waiting.

Max was going. Crip wouldn't try to talk him out of it. That would be a waste of breath.

Crip hugged Deena and shook hands with Max. "The battle is joined," he said, barely above a whisper.

"To victory, our victory," Max replied and signaled that it was time to go. The small group stepped into the brush and quickly disappeared from view.

"I can't help but think we're sending her to her death," Crip said.

Eleanor stood by his side. "She's a soldier, and she's fighting as hard as she can to help the Borwyn win more than a battle. She's going out there to help you win the war. *She* has determined that the risk is worth it."

"You make too much sense. I'm going to join my people and see what kind of training we're failing at because we're too loud." He waved and headed toward the bunker being used as a barracks.

"They should be preparing to move. We'll bring the carts up shortly," Eleanor called after him. "And then everyone will be on shovel duty."

Digging new bunkers, Crip thought. It was all part of avoiding the wrong battles to better shape the right ones. Crip stopped and caught Eleanor before she started the process of moving the camp.

"Do the Malibor have ground attack missiles?"

"It's been a while since they used one on us. We don't think they have them for use against the rebels in the forest, but they do have other gunships, ground attack ships that aren't like yours. They still have those. They fly out here every now and then."

"Have you seen any since we landed the gunship?"

"We have not."

"Maybe they haven't spotted our ship. That would be illustrative." Crip chewed on his lip with his head hanging as if focusing on something on the ground.

"What do you mean by illustrative?"

"They aren't watching the skies over the forest, otherwise they would have seen us. Maybe they don't have operational radar, or it's only pointed toward space. They've decided the Borwyn aren't a technological threat. Horses and no aircraft or spacecraft. They continue to underestimate us. No wonder they fought five civil wars in fifty years."

"I have to arrange the logistics of the move. We'll talk later. The philosophy of the Malibor engagement. Maybe we'll find a weakness." Eleanor waved and walked away.

Crip found it hard to not think about Deena and what she'd encounter in Malipride. He wanted to see her again, for his friend Max. Was the war worth fighting if the people who helped win it didn't come home?

He wanted them all to survive, knowing very well that they wouldn't.

"It's time," Jaq said. She turned in a three-sixty. Eager but tired faces looked at her from every position. It was good to have the bridge crew on the command deck once again. She finished by studying the board. Most of the status board showed green and yellow. There were more reds than she liked, but not as many as she expected. "Shepherd?"

The religious leader, who had also been working with Doc Teller to minister to the crew's physical as well as spiritual needs, spoke in a deep tenor. "May Septiman protect us from the claws of our enemy while guiding our hands to smite the Malibor, erase them from our existence!"

Jaq raised an eyebrow at the unusually combative terms.

"In Septiman's name, we pray," the shepherd ended.

"All hands, battle stations. Secure the emergency bulkheads. Secure the ship and prepare to fight. The battle is joined."

"Victory is ours!" the bridge crew shouted with a vibrance they'd lacked over the past two weeks.

"Launch the landers," Jaq ordered.

"They are underway," Brad confirmed. He had sent them out fifteen minutes prior. He hadn't wanted to stress the landers by accelerating more than necessary.

"Final report from *Starbound*," Amie reported. "Cruiser course and speed are constant. Arrival time is confirmed:

sixty minutes to clear the horizon. Gunship no longer registers."

The horizon was a moving target, depending on where *Chrysalis* could be found.

The Malibor's arrival was set. They hadn't changed course or speed during their entire transit.

"Why haven't they changed course or speed?" Jaq asked.

"It's a bit disconcerting, isn't it? I can't believe they have taken zero countermeasures. They may not know exactly where we are, but they have to know we're out here, especially since their ships aren't returning home."

"Decoy?" Brad suggested.

"I've been thinking about that but discounted it until they reached Farslor. I kicked the idea down the corridor, but it seems I'm out of corridor and have to address it."

"Where'd that gunship go?"

"Captain?" Ferd wondered. "We're ready to get underway."

"All ahead slow, point-five gees. Accelerate to one gee as we enter the moon's gravity well, then execute the slingshot maneuver," the captain ordered. She grabbed the mid-rail to hold herself steady as the ship accelerated. She sighed.

Brad eased up next to her. "I don't know about you, but I like gravity."

"Sometimes, the body demands it. Have DC teams ready in case something shifts in a way that could break something."

Brad returned to his seat and made the call over the ship's intercom.

"Half a gee, continuing to one gee," Ferd reported.

"Tracking into the gravity of Farslor's moon," Mary said.

Ferd added, "Acceleration increasing. Recommend seats. We'll reach three gees within five minutes and it will climb."

Jaq gestured for Brad to make the call.

"All hands, into the gel. We race toward destiny, and you better have your wits about you when we get there."

"Test fire into the moon?" Jaq asked. "One last alignment check. Five single shots."

Alby rogered the order. He'd been ready for it. They had already fired from a stationary position into the moon for a ninety-percent solution, but Jaq wanted ninety-nine percent accuracy if they couldn't achieve one hundred percent of rounds on target.

Taurus ran the E-mags using the programs that Dolly and Donal had modified. "Prepare to fire. Target is Crater Zeta Three, pinpoint dead center," she stated.

"Target acquired," Donal replied.

Chief Ping added, "Ready to report results. Active scanners pinging the moon's surface."

"Fire!" Taurus called. The low rumble of each cannon throbbed as the ship's heartbeat. They rotated through each battery twice while the ship continued to accelerate.

"Sending adjustment information to weapons," the sensor chief said while watching his scopes.

"Confirmed." Dolly Norton was a prodigy, only thirteen, but she worked a normal shift on the bridge. Her position with passive sensors was only part of what she did. With Donal, they'd reprogrammed the targeting system to better integrate the fantastic speeds at which Chrysalis traveled to engage the enemy. It was extremely complex aiming a weapon from a ship moving at a million kilometers an hour through spatial anomalies at a target that was also moving.

It wasn't for the weak of heart. Donal brought the experience and the programming. Dolly brought the math. Donal could hold his own, but it took both of them to optimize the system.

"One more shot to confirm adjustments," Taurus said, eyes focused on her screen. "Fire."

The batteries thrummed from one to the next.

The energy gauge had started at ninety-nine percent. Acceleration and a test fire were already draining their cells. Ninety-five percent showed on the screen. That didn't bode well for an extended battle, something Jaq already knew. She thought she'd prepared herself for it, but the reality of it was already bowing her back under the pressure.

"End test fire," Taurus reported. "Efficiency?"

Slade Ping double-checked the numbers. Dolly double-double-checked.

"Ninety-seven percent," Slade announced. "Ninety-seven impacts in a ten-meter circle out of one hundred at a range of ten thousand kilometers. The bulk of the impacts are within two meters."

"That means at a range of fifty thousand kilometers, we'll be down to fifty percent impacts?" Jaq suggested.

"Yes, with a pattern that encircles the target should they conduct any last instant maneuvers. At fifty thousand kilometers, the impacts would be nearly instantaneous, less than six seconds at five hundred thousand kilometers. We'll hit what we're aiming at, Captain," Alby answered, stepping up to speak for the weapons and sensors teams in his role as the battle commander. "With high confidence."

The ship buffeted slightly during acceleration as it wasn't holding a steady line into the gravity well.

"Compensating with thrusters," Mary called over her shoulder while she hammered at the buttons on her screen.

The energy gauge dropped another percent.

Jaq groaned.

Acceleration slowed. A red light flashed for the ion drives. "Main engines are offline," Ferd said. He worked his screen, but the problem wasn't there.

"The bio-pack," Jaq whispered. She looked at Brad. Acceleration had dropped to one-point-five gees.

"On my way," he said, throwing himself out of his seat and running under the burden of the acceleration load on his way to the central shaft. The shaft had closed and he had to summon the elevator. He didn't think he could take the ladder to engineering at one and a half gees along with the buffeting that started to increase without the additional thrust from the main engines.

The elevator showed up quickly since no one else was out and about, not while they were at battle stations.

He pressed the button and descended toward the aft end of the ship. Deck Two. He hurried through the hatch and into engineering. Teo had already removed the cowling and was inside the ion drive while Bec leaned against it. The two were talking.

"Fuchsia isn't light green. It's more of a pink."

"Then why don't we just call it pink?"

"What is going on?" Brad demanded.

"Hey, Dad. I'll have this back online soon," Teo called from inside the unit.

"I don't want to interrupt your train of thought," Brad said, "but we're going to die if you don't get the engines back online."

"Is that supposed to help me work better?"

Brad leaned into the ion drive to find Teo massaging the bio-pack, kneading it between both hands.

"What are you doing?"

"The system heated up and overloaded one side of the pack. It didn't transfer the signals properly. I'm separating the gel and moving the bits around. Notice the multimeter." She pointed with her nose. "When the resistance reaches one, it'll be ready. Getting close."

"That looks really bizarre, Teo."

"You probably shouldn't watch as I'm stimulating the gel," she quipped. "Get ready to resecure the cowling."

Bec and Brad helped pull Teo out of the engine. They lifted the cowling into place and used the auto-drills to screw the bolts in. Teo moved to the control panel and waited for Bec to give her the thumbs-up.

With the cowling in place, she tapped the screen to bring the engine to life. "Half a gee added acceleration. The ship pushed forward across the gravity well." Brad struggled to the wall comm. "Engines restored. Ease them up to full power. I'll stay down here until we're around the moon, then I'll get back to the bridge."

Jaq acknowledged, and Brad worked his way to an open seat. Bec never liked having spare bodies in engineering so there were only three seats, the third being installed after Teo arrived.

The ship surged to one gee, giving it an actual acceleration of two and a half gees and climbing.

Brad would have been okay through two gees, but not beyond that. At three and climbing, he was working hard to breathe normally.

"I'm feeling my age, Teo!" he shouted.

Teo would have laughed, but they were no longer getting the age-defying food and water from New Septimus. If it tasted good, it wasn't good for them, even though there was nothing bad in the food.

Chef had said something about bacteria that was particular to New Septimus, which accounted for the bad taste, but it worked with the system. They needed to get back there and collect greater samples if they were to replicate it for ingestion in a way that didn't befoul the food.

The chemical analysis team on *Chrysalis* had other priorities. They had identified the bacteria, but never had the opportunity to take it further.

None of that mattered if the next hour didn't go their way, however.

Brad wasn't religious, but even he said a prayer to Septiman.

CHAPTER 26

History never favors the oppressor.

Jaq tore her eyes from the energy gauge.

"Slade, where did that gunship go?" she demanded. "What's your plan for finding it?"

"Fore and aft sensor sweeps along with lander packages. Although their systems are low power, they should give us enough of a look to keep a gunship from sneaking up on us. In thirty minutes, we'll paint the sky with the full array of the electromagnetic spectrum."

Jaq's chest tightened from more than the gee forces. "What's the power drain for that level of activation?"

"We can dial it back to fifty-percent power because we don't need extreme range. That will still draw five-percent reserve every ten minutes."

"Fifteen percent total. You'll have to wait for forty minutes before engaging, then activate at twenty-five percent. At fifty-five minutes, increase power to maximum on all systems. Manage the power usage, Slade. During the engagement, if we have all the ships accounted for, dial it back. Save our power for the E-mags."

Chief Ping acknowledged the order, keeping his focus on his screens.

Jaq glanced at the empty seat beside hers. She'd gotten too busy working on the E-mags and afforded herself the minimal amount of sleep. She hadn't gotten the private time with Brad that he'd been after. She wasn't opposed, which was a big step for her, but her priority remained the ship.

As Crip had told her, make sure life was worth living.

"Lander information is updated. Blackout in ten seconds," Slade announced.

As they headed around the moon, the line of sight was blocked. They'd get around it quickly enough. It gave them time to analyze the newest data packets.

"Alby, how does a gunship disappear?" Jaq asked.

"It doesn't. They show up on scopes, even if they're dead, but that's active. Did it shut down and coast?"

"That doesn't give it an advantage. It'll show up near the cruiser on a ballistic trajectory and need to power up to fire back. No. I think it's something much simpler. It's hiding."

"Behind the cruiser?"

"Behind the cruiser or maybe even attached to the cruiser. Two weeks flying in a gunship wouldn't be optimal for the crew's mental health. Maybe they linked up with the cruiser for a little R-and-R. Sometimes the simplest answer is the right one."

"Comes down to how we can confirm or deny the

hypothesis." Alby struggled to turn his head enough to look at Chief Ping.

"Active sensor sweeps will give us our answer in less than a second," Slade confirmed.

"That means we'll know the instant they clear the horizon. Do we think they know we're here? Are they disciplined to carry out the subterfuge of hiding a gunship only to break it free at the last instant to attack us along multiple vectors?"

"Their deliberate speed and lack of course change suggest they do not know we're here. If they did, they would have sortied everything they had left to come out here and finish us."

"If they'd done that, then they would have. Presumption is that they don't know we're here, but that changes nothing. We hit them the instant they come around Farslor, nose on to minimize our profile. We cannot give them a look at our aft end. The ion drives cannot be exposed to their guns. Engine status?"

Ferd replied, "All systems nominal. Currently all ahead slow. Gravitic assist ongoing."

Chrysalis dipped closer to the lunar surface and continued accelerating.

"All ahead standard. Bring us to five gees."

They approached four until the engines increased their output, then the ship launched beyond four and climbed steadily.

"Will pull out of the gravity well starting in ten, nine..." Ferd counted down. The ship rapidly accelerated. The energy gauge ticked down. It was at eighty-five percent and dropping.

They wouldn't bring the E-mag systems online until the last second as Jaq attempted to shepherd their limited power reserve.

Jaq activated her comm link to engineering. "Teo, thank you for your work on the ion drives, bringing them online and giving us the power to prosecute this engagement. We'll power the drives down momentarily, but if we need them again, we'll need them for flank speed."

"We'll be ready," Teo replied.

The gee forces increased beyond five as the ship bulled a course away from the moon and out of its gravity well.

Jaq gritted her teeth and grunted to keep her blood from welling inside her body cavity. It wasn't threatening her consciousness. Her vision wasn't narrowing. But she needed her wits. They'd planned this engagement for a long time, but their survival depended on the last-second adjustments.

The crew grunted along with their captain. The bridge started to smell of sweat.

"Idling the ion drives. Speed one hundred and fifty-seven thousand KPH," Ferd reported.

"We're ahead of schedule," Mary said, highlighting their course on the main board. They'd meet the Malibor cruiser at a different point around the horizon than they'd planned, and the shot angles might skip through the planet's atmosphere. That had been the captain's original plan, the one that was more defensive in nature.

Brad had changed her thinking. By being more aggressive, they reduced their exposure. Hit them fast and hard. It made sense.

They were traveling at about the same speed as the

Malibor cruiser that had been underway for two weeks. *Chrysalis* had been accelerating for less than thirty minutes.

"Something's wrong," Jaq muttered. She looked over her shoulder for Brad, but he had not yet arrived. She studied the screen, the same thing she'd done for the past week. The projected course hadn't changed. Their position was finally changing, no longer guesstimated but actual. "What are you playing at?"

A thump next to her signaled Brad's arrival. "I'm home, honey. What's for dinner?"

"You are incorrigible," Jaq called over her shoulder. "They should have changed course by now. I think the gunship is attached to the cruiser."

"Just means we can kill two with one shot. Sensors and targeting systems are aligned and operational. We'll pump so much obdurium into them, they won't even realize they've died," Brad replied.

Jaq nodded easily with the return of zero-gee. She climbed out of her seat and checked the time. She had about thirty minutes of freedom before she had to return to her seat.

"Engine status," she called.

"Nominal. No changes," Ferd reported.

When they engaged the enemy, they'd need the engines to work. "Brad, your opinion on the engines."

"I think they're as good as they're going to get. The biopack isn't ready for full deployment. It has bugs that need to be worked out, but Teo knows what they are and is manually mitigating them."

"What does that mean?" Jaq asked in alarm.

"It means she was massaging the bio-pack when I got

down there in order to optimize the electrical flow. It was consolidated on one side of the pack and needed a little manual squishing and squeezing."

Jaq shook her head. The alternative had been no engines, thrusters only. Static positions were a monument to failed military interventions. They had to move if they were to win the battle and eventually the war. If that meant an experimental bio-pack in lieu of a circuit board, so be it.

"It'll have to do. Keep those magic fingers warmed up, if that's what it takes." Jaq glanced at Brad to see if he was kidding, despite it not being the right time for jokes, but he maintained a sincere expression. He returned to studying his screens.

"Emergency bulkhead on Deck Nine has failed in the open position. DC crew is deployed. They have twenty minutes to get it sealed," Brad said.

Jaq chewed her lip. "What surprises do they have in store for us?"

"I think the surprise is that we're here. They might be headed to the last-known location of their troopship or their ship *Hornet*. You said the simple answer might be the right one."

"The Malibor exist to make my life hell, but Septiman isn't going to allow that, is He, Shepherd?"

"Septiman smiles on His servants," the shepherd intoned before descending into a mumbled mass of words that could have been a prayer.

"See?" she told Brad.

He shrugged it off. "If they can hide one gunship, what if they hid more? Last count, they had ten of them left. What if they sortied an armada that only looked like one loser cruiser barely able to make speed?"

"That is the smartest thing I've heard and the only explanation that makes sense." She reached over to pull him to her for a quick kiss and then pushed him back into his seat. "Taurus, prepare for multiple targets. Fifty percent to the cruiser, split the rest, swivel the cannons and be ready to kill the ships the second they appear. We'll have a better angle on them. The cruiser will have railguns on gimbals, but the gunships will have to face us. Prepare for five targets. One cruiser and four gunships."

"Captain?" Alby blurted before settling down. The clock was ticking. "We have eight functioning batteries, ten total cannons. That means four on the cruiser, the double barrels, and one cannon per gunship, if we see up to four. If they have more, I'll allocate one of the cruiser-designated cannons to a fifth or sixth gunship. I really hope they don't have six, or even four."

"Me, too." Jaq faced the screen. "Fire at the cyclic rate. We will only get one shot at this. Don't worry about the energy gauge. It'll be enough. Slade, are we getting any new data from the landers? I want to know where the cruiser is and even more importantly, I want to know if Brad is right about those gunships."

Slade winced. He didn't have the answer the captain was looking for. "The landers are flying too slowly. We needed to launch them two hours earlier to put them in the best position. They continue to accelerate, but we are almost abeam. They have a slight advantage in angle on the horizon, but that will give us ten, maybe fifteen seconds' lead time."

"How did we get that so wrong?" Jaq snapped. She clenched her fists, but only for a moment. She forced her hands open. "Never mind. Ten seconds will be enough. If we fly past the cruiser without having killed it, then the landers will play a critical role in taking out the enemy ship. We can't have it chasing down *Cornucopia*."

"Conserving fuel for just that possibility. Benjy will maintain direct line of sight to steer the landers into the cruiser, if—and that's a big if—we don't destroy it first," Brad replied. "Everything is on track. If we can see them, remember, they can see us. The landers giving them ten seconds changes nothing they can do while giving us all the time we need to slew cannons, check aim points, and fire."

"You make it sound easy. Taurus, you ready to do all that?"

"I was ready yesterday," she replied and then made a face. "That didn't sound as impressive as it was in my mind."

"We get you. Donal and Dolly, if we need skip shots, are they going to work?"

Dolly nearly shouted her affirmative, but Donal was more reserved. "Now would be a really bad time to tell you anything other than a resounding yes, so that's my answer."

Brad snorted.

Jaq looked appalled. "Is it a resounding yes?"

"That is my answer, Captain. Go get 'em, team!"

She looked to Brad for support.

He scoffed. "You've got good people, Jaq, and they're doing the best job they are capable of doing. Of course the skip shots will work. Relax."

In the entire history of humanity, telling someone who was stressed to their limit to relax had never been successful.

But Jaq was different. "You originals are strange. I can't believe we came from your generation." She checked the gauge. Eighty-one percent. The energy drain had slowed with the shutdown of the engine. The weapons had not yet fired. The sensors had not yet engaged.

They were going to burn through their power soon enough, but for the moment, she could relax, but not because Brad had suggested it.

She clasped her hands behind her back and attached her boots to the deck. Time counted down.

It dragged.

"Emergency bulkhead status?" Jaq asked.

"Repaired and the damage control team has returned to their stations," Brad replied.

"Another job well done. Like you said, they *are* good people. Everybody strap in. It's time to make war."

CHAPTER 27

The wound of honor is self-inflicted.

Jaq watched the main screen. The bridge crew hovered their fingers over activation keys, ready to begin the sequence of events that would drain the ship's power precipitously.

Engage *and destroy* the Malibor.

One cruiser and at least one gunship. If *Chrysalis* could destroy them, that would leave the Malibor inventory with only one cruiser and nine gunships. Judging by the state of those that had been pickled in orbit over Farslor, the remainder of the Malibor fleet was barely operational. The cruiser could only reach a top speed of a hundred and fifty thousand kilometers per hour. Maybe they couldn't accelerate. Maybe they couldn't slow down.

Fifty-four minutes had passed since they got underway. The hiccup with the ion drives was well behind them. They'd made up for it with an increase in speed. They were slightly ahead of their projected course. There remained an estimated six minutes to contact.

Jaq climbed into her seat and activated the intercom. "Prepare for combat. These are going to happen at the speed of light over the next five minutes. Keep your wits about you. Do your jobs as you know how to do them. Seal any breaches as quickly as you can and prepare for the next task. Save the ship at all costs. The better we're prepared for damage, the more likely we won't suffer any. We are going to deliver a decisive amount of obdurium on target. The Malibor will, once again, not know what hit them. The battle is joined." Jaq spoke emotionlessly. The anticipation of the battle had her wound tightly, but her control would keep the crew under control.

"Victory is ours," the bridge personnel replied.

"Sensors are pinging at one hundred percent. Nothing on the scopes," Slade reported after a few seconds.

"E-mags are powering up. Targeting systems are online. Running through pre-fire diagnostics," Taurus said, never looking up from her screen.

"Prepare to accelerate at all ahead flank," Jaq ordered the flight crew.

Ferd confirmed the order.

Mary asked for clarification. "Vector?"

"The one that will provide our lowest profile to enemy guns. As soon as we have information regarding their position and disposition, don't wait for my order. Keep us oriented to maximize our firepower while minimizing theirs. Flank speed to escape engagement zones."

"Understand. Watching the screen and ready to respond," Mary said.

Time still dragged. They watched every second as it counted down.

"Nothing new from the landers." Alby filled the uncomfortable silence to let the captain know that the void of information remained unfilled.

Jaq fidgeted in the zero-gee while remaining strapped in her seat. At any moment, they could be forced to fire the drives. They wouldn't be able to wait for anyone to get back in their seats.

The energy gauge ticked down to seventy-three percent. It wasn't drawing energy as fast as she feared.

Jaq thought her head would explode with the anxiety-filled slowing of time.

Fifteen seconds before they were to clear the horizon, the lander information populated the main screen.

"Targets!" Alby shouted.

A cruiser and four gunships in a tactical formation. The cruiser led the way while the gunships flew in a vertical line, parallel to Farslor's horizon.

"They knew we were here," Brad said.

"Fire!" Taurus called out. The ship thrummed with the violence of ten E-mag cannons unleashing their maximum rate of fire.

"Impact," Brad growled as the rounds streamed into the biggest target—the cruiser. Rounds chased the gunships, who were already corkscrewing through space.

"Accelerating into the ambush," Mary announced. The

ship lurched forward under the instantaneous application of one-hundred-percent power.

Ferd managed thrust control while Mary pointed the nose at the gunships to pass behind them by the time they arrived. The gunships were still traveling at a hundred and fifty thousand KPH while changing orientation related to *Chrysalis*.

The energy gauge dropped faster than a percent every second. Jaq had to tear her eyes from watching it. Everyone was busy, except for her and Brad.

Acceleration forced them deep into their seats. The ship angled toward Farslor's upper atmosphere. The E-mags continued to hammer away.

"That one percent is working in the Malibor's favor," Brad grumbled about the targeting margin of error.

The gunships were bracketed by fire, but with only two barrels per ship and their erratic maneuvers, none of them had been dealt a killing blow.

The cruiser wasn't firing back.

"Target only the gunships. The cruiser is a decoy," Jaq cried out.

Brad groaned his disagreement but didn't say anything. He wanted to see the cruiser as a cloud of debris. It continued away at a hundred and fifty thousand kilometers per hour but without being a threat to *Chrysalis*. That was what mattered most. It took him a moment before he admitted as much. "Good call."

"Fire and fire," Taurus said, more to herself than anyone else.

"Adjusting calculations," Donal interjected.

Better make it fast, Jaq thought, but avoided saying it out loud.

The main screen showed the four gunships separating and twisting to get away from *Chrysalis* while trying to bring the nose of their ships to bear on the Borwyn.

One gunship exploded and turned into a cloud of sparks and shredded metal.

"Three targets," Brad corrected. "Maximum firepower."

The E-mags spat their relentless assault on the space between the opposing forces.

"Fire adjusted," Donal said.

A second gunship exploded.

"Yes!" Brad growled.

The tactic of accelerating was working to foil the aim of the last two gunships, but those few seconds of respite were at an end.

The E-mags were going to struggle to slew to the targets as *Chrysalis* raced behind them. Jaq consoled herself that they hadn't been hit yet. One on five and *Chrysalis* was dominating the Malibor. Jaq's lip twisted upward in a snarl. How dare they think they could defeat the Borwyn.

The gunships rotated to bring their noses toward *Chrysalis*. Their railguns belched fire that flashed across space as they continued to rotate. The gunships were spinning faster than the E-mags were slewing.

"Hit them. Hit them!" Jaq told the trails dancing across the screen.

The board didn't have time to populate with red or green lines showing imminent impacts or misses.

They'd closed the distance and all shots arrived almost instantaneously from when they were fired.

The delay had taken the captain's attention away from the energy gauge. She glanced at it to find it read forty percent. Far better than she thought.

E-mags, six cannons each, zeroed in on their targets. The lines converged on the enemy as the gunships brought their weapons to bear. They had an angle on *Chrysalis*.

The first round hit the Borwyn cruiser like thunder from a god.

The gunships exploding on the screen elicited no cheers as the death throes from their railguns pounded *Chrysalis*. The ship reverberated from multiple impacts that laced up and down its sides.

The impacts stopped quickly with the demise of their firing platforms.

"Idle the engines," Jaq said.

The acceleration had been brief but intense and added to the acceleration gained from Farslor's gravity. They had reached nearly two hundred thousand kilometers per hour.

Two new red lights appeared on the status board. They'd lost environment in two of the outer sections.

"DC teams to stations. Assess the damage and fix the ship."

Thirty-seven-percent power remained.

Jaq popped out of her seat and floated into zero-gee.

"Slade, how long before the Malibor see us?" Jaq asked.

"They can probably already see us," the sensor chief replied.

Jaq nodded. There was nothing she could do about it. They needed to shepherd their power.

"Jaq, that cruiser will have power plants. I bet it's unmanned..." Brad winked at her.

A flash on the board showed an explosion at the nose of the cruiser.

"The landers!" Jaq faced Brad.

He activated his comm. "Benjy, stand down the landers. Don't destroy that ship."

Benjy's voice crackled back, "Will do, but I've got some great angles for another few seconds. You won't be able to change your mind."

"I won't. Stand down the remaining landers."

"What are you suggesting, Brad? We take over the Malibor cruiser and add it to the growing Borwyn fleet?"

"No need to grow the fleet. We link up with it and cut the power plants out. We replace ours and we're back up and running in no time."

"We don't have the power to chase it down." Jaq gestured toward the board.

"But *Cornucopia* does. For that matter, so does *Starstrider*."

"The only drawback with your ship is that it's being used to power us, and you can only fit three people in there." Jaq didn't sound like she was arguing. She wanted an answer that she could embrace because she wanted *Chrysalis* back to being fully operational.

"*Cornucopia* is a long way away. If the ship is nothing more than a drone, it'll continue on its present course at its present speed. *Starstrider* can link up with it, a dashing captain can board the cruiser, and he can shut it down."

"Can we do without *Starstrider's* power?"

Brad shrugged. "You *can*. But do you want to?"

Jaq nodded before shaking her head.

"We need to stop and come back for the landers, and then we need to run down that cruiser," Jaq said. "Watch the gauge. Stop our forward momentum. Three gees acceleration. How much power will that burn? Inform the damage control teams."

"Three gees for thirty-one and a half minutes will burn twelve percent under current usage rates," Ferd said.

"Are sensors still radiating?" Jaq asked. At Slade's nod, she ordered, "Shut them down."

"We'll be blind."

"There are no other ships out here. Passive only," Jaq replied.

Slade tapped two buttons. "Sensors are offline. Big ears are listening for anything that might want to tell us it's out here."

Jaq waved over her shoulder. "Keep your eyes on that energy gauge. Twelve percent, huh? Can we still slingshot around Farslor?"

"If we burn right now, but it has to be now."

"Do it," Jaq said. "All hands, secure your tools and into a seat. We'll be accelerating right now to preserve energy. We're heading around Farslor to come back to that Malibor cruiser. They're going to give us their power plants. Department heads report in when your people are accounted for."

The ship rotated using thrusters and accelerated to all ahead flank to drive the ship onto its new vector.

"Hang on!" Jaq shouted at the intercom. They hadn't given the damage control teams time to get to a safe place. She tapped the control to talk with Medical. "Doc Teller, prepare for impact injuries."

"You've got one down here. I'm going to need zero-gee if I'm to get around. I fear I've sprained my ankle," he said, punctuating his words with gasps of pain.

"Calculating new course to intercept the cruiser," Mary confirmed.

"Accelerating through three gees," Ferd announced.

The energy gauge showed thirty-four percent. All things being equal and math being math, a slingshot maneuver should save their energy. Twenty-two percent or greater? She smiled. Jaq had expected to be in the single digits, counting down. Would they win before reaching zero?

The horror stories she had told herself before the engagement had nearly paralyzed her.

"Contact?" Dolly said, somewhere between a statement and a question.

"Radiating," Slade said without asking permission to use the active sensors. It took a couple seconds for the system to power up.

Instantly, a red line of fire appeared on the main screen.

"Gunship. Twenty degrees off the nose."

"Bringing E-mags online," Taurus reported in a voice one octave higher than usual.

A heavy thud made the ship shudder. A single railgun impact.

Chrysalis continued her acceleration around Farslor. Speed had been her friend in nearly every other engagement.

Five gees pressed them deep into their seats.

"E-mag Battery Seven is offline." Taurus tapped two buttons. "Fire."

Four E-mags fired at the cyclic rate followed quickly by five more. The cannons sent their obdurium projectiles across the upper atmosphere with deadly precision. The gunship had been slowing, not even a hundred thousand KPH as it waited to ambush *Chrysalis* running from the four-gunship attack.

Jaq's carefully preserved power stores evaporated in the blink of an eye. Twenty-five vaulted down to twenty and then nineteen.

The E-mag rounds trailed toward the gunship and through, but it kept flying.

"How is that possible?" Jaq asked.

The railgun fire stopped.

Chrysalis flashed through the upper atmosphere and past the gunship, which was slowly breaking in half.

"The gunship is dead!" Alby declared. "Leaves one cruiser and five gunships, Captain."

Jaq would have nodded, but they were straining under five gees.

"Pull back to three gees. Power down the sensors and weapons."

"Captain?" Slade wondered, asking at the same time as Taurus.

"If we run out of power, no amount of awareness or readiness will save us. Passive only. We are committed to intercepting that Malibor cruiser. I don't want to run into it with a dead ship."

"Roger," they both said. Taurus powered her systems down completely. Slade conducted one final three-hundred-and-sixty-degree scan. He took the active system offline after his final pass.

Fourteen percent.

Silence reigned on the bridge while Jaq stared at the red lights flashing on her board. Two sections were vented to space, but they were outer areas where crew weren't allowed during combat. The one impact from the final gunship hadn't made its whereabouts known.

"Where did that last round hit us, Brad?" Jaq asked.

"We'll find out as soon as possible. I don't have a good feeling about it."

Jaq had the same thought. "Department heads, report damage and personnel status."

The reports took too long to arrive. Jaq was almost willing to try moving under three gees when they cleared around Farslor and powered the engines down.

"Yes!" Ferd cried out. "Ten percent and a hundred and seventy-five thousand KPH. We'll intercept the Malibor cruiser in less than an hour. We have enough power to slow down, then match course in order to link up with the ship."

"We'll take that one step at a time," Jaq said. "Just in case they planned on us doing exactly what we intend to do."

CHAPTER 28

When you fight, you must fight to win.

"This is it," one of the escorts said.

"Thanks for bringing me. I guess I have to take it from here," Deena replied, looking at the field beyond the trees and the city wall in the distance.

She remembered it only too well. It had been nearly two years since she was last in the city. Two long years. She wondered where her father was.

There was no way she could make contact with anyone from her previous life. If she did, she had a cover story of space sickness and they'd let her go. She wasn't sure what the fleet was like right now. When she joined, they had all their ships and no enemies.

Then the Borwyn heavy cruiser showed up and wreaked devastation on the Malibor fleet.

Max hugged her fiercely. When he let go, his eyes glistened, but he didn't say anything in an attempt to not appear weak. He waved one last time, and with the escorts, they faded into the brush and disappeared from view.

Deena was alone. For the first time in her life, there was no one around. Her pulse quickened. Her breath came in ragged gasps. She tried to step into the open but found her legs weren't cooperating. Deena stood in the tree line, not going forward, not stepping back.

Walk straight ahead like you belong there, she counseled herself. She closed her eyes and thought of Max. He'd had faith in her. They had talked about this mission. It was the most dangerous thing she would ever do. Surviving the destruction of *Hornet* was nothing compared to this. She'd have to be on her guard every minute of every day.

She patted her pocket, where she carried all the money that Glen had recovered from the dead Malibor soldiers. They still used paper money. She recognized it. She didn't have any of her own since she hadn't been carrying it when she found herself trapped near the bridge of her Malibor ship.

The ground troops had been rich compared to the cash she had in space.

She figured it would get her over the worst of it. She would take a job that paid cash, a waitress in a restaurant close to fleet headquarters. That was the plan, anyway.

It started with the first step. She opened her eyes. She had to cover a few kilometers of open ground. At least no one would be shooting at her, she hoped. She was unarmed. She carried a Malibor military canteen. They had been common when she was in the city and popular among the youth. She didn't know why. Maybe it made them look bad.

Deena took a sip, capped the canteen, and tucked it away. She strolled into the open, taking it easy at first to make sure the panic attack didn't return. The more she walked, the better she felt. She looked for the gate where she'd have to convince the guards to let her through. Her Malibor fleet identification was the only personal item she had from her time aboard *Hornet*.

What she didn't need was an extensive search of her small bag. The radio was disguised as a Malibor radio, but it didn't work. She had to take it apart and reconfigure a number of wires before it was operational on the frequency she needed.

She found the going easy. The sky was clear and temperatures were comfortable. It was Septimus. She understood how it had affected the crew who had never had the opportunity to live in a place like this.

They had called it paradise.

It could be again for the Borwyn. But first, it would take her doing her job, and it would take Jaq and *Chrysalis* to do their job and finish destroying the Malibor fleet.

"Any time now, we should be hearing from *Chrysalis*," Crip said while he and Max stared at the radio. They'd sent their report, cryptically referencing Deena's deployment to the city, the training, and the gunship. Nothing Septimus-shattering, only a status report. The war continued, and the Borwyn were shaping the battlefield to take advantage.

The Malibor were on their heels and the Borwyn kept punching.

Unless they weren't.

"What do we do if *Chrysalis* is gone?" Max asked.

"Then we press on, hitting them in the city, in the spaceport, out here, anywhere they are. With or without *Chrysalis*, we are still at war with the Malibor. They stole our home. We're going to take it back."

Max clapped his friend on the shoulder. "I couldn't have said it better myself." He stared at the radio.

Larson adjusted the controls. "Our signal is good."

"I know. Something has happened, either to the scout ship or *Chrysalis*," Crip replied.

"What about Deena? When will we hear from her?" Max pressed.

Crip didn't know. She was to contact Glen's people, First Company of the Borwyn Assault Battalion. Crip had asked about the other companies but only received a waffling answer. He was starting to suspect that if there were other companies, they were light on numbers. Glen's company was the only functional unit left.

After fifty years of fighting in the forests west of Malipride, the will to fight had waned. The Malibor were happy sending fighters every now and again to keep the Borwyn where they were and on edge.

It didn't hurt the Malibor to have Borwyn running around the forest.

They needed to wreak havoc from within the city. The Malibor wouldn't expect that.

Glen joined them. "Anything?"

"Nothing. Did your people get back from dropping Deena off?"

"Not yet. They were to wait until she reached the city and made it inside before returning. I wanted to know that she made it without any problems."

"Good call." Crip glanced at Max, who was listening intently and scowling.

"Sir," Larson interrupted. "Message from *Starbound*."

"Relayed?" Crip asked.

"No. Originating from *Starbound*. It is as follows: *Chrysalis* engaged one cruiser and five gunships. That is five gunships. All gunships destroyed. *Chrysalis* last seen accelerating out of Farslor orbit toward deep space on a trajectory we calculate will intercept the cruiser. Comm is silent. Expect it is damaged. *Chrysalis* is the Borwyn fleet's flagship and has singlehandedly destroyed nearly the entire Malibor order of battle. Cheers to the stalwart captain and crew. Two cruisers are in the shipyard undergoing repairs. One cruiser is orbiting the station. Five gunships are docked. The large unidentified ship remains under construction. *Starbound* going dark. Next comm in ten days, same time."

"We can't talk to *Chrysalis*?" Max wondered.

"Sounds like nobody can. Three cruisers and five gunships. Chrysalis has been busy. They reported two and ten before they destroyed five and went after one. But this report says there are three cruisers plus the one they're going after. Who's right?" Crip recounted three times based off what he knew. There was a gap between when they left the ship before it engaged the ships around the space station.

"That's good, isn't it?" Glen asked.

"The ship has been damaged," Crip deduced. "Much more than anyone is saying." He rubbed his chin in thought. "Send this..."

"Can't," Larson interrupted. "They've already cut the connection. That little bit where they said they were going dark? They meant it."

Max blew out a breath, still staring at the radio as if more information would appear.

Larson powered the unit down and started packing it. The movements added a finality to the event.

"The battle is joined," Crip whispered. He took a knee and mumbled a prayer to Septiman.

"Crip," Max started, "that makes what we do down here that much more important. But it also means we have time to do it right."

"That means we give Deena time to casually gather the information and not be overzealous. She'll be okay, Max, but we'll have to demonstrate a level of patience that we're not used to." Crip groaned. "Call the combat team together and we'll bring them up to speed. We're going to have to hurry up and wait together."

"Another test of our mettle?" Max asked with a chuckle. "We are constantly being tested. The good news is that unlike Farslor, we haven't lost anyone on Septimus."

"And that is good news indeed. Gather the team and let's talk to them. Please join us, Glen. This involves you, too, since we're going to be here for a while longer."

———

"Ho there!" a voice called from a point above the gate. Deena couldn't see who was speaking.

She waved and smiled but kept walking.

"Where are you coming from?" A Malibor guard appeared. Gruff, unkempt, the soldier class in an era when there were no wars—not according to the Malibor. The Borwyn in the western forest were nothing more than a nuisance. That was why they took their civilian adventures to the east, but now they'd seen the sting in those forests, too, when the missing group of hunters had been reported.

They probably kept that information from the general population. They didn't want to stoke fear, only hatred of the Borwyn. She'd been taught to hate the Borwyn, too, who turned out to be decent people with a healthy respect for life and a way of treating everyone as their own person.

No race was good. No race was bad. Individuals were generally good, but the governments were bad. The Borwyn had no government besides a ship captain doing her best to reclaim what had been lost.

"I got lost and spent the night in the wood. I thought it would be a grand adventure, but it sucked." She ran her fingers through her tangled hair.

"I didn't see you leave when I was on shift yesterday."

"I left by North One," she answered, knowing that gate led to fields of grain and vegetables managed daily by farm crews.

"And you ended up here? That was an adventure. Go rest your feet, beautiful, and then come on back. Maybe we can have a drink or something when I get off shift."

"Maybe, kind sir. We'll see if I wake up in time." She had

no intention of coming back or ever laying eyes on that guard again. The door lock clunked free, and she pushed it open.

She walked through and dutifully closed the door behind her. She waved up at the guard and walked into a small area that would be a kill-zone for an enemy coming through that door. It stunk of animals. That indicated which purpose it had served and which it had not. She picked her way across and under a portcullis to get into the city. Once there, she looked for the nearest station.

Inside Malipride, there was public transport for the masses. Only the very rich had personal vehicles. The sidewalks were wide while the roads were narrow with only two travel lanes, one for each direction. Pullouts every two hundred meters were for the buses that ran their routes every fifteen minutes. They sported solar collectors as roofs to keep their energy storage banks filled.

One trundled away as she walked up. The good news was that she'd only have to wait fifteen minutes for the next one.

But where would she go? The military headquarters was at the southern tip of the city, along with the spaceport. Deena needed a place to stay and a job. She'd find a room to rent first, and then get a job.

She laughed quietly. The indignity of it all, but what made it better was the mission. She was undercover to free the Borwyn. In her mind, that meant she would also free the Malibor people from the clutches of a government that believed war was the answer to every question.

Deena planned to be the best server they'd ever seen, wherever *they* were. She'd start with the place closest to the base and then move outward. She wouldn't live in that area so she could maintain some separation from lovesick soldiers like the one who guarded the gate she'd just gone through.

She waited the fifteen minutes and the next bus trundled along. She climbed aboard, paying cash for the trip using the smallest bill in her possession. She waited for the change while the driver took the time to look offended and made disgusted noises. Eventually, he produced the small coins and slapped them into Deena's hand. She'd been ready. It was the same game they all played. Had she dropped the coins, he would have started off, sending her stumbling toward the back so he could recover the coins later. It was a pittance, but the drivers weren't the highest paid of the city employees.

Deena hurried to a seat and looked out the window. She wasn't sure about being back in the city. When she went to space, she hadn't thought about returning to Malipride. She thought the space station might have what she was missing in her life.

Then again, she didn't know. She was young. How long would she have been gone on *Hornet* if she'd been able to make a career of her service, even though the track record up until *Chrysalis's* return was that the Malibor fleet would be used against other Malibor. Was she ready to kill her own people? She had been before because that would have been part of the job. Now, she was looking at how to save them by destroying only that which needed to be destroyed.

It was a dichotomy of philosophy. Join the enemy because they were friends to save those who had been family but were really the enemy. She tried to wrap her mind around it, but the easiest answer was to knock down the tasks before her, one by one.

The bus traveled three stops to a hub where Deena changed to a route that went south. It took a circuitous track to get there, but after forty-five minutes, she climbed off.

The base started another hundred meters ahead. She hadn't intended to get off this close since she was looking for a place to stay first. A sign in the window of the restaurant located no more than ten steps from the bus stop caught her attention and forced a change in plans.

She strolled in, grabbed the help wanted sign, and carried it to the counter.

An older man looked her over without leering. It helped put her at ease. "I need a job."

"I've got a job." He scowled. "What's wrong with you?"

"My stepfather was hitting on me and I had to get out of there. I have the clothes on my back, this small pack, and nothing else besides the money I took out of his wallet on my way out the door. I want to work for cash. My stepfather has access to the system and if I'm in it, he'll find me."

"You need a place to stay?"

"I'm not shacking up with anyone, if that's what you were thinking."

"Nah, what kind of creep do you take me for?"

Deena raised one eyebrow.

"It's clear to me you've been in the biz before." He looked at the few customers to see that none of them were watching. He leaned close and whispered, "Cash under the table, but thirty percent. I keep seventy as room and board. You can eat here and stay here."

"Suits me just fine. When can I start?"

"How about now? Learn the menu and get them to buy drinks. More and more drinks. That's where I make my profit since they're all watered down." He laughed loud enough to draw the looks he had been trying to avoid.

The owner tucked the help wanted sign under the counter and gestured for Deena to follow him.

Up a narrow staircase to a second floor with an office, a communal bathroom, and a second room that was barely bigger than a closet.

Deena crossed her arms and stared at the man.

"What?" he grumbled.

"For a room that's nothing more than a closet and a communal bathroom? You keep thirty percent, and I get seventy."

"We'll renegotiate after I see if you can serve the customers and upsell the booze."

"We'll renegotiate right now. Look at me. You don't think I can sell booze to soldiers?" She stood back to strike a pose.

"You have a point. They'd have to be both blind and deaf to not buy a drink from you. Okay, forty percent for me."

"Done." She held out her hand and they shook. "What's your name?"

"You can call me Boss. See you downstairs in five. Clean yourself up."

Deena looked at her hand that was now sticky. She found a bathroom that didn't have a locking door and a ratty shower that may have never been cleaned. She'd take what she needed to clean it and make it a place where she'd wash off the grease and filth of a day half in a kitchen and half on the floor.

The lack of a lock bothered her, but the doorknob could be braced from the inside. She'd use the lone chair in her room along with adding a sign to the outside knob that would say "Occupied." She put her stuff in the room and locked it with the key that was already in the lock. She stuffed the key into her pocket and headed downstairs, where a dirty apron awaited.

"Have you never heard of cleanliness is the way to Septiman's good graces?"

"You're not a holy roller, are you?" he shot back.

"No. I'm just allergic to death from the filth of this existence. We're cleaning this place when the last customers are done. Do you hear me?"

"Holy mother of Septiman! I've hired my wife." He looked shocked. "We don't have to clean it all tonight, do we?"

"We can pace ourselves, but it's been a while since you've had help, hasn't it?"

"Too long. I've let some things go, but I can't be here every hour of every day. That was killing me. The doc said I had to take time off."

Deena rubbed her finger and thumb together in the traditional Malibor slight of the world's smallest violin playing the crying concerto. She clapped him on the shoulder. "We'll get there. No cash out of hand and you gained yourself a loyal employee."

"Order four is up!" a voice called from the kitchen.

"Your only other co-worker. His name is Festival. He's a bit off."

"Ooh! What do we have out there? Is that fresh meat?" he called through the window.

"See what I mean?"

"If I come in there, it's going to be to punch you in the face. Do you understand me?"

"Hiring a feisty one," Festival said. "I like 'em feisty."

"I'm going in." Deena took an angry step toward the door. The boss grabbed her arm and pointed at order four. He pointed at a table close to the door. "Table four."

She redirected her efforts to serve the late lunch crowd. After a short conversation, they ordered two drafts.

The boss beamed. While he was pulling the beers, Deena went into the kitchen and punched Festival in the side of his head.

He cowered after she hit him. In the fleet, she'd learned how to deal with bullies, even though she had to take greater care when denying favors to officers. But here? She had no intention of playing nice. This was the heart of Malibor, where the strong got ahead.

Deena had to look away when she realized how easily she had slipped into the role of being hard and mean. She took a deep breath. It was for a better purpose, and maybe playing the tough role, she could teach these people to be decent human beings. There weren't enough strong women in their lives. If the boss's wife was so demanding, why wasn't she here helping him?

Deena strolled back to the dining room and received a round of applause. The boss nodded while the customers clapped. She bowed before getting to work. She dug underneath the counter to find the cleaning materials. She started with the empty tables, much to the boss's approval.

The others bought drinks, too.

"Let me tell you a story my brother told about his time in the fleet…" She didn't have a brother. It was her story, so she could embellish as needed.

More drinks.

Deena was in a hurry for the shift to end so she could activate her radio and send the message that she'd arrived. The message would be a simple two clicks. That was the code that she arrived with no issues. One click would have indicated a problem. Three clicks would have meant that she wasn't set up but there were no problems. Two clicks were what they wanted to hear, and she was happy to deliver it as soon as she finished for the evening.

Two hours after they closed, she found that she could barely lift her arms, but the boss paid her in cash on the spot. She wondered why it was so much.

"You did the work of two people. Sixty-forty for two people is that much. Take it, and see you tomorrow."

"I'll need to take off sometime during the day. I need clothes, and it wouldn't hurt you to serve a vegetable in here every now and then."

"Don't get uppity. Customers like my fried everything menu."

"We'll see over time, maybe try a salad or two. You'll be amazed, especially after I tell a couple round customers that they may be getting fat and should probably order a salad."

"You have a lot of faith yourself, don't you. I see why your stepfather kicked you out."

"He didn't..." She saw the look on his face that he was trying to get under her skin. "I'm calling it a day. See you tomorrow."

Deena waved and headed up the stairs. He went outside and locked the door behind him. She discovered that she didn't have a key to get out. That was a task for tomorrow. She'd wrest a key from the boss man even if she had to steal his. But first, Deena had to send a short transmission from a radio that she also needed to hide.

CHAPTER 29

Pain lets you know that you're still alive.

"What?" Jaq couldn't believe that the comm dish had been taken out. It was small but wasn't armored because that interfered with the signal. It had taken a round right through its heart.

"We have to go outside to replace it. Based on my last experience outside the ship while traveling at a high rate of speed, I would prefer we not do that," Brad replied. "But I can take *Starstrider* and use the scout's comm. I can also run ahead and gauge the status of the cruiser. Will you have to board a hostile ship? Until we know that, we can't recall *Cornucopia*, either."

"It's a good question, Brad, since we don't have any weapons besides a few axes and pikes that we can use as spears. It's not an impressive array. If they have two people on board with blasters of any sort, they'll repel our attempts and kill our crew." Jaq groaned and grumbled before making the only decision she could. "Take *Starstrider* out. We'll make do without the supplemental power. We still have ten percent remaining to run life support and tap the thrusters to align us with the cruiser, should we be able to link up and board it."

Brad saluted and hurried out.

"Amie, get a parts list for a spacewalking repair crew to fix our transceiver."

The communications officer looked confused.

Jaq explained, "For when they can go outside. We're not sending anyone out under speed unless it's an emergency. This is not worth risking any crew, not when *Starstrider* can use their equipment. When it was just us, we looked at things differently, but not now. We have a fleet!"

Amie nodded her understanding and accessed the radio to call Maintenance and Stores. Once those efforts were in motion, she returned her energy to collecting and consolidating status reports. The rest of the bridge crew had once again deployed on damage control duty. The challenges of restoring wiring, cabling, and piping from the attack weeks earlier was ongoing. The newest impacts caused minimal damage, but it only added to an already substantial workload.

They needed a month, access to *Cornucopia*, and unlimited power. The power was the biggest limitation under which they worked. They couldn't fabricate new power, so all workarounds were manual, cobbled together from parts on hand rather than using the right part printed when the circumstances allowed. Circuit boards and processors had to be programmed independently after insertion into a new system.

It would have been overwhelming, but the crew was tackling the challenges one at a time.

"Short-range comm is open," Amie stated.

Jaq looked at her console, waiting for Brad to check in. He was taking too long. "Brad, check in, please."

"You missed me, love of my life," Brad replied. At least it was only Jaq and Amie on the bridge. The comms officer laughed. "Heading out to get a clear angle to *Starbound*, and then it's off to catch the cruiser. I'll send a report to *Cornucopia*, too."

"Sounds good. I'll be off the bridge. We have a lot of work to do to be ready in case we get two power plants."

"Better gather some fighters together. I think even if the cruiser has people aboard, we still need to take their power plants. We don't really have a choice."

Jaq hung her head. She had never wanted to be the space pirate, but Crip and Tram had convinced her that it was a viable tactic if they wanted to win the war.

"Concur. We have to take that ship. I doubt they planned for what we're about to do, assuming someone is on board. They were ready to die for their plan, plus we hit them pretty hard. The ship might already be decompressed."

"I like how you think, Jaq. I'll report when I get there."

"Whatever you do, don't you board that ship by yourself!"

The channel closed instead of a reply.

Amie caught Jaq's glare. "You know him pretty well," Amie said.

Evelyn stood when Crip was ready to address the group. "I have something to say."

Crip nodded and motioned for her to move to the front.

She moved easily through the group but when she got to the front, she faced Crip. "We appreciate how you've integrated us into the team. We like the pulse pistols, but feel our bows have better range and accuracy. And finally, you men need to stop protecting us. Don't make us fight you."

Crip rubbed the stubble on his face. "I thought you had something important. We know all that stuff."

Evelyn glared at him.

"Are you sure you don't have kids? Because that look is what you do when they're acting up." Crip waited for her to lighten up. She pursed her lips but remained silent. "Serious talk. I'm perfectly fine with bows instead of pulse pistols, but when we get the rifles, you'll upgrade to them. We've been teaching you how to shoot them in case we fall in combat. You can pick it up and resume firing at the enemy. As for the men protecting you, I'm sorry. It's what we do."

"You're fine, but they need to stop!" Evelyn nearly shouted.

"Thanks for the confidence in me. I've done the same thing to Taurus. It's in our nature to protect our loved ones. Your people have made an impact on us. We can't throw you to the Malibor. We put ourselves in the way first, not because we're better, but because we have body armor and weapons that can blow an enemy away with a level of violence the Malibor aren't used to. I think a separate strike team using nothing but bows will provide us a tactical advantage. A hammer-and-anvil approach—nothing against our two teammates with those names. The hammer hits the anvil with the enemy in between. Ambush the Malibor."

"We can get behind that. We'll establish our own squad."

Crip looked at the faces of his original combat team. "What did you guys do to chase them away?" he snapped.

They were shocked. "I thought things were going great," Hammer replied. He looked around hopelessly. The others did the same.

Evelyn laughed. "Is that what you think?"

"It seems like something we would do," Crip replied.

"Your people are great. But when it comes to the fight, we're all in. We can't do that if your hulking mass of men is in the way."

"Aren't you going to be on the gunship?" Crip realized.

"Yes, but I'm the spokesperson for this group because, well, like you, I'm old."

Crip was on his heels. The women on the ground giggled. Fantasia clapped.

"Hey!"

Glen eased back until Crip caught his eye. Crip shook his head at the man.

"We're in this with you," Glen interjected. "We all fight together. I recommend two squads, a mix of men and women, but no partners. You don't get to fight beside your mate because you'll make bad decisions. All that being said, that last engagement is probably the extent of the Malibor incursions this year. Winter isn't kind here in the forest. It's rainy and cold."

Crip wasn't looking toward winter. He had a shorter timeline. "We're going to wreak some havoc on Pridal. The silent death of an arrow will come in handy. How do they guard the gates?"

"Deena will provide a definitive answer to that," Glen replied.

The radio operator waved his hand to get their attention. "We've heard from her. Two clicks." He punctuated his report with a thumbs-up.

Max beamed in relief.

"That is good news." Crip had also been carrying too much stress about her, both for Deena and his friend Max.

"We can broadcast all we want, but her transmissions will be extremely limited. We can't let them triangulate her position," Glen warned.

"Are they that wary? That takes an effort, and I suspect their focus isn't on random radio signals," Crip replied.

"We use radios out here, but short-range or directional only. We don't send signals toward the city. I'm not sure we ever have, even before my time, and I've been doing this for three passes now. Talking with Deena will be the first time we'll have ever radioed someone in Pridal."

"Then what's the chance that the Malibor have people dedicated for radio detection finding?" Crip wasn't a believer that RDF was the counterintelligence the Malibor would engage in. To them, they weren't at war on the ground. The war was in space, and they were losing. Spending their days listening for signals that hadn't been there for decades wasn't a quality investment of their time.

"We don't want to take the risk. We're in this to win, and we *will* win, because we're better than the Malibor in all aspects of this war. The only advantage they have is they control the city with their million people."

"That's a lot of people. We have a couple squads, you have a company, and there's a phantom assault battalion out there somewhere."

Glen nodded, tight-lipped. "We have the bulk of the combat power in First Company. The rest are in support, like foodstuffs and supply."

Crip didn't like being lied to, even if it was by omission. He had divined the truth, but it would have been better had Glen been forthcoming. Crip leaned close and whispered, "Please don't lie to me again."

"We couldn't take the chance, not with a Malibor on your team, and I know, she's not a Malibor, but it didn't hurt anything she knew."

"I think you screwed up your messaging. It'll probably be better if they think you're no threat." Crip held up a hand to forestall further conversation. He'd talk with Glen privately about the value of trust. He faced the group. "Two squads. Max in charge of one and I'll be in charge of the other."

Crip motioned for Max to separate the group in two, leaving out Tram, Kelvis, Evelyn, and Pistora. Max made it easy, tapping heads and saying one or two. He put Hammer and Anvil in the same squad and Mia and Ava in the other. He didn't want the brothers looking out for their partners.

"Everyone who's in First Squad, over here." Max twirled his arm in the air.

"Everyone else over here," Crip said. He sized up his people. He trusted them all. He had both Danzig and Fantasia. "How did I get you?"

Fantasia laughed. "How could they put me with anyone other than my dad?"

"You'll be the reason I go gray," Crip replied. "We're going to run through formations and maneuvers first thing tomorrow. Bounding overwatch, covering fire, single envelopment. Simple stuff."

When Crip looked for Glen, he was gone but Eleanor was there.

"It wasn't my idea," she said.

"I understand." Crip didn't want to drive a wedge between her and the commander. He didn't want to have any issues with Glen Owain either. Maybe the issue was best left in the past. Glen and company hadn't done them wrong in any way. They fed them and welcomed them. "I more than understand. It's not as big an issue as I initially thought. Actually, it's a non-issue. Moving on. Tomorrow, we start more training but in our individual squads. We'll integrate the archers as their own element. We'll figure out when best to employ our advantage."

Eleanor gestured toward the group before Crip and the squad by Max. "Your advantage is in your commitment. I thought we were dedicated to the war, but not like you. You came to Septimus on a one-way trip and picked up wives along the way, and they're now fully engaged with fighting the Malibor, too. It's quite amazing."

Crip found it hard not to appreciate the kind words. "With peacemakers like you and Glen, how can we lose?"

"We all die?" Eleanor replied.

"Meteoric highs to terrestrial lows in the space of two heartbeats." Crip scratched his head and changed the subject. "How do we get information from Deena if she can't broadcast?"

"We have a select code that she memorized. We use it to communicate between the companies when the topic is sensitive."

Crip expected a high level of professionalism from people who had been at war all their lives. Theirs was a way of life that kept them out of the Malibor spotlight. They fought when they had to fight, but they avoided conflict. Being ready for it was critical to ensure the survival of their fighting force. It wasn't the way Crip would have done it because he embraced the attack. Jaq had shown him how effective attacking could be.

Punch the enemy in the face and keep punching.

But *Chrysalis* had one purpose and that was to make war. Despite the generations that had been born aboard the ship and grown up there, it wasn't about survival. The Borwyn on Septimus were trying to survive. Maybe they assumed the Malibor would kill themselves in one of their civil wars. With the sanctity of their mountain intact, they could afford the luxury of time.

Chrysalis, Jaq, and her crew never had that luxury. They needed a purpose greater than existence.

All or nothing.

And Jaq was still in the fight. *Chrysalis* had survived yet again at a significant cost to the Malibor. Maybe the war would be over sooner than Crip thought. He relished the day he could bring Taurus to the planet surface, when they would be unencumbered by the fear of dying.

Septimus is paradise, Crip thought.

"Thanks, Eleanor. We'll keep looking for opportunities to cause the Malibor grief until *Chrysalis* can dictate the terms of their surrender." He looked around. "Max, next time we talk with *Starbound*, remind me to tell them about the warrior from Fristen who was leading the latest Malibor infiltration team. We haven't taken a good look at Fristen. They might be a problem."

"As in, how did he get here?" Max asked. "That's a good question. There might be ships we haven't accounted for." Max grimaced.

"The Malibor order of battle of remaining ships keeps changing. Jaq needs to know that someone might be coming up from behind if they decide to attack the ships here."

Max nodded.

Eleanor asked, "Is there anything else you need, Crip?"

"I think we're going to call it a night. It's been a long day."

She gripped his shoulder for a moment before nodding and walking away. He watched her go.

"Deena is in. *Chrysalis* is flying away. Now, we wait," Max said. "The question is, how long? Winter is coming. We thought we might be here for a month or two while *Chrysalis* took care of business—" He nodded toward the sky. "—but that's not happening. How bad do you think it is?"

"Bad. *Chrysalis* has had weeks to repair itself, but the Malibor hit them. And now it'll be a while still. Have you ever seen snow?"

Max shook his head. "Can't even imagine what it looks like or feels like."

"I'm afraid we're going to find out. I hope Deena has someplace warm."

CHAPTER 30

Fate is a fickle master.

After transmitting his messages, Brad accelerated after the cruiser. Launching from *Chrysalis* at two hundred thousand KPH meant that he only needed to gain separation from the Borwyn flagship. He added two gees of acceleration to put him at the cruiser a half-hour before *Chrysalis*. That would give him the time to finish what he needed to do.

Cornucopia was making a wide turn to slow and get back to *Chrysalis*. Brad told them to watch the cruiser to see if it would turn. He suspected it wouldn't because it couldn't. It was on a solid hundred and fifty thousand kilometer per hour ballistic track through the Armanor system.

No one would have volunteered for such a mission, definitely not any Borwyn.

Brad told himself that the four gunships had been attached to the airlocks and the gunship crews operated the cruiser to get it up to speed. They'd separate them one at a time on the flight to never reveal that there was more than one gunship flying with the cruiser.

It made sense, but then again, Brad was arguing with himself. He didn't see a counterargument that would hold water.

He was going in, despite Jaq's warning not to. She knew he was and that's why she'd said it. She should have saved her breath, for all the good it did.

At least he'd come prepared with a boarding axe and a stunner that the combat team had in their ready room. He couldn't find anything else that looked like a weapon. He hadn't had much time.

He adjusted his course once he hit the desired speed. He'd spin the ship around and slow once he closed on the cruiser. He wanted to see it with his own eyes first.

Starstrider flew smoothly, despite the panel being taken apart below the flight deck where he'd helped them install a direct link from the ship's power to *Chrysalis*. He'd unhooked it hastily and tossed the cables out the hatch. It left a mess, but he couldn't be bothered with that, or could he?

He had an hour before he got close enough to see the cruiser with his naked eye.

He sighed, set an alarm, and floated free to collect the items that had gathered at the back of the central cabin after acceleration. He brought them up front, secured them in a net that he hooked to the bulkhead, and got to work.

Brad found that it took less than thirty minutes to put everything back together. In a different day, he would have put it off for weeks, only to be surprised that it took less time to do than the time spent avoiding it.

He cleaned up and treated himself to a Malibor ration.

"How can you people be so evil yet have such good food?" he asked. "Because the people preparing the food aren't the evil ones. They are geniuses who we should put on pedestals once we win this war." He threw his head back and gave his best evil laugh.

He looked around to see that there was no one there. The days of entertaining himself while on patrol had ended a decade earlier when Hammer and Anvil joined him. Now, they were on Septimus with their girlfriends.

Brad felt in his very soul that the Borwyn were on the right path to reclaim what they'd lost. Too many originals still lived to give credence to Malibor lies that they were the original race that occupied Septimus. No. It was the Borwyn, and they were coming home.

The Malibor chefs could stay behind. They were more than welcome to ply their trade with a Borwyn people ready to eat well. New Septimus deserved it after decades of consuming their own bacteria-infested food. Good for them but at a terrible price.

They lived longer. Brad was aging faster eating good-tasting food once more. He considered the trade-off to be worth it.

He secured his trash and returned to the flight deck. The Malibor cruiser was coming into visual range. Running lights were on as if it were a commercial freighter heading for its next stop.

Until he closed with it, he couldn't see anything else. It was on the exact same course as it had followed from the moment it left Malpace. Nothing was new. It wasn't like he'd see people in the minimal number of portholes. It was a warship, which meant it was armored and not intended for casual viewing of space. The bridge would be somewhere in the center of the ship for highest survivability.

Brad thought about how little he knew about the Malibor cruisers. They'd been watching them for nearly fifty years but had never seen inside one.

He inverted his ship and ran the engines up to three gees to slow down the scout ship. Brad watched the closing speed. With the arrival of *Chrysalis*, Brad had done more close-ship maneuvers than he had in the previous decades combined. He considered himself quite the expert, like landing his ship in the cargo bay. That was a tight squeeze and he'd done it without any issues.

"I still got it," he said with a toss of his head. If he had been able to walk around, he would have done so with a pilot's swagger.

He slowed until he matched the speed of the big ship, staying abeam the aft end. Thrusters brought the scout craft around to align it with the cruiser. Brad eased it forward, crawling along the hull to the aft airlock, which he figured was closest to the power plants. He didn't care about anything else on board the Malibor cruiser, except to satisfy his curiosity.

The ship wasn't streaming atmosphere, but it had been a couple hours since *Chrysalis* hammered it with obdurium projectiles. He could see where the E-mags had scarred the ship across its diameter and not down its length. No other significant damage was visible. It had been hit hard, what Brad would have considered killing blows, but it didn't send a power plant critical or overrun the engines until they exploded.

Brad had his priorities.

First and foremost was getting the power working on *Chrysalis*. They were still fighting a war.

He didn't hold his breath for the cruiser to be carrying any weapons. It would have fired if it had any operational. Brad angled his ship in and closed the last few meters to connect with the airlock. The hatch sealed.

Brad put on the spacesuit he'd liberated from outside the cargo hold.

He clicked the helmet into place and activated the environmental control. He double-checked the battery, in case the ship had vented its atmosphere to space. It would be cold inside.

With the air flowing, Brad cycled the atmosphere from inside the cabin until it equalized with the airlock. Brad connected his boots to the deck, hefting the axe in his left hand and the stunner in his right. He popped the hatch and opened it, staying to the side and peeking through.

It was dark inside the cruiser, for as much as he could see through the small window of the airlock. He reached inside and activated the hatch. It had a small manual override and hand crank. He released it and started cranking. It didn't give him any visual cues about what lay beyond. If there hadn't been any atmosphere, the airlock wouldn't have allowed him to use the hand crank. He continued to rotate the handle. It wasn't as easy as he expected it to be.

It made him wonder if the cruiser had been dug out of a scrapyard and pressed into service.

Spinning and spinning until he was about ready to pass out, finally, the hatch was open wide enough for him to squeeze through. He looked casually through to see someone in a spacesuit looking back at him.

Brad recoiled and bounced off the hatch before he recovered his bearings. He shook his axe at them.

"Prepare to be boarded," he bellowed. The person floated haphazardly. Brad moved one step closer and then another until he discovered it was an empty spacesuit. "You about gave me a heart attack. Don't do that!"

Brad suddenly felt his age.

"And now you're talking to yourself, too," he cautioned. "You need to find yourself a good woman and settle down."

He knew the answer to that. He had a good woman on the hook, an intellectual and leader of renown. There would be statues made and schools named after her. If he played his cards right, he'd be by her side for all of it, but then again, he wasn't winning any points by defying her order not to board the Malibor cruiser.

"It has to be done," he argued. He stepped across the threshold and into the enemy ship. He flashed his suit lights left and right, but it struck him as a dead ship. The suit was an anomaly, pulled toward the airlock with the release of any final vestiges of air.

Once he was sure he was alone in this one small section of the cruiser, he examined the suit. It appeared to be less than spaceworthy, ratty even.

It had been left behind because it was useless. It wasn't there because someone didn't get to their emergency equipment in time.

He pushed it aside and looked for a central corridor that led to the next decks down, where he expected to find the power plants.

Brad discovered the ship was very cold. It hadn't lost its atmosphere during the recent battle. It had been without it for a very long time, and the cold was extreme. It was every bit of ambient in space this far from Armanor.

He dispensed with walking and unhooked his boots from the deck. He pulled himself toward the central axis, where he found a vertical corridor similar to what *Chrysalis* had. He shouldn't have been surprised. The Borwyn and Malibor had been friends at one point in ancient history. It made sense that their ship designs would be similar.

Brad flew down the central shaft, but he was stymied by an elevator one deck down. He couldn't get around it in his spacesuit. A person not in a suit would have been able to squeeze past on ladders attached to the wall. He connected his boots to the sidewall and tried to pull the elevator. It moved relatively easily in zero-gee.

He pulled it up one step at a time until it was even with the deck where he'd entered. Brad moved into the corridor and pulled the elevator up until it was above him. He looked into the shaft, noting there was only one deck below where he stood. That was where the elevator had been stuck. It probably went there during the initial acceleration and there was no one to move it back.

He relaxed, but not enough that he'd leave the elevator over his head. He wedged his axe into the travel channel. He clipped the stunner to his gear belt and launched himself downward. He grabbed the rail surrounding the exit and corkscrewed himself into the corridor, breathing a sigh of relief at his escape from the load over his head even though it wasn't really a threat in zero-gee.

Brad checked the time. He was running out of it. *Chrysalis* would be along shortly. They were probably already trying to contact him, but the suit he'd taken didn't have a functioning comm unit.

He laughed because he felt like a little kid who had gotten into trouble and was dreading telling his parents. He'd come this far. Might as well find the answer he was looking for.

The power plant and drives were in two different spaces, but on opposite sides of the ship. The drives were old, but undamaged. They must have worked well enough to drive the ship to its current speed. Maybe a relay burned out or some other easy fix.

Brad left and hurried to the power plants. The hatch to the space was closed, and the central wheel to open it wouldn't budge. He hammered on the hatch in frustration.

He was out of time and had to return to *Starstrider*.

Brad had pushed off and turned to head to the central shaft when he felt it as much as heard it—two clunks, as if there was someone on the other side of the hatch hitting it with a spanner. Brad removed the only tool available to him, the stunner. He used the butt to hammer three times. Three thunks answered him.

Someone was on the other side. He put his stunner away and pushed off. He had to go. When he returned, it would be with a team from *Chrysalis* with the equipment to determine what was on the other side of that hatch and a way to open it.

"Is that what I think it is?" Jaq asked.

The bridge crew had returned to their stations. Alby knew she was talking to him, but he was hesitant to answer because he didn't have the answer she wanted nor did he want to get between her and Brad.

"Watching my screens, ma'am. Don't see a thing. Space is clear."

The captain jabbed her finger at the screen. "I knew you were going to board that ship."

No one fed her anger, as short-lived as it was.

"You knew he would," Amie offered.

"I did, and I let him go anyway."

"What would you have done?" Amie asked.

Jaq smirked. "The same thing, I guess." She looked around the bridge, and everyone made it their business to be doing something other than watching her. At least they had the good sense not to laugh. "For the record, I'm furious with him."

Alby rolled his eyes.

"I saw that."

"*Chrysalis*, this is *Starstrider* on the short-range comm, are you here yet? I was resting my engines and not boarding the Malibor cruiser."

"You were. What did you find?"

"There's someone trapped in the power plant space. The drives look functional, and the rest of the ship is dead dead. No atmosphere. The running lights are on, so there is some power. The engines ran it up to speed, which tells me the power plants can generate energy. Dock at the starboard airlock so you're closer to the power plant. It's on that side of the ship, opposite *Starstrider*. I'll return to the cargo bay as soon as you're linked up so my ship can resupply power."

"Thanks, Brad. I'm glad you're okay. We're almost out of juice. An infusion would be nice."

The energy gauge read three percent. Everything was offline except computers, thrusters, and air handling. Ferd and Mary deftly handled the maneuvering to bring the ship alongside the Malibor cruiser, align the port-side roller airlock with the cruiser's starboard airlock. The ships touched and the magnetic locks engaged.

"Powering down," Ferd declared. He held his hands up to show the controls were offline.

Two percent remained.

Starstrider detached and rolled around the ships to maneuver into the cargo bay that had been left open after he departed. It took way too long to manually close it. He could sympathize since he didn't bother closing the airlock door, but with the pounding the cruiser had taken from *Chrysalis*, it was already vented to space.

He sent a short message to *Cornucopia* to join them. He gave the location, course, and speed. They'd have to calculate a better intercept course to come alongside.

Brad reveled on flying his ship into the tight space. He landed, engaged the magnetic clamps, and declared victory. There was no one in the cargo bay to greet him. He was still in his environmental control suit. He left his ship to find that he was the one responsible for manually closing the cargo bay door. Before he committed to that, which he saw as punishment for his transgression, he reconnected the power. It made him wish that he hadn't cleaned up so well since he had to remove the panel he'd just reinstalled an hour earlier.

With power reconnected and the engines running, Brad clomped across the hold to the manual access. It was a large crank in the same style as the one he just used to open the Malibor airlock.

He started cranking and cranking, changing hands, changing stances, and doing everything he could to get it done. When it finally thunked shut and the locks engaged, he access the environmental panel to flood the space with the air that had been sucked out before the doors had been opened.

When the light showed green, he took off his helmet and breathed the air of his second home.

Brad took off the suit and carried it under his arm as he crossed the hold to the hatch, spinning the center wheel to open it.

He found Jaq waiting for him on the other side. "I get it. I've been duly punished for violating orders." He rubbed his arms.

"That? No. We didn't have anyone to spare or enough power to cycle air in and out. No, you were always on your own with that one. Your real punishment? My quarters as soon as we have a crew working on removing the power plants." At Brad's look, she explained. "If you can't beat them, join them. You're too much like me to give orders that don't make sense, even though from a logical standpoint, you shouldn't have boarded without backup."

"I know, but I had to. Just like the cargo bay. There

wasn't enough power or personnel to spare." Brad didn't look guilty.

"We need those power plants, Brad. It's a shortcut to get us back into the fight. The longer we take, the more they can prepare for the next battle. With each engagement, they learn more about us and improve their attacks. Five gunships almost did us in. They were a few more shots from tearing us apart, but they were slow executing their plan."

"I've got worse news, Jaq," Brad said while putting his suit on the rack and plugging in the power pack, even though there was no power to those stations at present. "*Starbound* says there's one cruiser at the space station, but there are two cruisers in the shipyard along with the big ship we don't have any intel on. The Malibor are working on all three of those ships."

Jaq screwed her face up. The math was easy. There should have only been one cruiser left but there were three.

"In the shipyard. That means they weren't destroyed. They survived our high-speed pass. I didn't think we hit them hard enough, but it was all we had. Damn."

"I didn't think you'd like that. But if they're in the shipyard, they won't be coming out to meet us. We can move farther out in the system and accelerate to a couple million KPH, then slip past Farslor and straight on to Septimus. They won't be able to react in time, and we'll destroy everything in their space dock."

"Speed is our advantage, but right now, we have issues. We have to plug a lot of holes and fix our external cannons before we attempt that kind of maneuver. If we can get the power online, it'll shorten our timeline."

"Then that's what we'll do. I'll lead the party into the cruiser, if you don't mind, but I need a spacesuit with a working comm unit."

Jaq moved down the line of suits until she found one she recognized. It was the one Crip had used. There was a repaired tear on the mid-section from his engagement aboard *Butterfly*. It was fully functional.

"Take this one," she said.

Brad pulled her in for a quick kiss, the kind of peck a married couple gives each other, something more from habit than out of passion. Brad got into the suit and clicked the helmet home.

"By the way, I left the boarding axe on the cruiser. It's holding the elevator in place so it didn't mistakenly race down the central shaft and kill me."

"Sounds like a reasonable trade-off. Don't tell Max you lost his axe." She pushed Brad and he sailed down the corridor. He raised his head and kept going to the central shaft, where he pulled himself in and disappeared.

Jaq released her boots and flew after him. She pulled herself up the central shaft. She needed to return to Medical, where a gunship round had penetrated and ripped through the bulkhead, peppering Doc Teller with shrapnel. He weathered it like a tough old man, but he was on light duty. It was easily enforced since he was the only member of the crew injured in the latest attack.

CHAPTER 31

The end is only the beginning.

Brad headed into the ship. Alby and a team from engineering were with him. They didn't have any soldiers, so they made do with what they had. Alby carried a stunner, as did Brad.

They reached the access to the power space, and Brad pounded on the door. A few seconds later, someone pounded back.

He pressed his helmet against the door and shouted, "Open the hatch."

There was no response but a couple bangs.

"IR scan," Brad directed.

The engineers scanned it with an old device that blinked in and out, but they gathered enough data to give Brad insight. "The space is warm. I think he's got atmosphere in there. We see what's probably only one person."

"I'll take it." Brad clomped up and down the corridor. "Drop these bulkheads into place and bring an air cylinder to help us equalize the pressure. Get us an extra spacesuit, too. I'll wait here."

The team rushed away to gather what they needed to create an airlock that they could use to open the door and inspect the space beyond.

"Jaq, Brad here," he called using his functioning radio. "There's air and heat in the power plant area. That tells me we have some functioning plants. Teo will get a lot out of them."

"She's on her way. She was a bit put out that you didn't bring her with you."

"She's supposed to be prepping the space to receive the new plants."

"Miffed, Brad. She was really miffed. I'm sure you'll hear it for yourself."

"Jaq, please give me some friendly advice. How do I keep women from being mad at me?"

Jaq laughed. "That's easy. You don't. Just try not to intentionally make them angry and you'll be fine."

"Dad!" Teo bellowed into her helmet. Brad couldn't hear her, but he could tell the word and that she was yelling.

"Gotta go, Jaq. I look forward to not being on this cruiser."

Teo stormed in and slammed her helmet into Brad's so he would hear her. "Why wasn't I on your team?"

"Because we're *your* people. You sit on the throne, and we bring you presents."

Teo leaned back where their helmets were no longer touching. She looked confused. "What?" she mouthed.

"We'll figure out how to get the power plants off this ship.

I'm assuming there are two. But we have to get past a Malibor who is in there with them. We're going to drop these bulkheads and create a poor man's airlock."

"But...I'm angry with you."

"That line is long and distinguished. Be honored that you're in it," Brad replied nonchalantly.

"You might want to secure your radio channel," Jaq said into his helmet. He accessed the wrist control and muted his radio.

"What are you really angry about? The fact that someone suicided right in front of you because they were working too hard and you missed any signs that they were losing control?"

Teo deflated. "We can't win. Every fight gets harder. And everything is a fight. It's a vortex of failure that I'm swirling down."

"We're going to patch up the ship, and then we're going to go to Septimus and destroy the rest of the Malibor fleet. I hear the planet surface is beautiful this time of year. Wouldn't you like to visit your brothers and their girlfriends?"

Teo snickered. "Of course I would, but there are too many steps between here and there. I can't see how to get there."

"Everything starts with the first step. Look back to see how far we've come. That makes how far we have left to go look not so intimidating."

"I'm tired," Teo admitted.

"We all are, but we our energy gauges aren't blinking red, not yet. They're a steady pink. That's a whole lot different. We need you, Teo, for a while longer, then you'll be able to settle on Septimus, too. They say it's paradise down there. Those aren't rumors from oldsters like me dredging up favored memories. Those are our people down there right now telling us the truth of it. Paradise. I'm tired of living on a ship or eating horrible-tasting food just to stay alive. I want to live, Teo!"

After a while, Teo nodded. "Me too, Dad. I want to do more than just survive."

Brad hugged his daughter in the bulk of their spacesuits until the team arrived with the equipment they'd been sent for.

Alby used the general radio channel to coordinate. "Everything we need, including a supplemental battery. It might be easier to drop those bulkheads with juice. We've sent an engineering team to look over the rest of the ship, carefully, in a group of three to see if there is anything worth taking or if there are any other secured spaces."

"They'll run into problems amidships where the damage from our E-mags is extensive."

"They're ready for that. Let's get to it." Alby gave the orders and in no time, they were pumping air into the space to bring it even with the power plant section.

Brad tapped with the butt of his stunner. A series of double taps before he tried to spin the wheel. It moved easily, suggesting it had been secured earlier.

Alby held his stunner at the ready while Brad shooed the group away from the opening in case the Malibor was armed.

The locks retracted and the door moved. Brad took off his helmet and tossed it behind him into the zero-gee.

Brad positioned himself behind it on the opening side and pulled it slowly toward him.

"Can you hear me?" Brad asked.

"Are you Malibor?" a voice replied.

"We don't want a fight. My name is Brad, and I'm going to open this door. Please don't shoot. You'll get yourself killed for no reason."

"I don't have a weapon," the voice replied.

Brad pulled the hatch open far enough to glance inside. An extremely young Malibor stood on the other side. He shivered with the rush of cold air from the corridor and held himself tightly. Brad pulled the hatch open the rest of the way and tucked his stunner into his belt pouch as he stepped into the opening and raised his hands.

"It is a bit chilly out there, isn't it?"

The lad nodded.

"Let's move in where it's warmer." The Malibor wore a haggard jumpsuit that was too big for him. Brad wrapped an arm around his shoulders and guided him toward to grossly oversized power plants. Together, they would completely fill the cargo bay he'd been using as a hangar. "Are you hungry?"

The boy nodded vigorously.

"We brought a suit for you. It'll keep you warm until we can get you back to our ship where you can get something to eat. Tell me, what are you doing here?"

"My parents work in the shipyard. I heard the cruiser was going to sortie out to destroy the Borwyn fleet. I was too young to join, so I stowed away. They didn't have very many people on board. It was easy to hide, but then they all left and turned everything off. I was able to get the plants running, but that's all. What happened to the Malibor?"

"They took their five gunships and attacked the Borwyn fleet. All five gunships have been destroyed. All crew aboard them were lost. This ship has taken heavy damage. You are the only survivor." Brad waved for the spacesuit.

Alby personally delivered it. It was way too big, but it would keep him warm. He wouldn't be able to use the suit's gloves or boots.

Teo moved to the power plants and started her examination.

"What are you going to do with me? I don't have much meat on my bones, so you won't get your meals from me!" he said with the first bit of defiance since they'd met him.

"We're not cannibals. We don't eat people. But we have good food on board *Chrysalis* and you'll be able to eat as much as you want. You'll get a warm place to sleep. Whatever stories you've heard about how evil the Borwyn are, I challenge you to start forming your own opinion right now based on what you see from us. We have no intention of killing Malibor just because they're Malibor. You seem like a decent sort. We'll keep you around, show you that we're decent people, too."

"But you're Borwyn." His voice sounded small.

"How old are you?"

"Ten years. Fourth grade and I'm the second in my class to ride on a spaceship."

"I bet you're the first in your class to survive a space battle."

"We all survived when the Borwyn attacked the station."

"That was an errant shot at a gunship using the station to hide, but we take full responsibility, and it is great to hear that we didn't hurt any civilians. I'm sure the captain will like to hear that, too. Get your helmet on so we can get your environmental control dialed up. Wait."

Brad produced a water pouch.

"When's the last time you had something to drink?"

"I don't know. A while, maybe."

Even though it had only been a few hours since the second battle of Farslor, he handed the water pouch over and the boy drank fully, nearly draining it.

"Helmet." Brad pointed.

Once it was clicked into place, Brad adjusted the controls to bring the boy to a comfortable temperature.

He activated his microphone. "Crack the seal on those bulkheads and vent this section to space. Let's get those power plants offline and out of here. I'm taking the boy to *Chrysalis* to get him something to eat, and then I'll return to help explore this big, ugly pile of junk."

Teo watched her father go from her position in the overheads. She'd already measured the units and looked for space between the ship's main spars where they could cut out sections to move the power plants. What she found surprised her. They'd already been cut once.

She swam around to check the deck, where she saw a smaller footprint had been occupied before the bigger units were moved in.

This ship had been repurposed for a single mission—to carry the gunships to engage *Chrysalis*.

With a marker, she detailed where the plasma cutters would create the opening. Once through, they'd find something similar until they left the outer hull.

With a woosh, the air in the power section vented. Temperatures plummeted further but wouldn't reach space ambient as long as the plants were online.

She studied the panel for a few seconds. They were simple, something the Malibor embraced since their crews weren't engineers first. They were soldiers, volunteers, and conscripts. Their systems were graphical and easy to follow.

"Lights going off in ten seconds," Teo declared. "And then the real work begins. We'll put these monstrosities in the cargo bay as soon as we get them out of here. Bring up those plasma cutters and let's go."

The energy gauge ticked down to one percent. Brad's ship provided the baseline power to the ion drive. In thirty minutes, they'd have another percent, and for the thirty minutes after that, they'd have freshly filtered and recycled water.

Thirty on, thirty off until *Starstrider* was moved out and the Malibor power plants moved in.

Jaq was pleased with the efforts of all involved.

As suspected, there were no functioning weapons on the enemy cruiser. The gunship crews had left it trashed with food bags and other waste. The fresh water was half-full, but the sewage was overflowing. At least the Borwyn crew had been in spacesuits and didn't have to deal with the stench.

Jaq detailed a team to transfer the fresh water, once tested, to *Chrysalis*. Same with the air tanks. The ship's atmosphere would have been stable, but *Chrysalis* had punched a bunch of holes in it. With power out, the emergency bulkheads didn't engage when they should have fallen into the closed positions. Maybe it was a design flaw or maybe the Malibor wanted them open so the ship would die more quickly when it was hit, giving the Borwyn their cheer until the gunships hammered *Chrysalis* into oblivion.

No matter the reason, compressed air was stored at various locations throughout the ship. These were intact. Another crew to recover them. It wasn't going to take hours but days to transfer what they needed.

At least they had a plan and newfound hope, something Jaq had been on the verge of losing after having to fight the Malibor with a broken ship that became more broken when it was stitched up by lucky gunship fire.

They only had to get lucky once. *Chrysalis* had to get lucky every time. It was providing more stress than the captain expected.

Brad appeared on the bridge escorting the Malibor boy.

"Who do we have here?" Jaq asked. She leaned against the captain's seat with her arms crossed.

"Captain Jaq Hunter, this is Zinod Weft, ten years old and recently of the Malpace station. He has noted that the rounds that hit the station on our high-speed fly-by did not kill anyone."

"That is some good news. I was worried that we'd hurt

civilians." Jaq walked slowly across the bridge and stretched out her hand to the boy.

"You're the captain?"

"Yes. I know. I'm shorter than you expected." Her joke fell flat because the boy was even shorter.

"We don't have any women in charge of our ships."

"No. Makes no difference to us if a woman or a man is in charge," Brad explained. Even though he'd tried to take over when he first boarded *Chrysalis*, it wasn't because of gender but because of his age. "Jaq is the most capable, so she's in charge, but the best leaders surround themselves with the best people who they trust to do their jobs. Did you see people working all over the ship?"

The boy nodded.

"And you see the captain trying to get into their business?"

"No."

"Exactly. She doesn't need to. Let's find you suitable quarters and let you rest. Can I get your word that you're not going to attack us in any way?"

"Only if I get your word that you'll take me home," the boy countered.

Jaq smiled. "You know, Zinod, we all want to go home to Septimus. We'll get you home as soon as possible. Do you know if the cruiser had any escape pods?"

"What are those?" the boy asked, which almost answered Jaq's question.

Brad gestured. "I'll ask our people to look. If there is one, we can drop him off on our next trip past the station."

"You can dock. They have ports that'll link up to any ship, even one this big."

Brad and Jaq smiled at each other. The naivete of youth. "That would be optimal," Jaq said. "Until we can do that, we'll look for other ways to get you back to your parents. I'm sure they miss you. We'll send a message to them."

Brad shook his head.

"We have a Malibor cruiser from which to transmit, the second we're ready to disconnect and be on our way," Jaq clarified.

"I'm sure it'll be fine." Brad didn't sound convinced. "Dolly, can you take our passenger to stores and get him bedding and a place to stay?"

With someone closer to his age, Brad figured the boy would better assimilate until such time as they could return him to his parents. Zinod Weft could very well be the beacon of peace. Not a negotiating tactic, just an honest delivery of a person the Borwyn found.

The Malibor would never believe it, and that's what would make it so effective. He was ten. He had disappeared with the fleet and returned after they abandoned him.

Dolly left her station and took the boy down the corridor. They were almost the same size. Zinod pulled himself shakily to keep up. He wasn't used to zero-gee. By the time he got back home, it would be second nature.

Chrysalis had too much work to do to make it sooner, with how badly they needed to get the work done and get back in the fight. The longer they took, the more of a chance that the Malibor would return those two damaged cruisers to service and maybe even press the big ship into functionality.

"Are you thinking what I'm thinking?" Brad asked.

Jaq raised one eyebrow. "That we're not going to be able to drop him off on our next trip past the space station because we're going to blast their shipyard to pieces?"

Brad chuckled. "That was close. If we don't get there soon enough, we'll face two cruisers in space versus easy targets in the shipyard docks. The longer we take, the greater the risk on a fly-by."

"That boy could be a key to keeping them from shooting at us. It would be a nice starting point to negotiate peace." Jaq looked to her team. Amie and Taurus were the only ones still on the bridge. "Do you have an ETA for *Cornucopia*?"

Taurus replied, "They were three days ahead of us. Brad ordered them to return only a few hours ago, so a day or two to slow down if they burn hard, then three days back plus another day to slow, but we're heading their way at a hundred and fifty thousand KPH. I wouldn't expect them for about four days, but I can't confirm that without active scanners."

"That's close enough," Jaq said. "About what I thought, too. I think we'll be back online by the time they arrive. Then we can strip the cruiser of any circuit boards, power systems, air, and anything else we think we can use. The drives are okay, but the ship is a dead hulk. We don't need their engines, although it would be nice to slow the ship and park it somewhere for later exploitation, if needed."

"We'll throw some retro rockets on it. I suggest we spacewalk to fix our transceiver. We need to talk with people."

"As much as I don't want to, I know you're right. Are you going to do it?"

Brad turned to Amie.

"Don't look at me. I'm too old for that garbage."

"You're younger than me," Brad retorted, but he'd already decided. "I'll do it."

"I figured, but we have time. I say we rest up before going out there and fixing it."

"You're going with me?"

"We don't have anyone else. They'll be stripping the cruiser or installing the power plants."

"Which means I need to move my ship." He caught the gleam in Jaq's eye. "I guess I can do that in a couple hours."

"Amie, we'll be in my quarters. Make sure no one bothers us for at least ten minutes."

"Two hours," Brad corrected.

They flew down the corridor and into Jaq's quarters. "It's been a while," she said softly.

"How long is a while? I've been alive for a long time. I suspect our definition of time is different."

"Forever. I never had the time nor inclination."

Brad was taken aback. He struggled to find the words.

"Until now." She unzipped her uniform. "Showers are up for another fifteen minutes."

"Who am I to say no to a shower?"

CHAPTER 32

The nature of a person can be changed, but it takes work.

Deena waved as the latest group of customers left. "What do you think, Boss?"

"I think it's nice to have customers back. Word of mouth travels fast. A hot babe working the tables."

"I'd like to think it's a person who embraces cleanliness and doesn't put up with any garbage. And I'm also nice to look at, but if any of them touch me, I'm going to pound them into next week."

"Where'd you learn to fight?"

Deena had her answers prepared. "When you look like me but don't like being touched, you learn to protect yourself. I've had good teachers." Thinking of Max and Crip made her smile.

"We could use another employee. We're swamped," the boss stated.

"Did I hear you say you were looking for help?" a young soldier asked.

"We don't take military who are moonlighting. You might get assigned to a different gate or sent somewhere on short notice. Too unreliable to schedule."

"No." The man waved his hands. "My wife could use a job, and I would never recommend a place like this except for you." He nodded to Deena. "The men respect you and keep their hands to themselves. If you can help my wife, I'm sure she'd be a great employee. She's smart and beautiful. I trust her, but I don't trust them."

Soldiers filled half the tables in the restaurant.

"Of course we'll take good care of her. You have my word." Deena saw the opportunity to ask questions about the base and the military within without looking like she was collecting intelligence. "She's hired. Do the paperwork, Boss man."

"Wait a minute! This is my place. There has to be an interview, and I say whether she's hired or not."

"Send her by as soon as possible. I'll teach her the ropes while Boss man decides to hire her. She can start first thing tomorrow."

"I don't know why I'm agreeing to this, sight unseen. Fine. Send her. We'll see if she can hold her own carrying trays and putting the plates in front of customers."

"If what's-his-dumbass in the kitchen says 'fresh meat' again, I'll pound him into next week. You might want to warn him or better yet, hire someone who's not a repulsive derelict."

"If we hire two more, I'll do the cooking. You can run the

seating operation. I got into this business because I cook well. I make good-tasting meals. We've lost that with a simplified menu that even he can cook."

"We'll find you another," Deena promised. "You, get the word out on base. Looking for another wife who will be taken care of. And you..." She looked at the boss. "Ask your wife to come in. I'd like to meet her. I bet she'll be willing to work the counter, check people in and out, when she finds the place is clean and the staff is friendly." Deena flicked his apron. "Can you wash that?"

"It's clean!" he shot back. "Those are stains that won't come out."

"Then buy a new one." Deena clapped the young soldier on the shoulder. "Send your wife to us. We'll do the rest."

Deena served up the next order and cleared dishes from the last order. She deposited all of it directly into the automatic dishwasher.

She wasn't hating her undercover assignment. There was a banal normalcy that came with a job. She had already pocketed enough money to rent a real apartment but thought it better to stay over the restaurant. She didn't need comfort as much as she needed friends and proximity. She watched the comings and goings of the soldiers, but that wasn't telling her what she wanted to learn.

She needed to know particulars about the refueling station at the spaceport. She needed to know when the Malibor would deploy to the forest to harass the Borwyn. She wanted to know if they had missiles, where they stored their munitions, and where the space fleet headquarters was located. It was all vital information that the Borwyn could use.

Being in a hurry wouldn't get her what she wanted, but having a friend who owed her and had a soldier as a husband would.

She looked forward to getting help cleaning the restaurant. They almost had it completely cleaned, top to bottom with an inventory of what needed to be replaced, like the tables and chairs. Despite the boss's claims that they added charm, Deena suggested that they needed to go. She planned to replace the chairs four at a time, buying them with her own money if she had to. Her cash payments weren't the only money that was skimmed. The boss maintained enough to keep the auditors happy, but not so much that he paid what he really owed.

Deena didn't care about any of that, but what was important to her was not falling under the scrutiny of the government. Keep the customers happy with good food at a good price and pay the government their share.

"Don't skim too much, Boss man."

"Hey! Them's fighting words," he replied.

"We don't need any government officials stopping by to check your records. They'll find me and that will highlight me to my abusive stepfather. I can't have that."

He nodded. "I get it. I'll keep my nose clean. Just when I started to turn a profit."

"You'll be fine. We'll keep growing the clientele. When are you going to fire what's-his-face?" She jerked a thumb over her shoulder.

"Need two more good employees. Three like you and this place will be filled from the moment we open until we close."

"Working it, Boss man. Soon. And we'll dominate the restaurant business in this part of town. Your neighbors will be envious."

"That'll be the day." He put the help wanted sign he'd been holding back under the counter. "But I can see it. You're making a difference, Deena. Pretty soon, I might even be able to take a day off."

"I tell you what, the day before the first workday of the week has low clientele. You're barely breaking even. I suggest you close on that day. Let all of us take some time off. I can work six days a week. But seven? I can use a day off."

She needed to see some things for herself and couldn't do that outside of the restaurant's hours because she'd look suspicious walking around at night or too early in the morning. No. She was better conducting in-person reconnaissance during normal hours with the usual crowds where she could blend in.

It was going according to plan. With the impending new employee, Deena had her way into the inner workings of the base without having to cozy up to any of the customers. That idea nauseated her. She wouldn't go that route no matter how much information she needed. They'd done without intelligence collection before. It had been looking like they would have to again until the young soldier interrupted.

The battle is joined, she thought.

To be continued in Starship Lost Book #5

The story is ongoing at a high rate of speed. Sorry for the cliffhangers, but I had to cut this tale at some point. The good news is that Starship Lost Book #5 will be out in less than a month, if it's not out already. The Borwyn's fate continues to play out.

Please leave a review on this book, because all those stars look great and help others decide if they'll enjoy this book as much as you have. I appreciate the feedback and support. Reviews buoy my spirits and stoke the fires of creativity.

Don't stop now! Keep turning the pages as I talk about my thoughts on this book and the overall project called *Starship Lost*.

You can always join my newsletter at https://craigmartelle.com or follow me on Amazon https://www.amazon.com/Craig-Martelle/e/B01AQVF3ZY/ so you get notified when the next book comes out.

AUTHOR NOTES - CRAIG MARTELLE

Written September 2023

Here we are again, another book, another crisis resolved, yet more remain. Getting home isn't as easy as returning. The Borwyn are evolving as they engage in more battles and see greater opportunity.

The engineering and technical aspects within these books remain sound. This is hard science fiction, space opera, and space adventure wrapped into one neat series. I planned it that way from the outset. I wanted the math to work. I wanted the relationships to be profound. I wanted the adventure to be gripping. And the military aspects? Those are my go-to. Nothing like a good space battle or land battle to keep the action genes thrumming.

As for me, summer has wound down and we race through our one month of fall toward winter. By the time you read this, it'll be the dead of winter—if you pick it up when it first publishes. I live in the Alaskan interior, about 150 miles from the Arctic Circle. We have six months of winter, a month of spring, four months of summer (with three of those months having twenty-four hours of daylight), and one month of fall.

During the winter, we hit the solstice where we have less than four hours of daylight, and it is grim daylight. The sun rises in the south, stays on the southern horizon, and then sets in the south. In the summer, the sun stays in the northern sky. It's odd and difficult for those not used to it to accept it as the norm. Everything depends on the time of year for little things like daylight. We are considered high desert here, and that means we don't necessarily get a lot of snow. Temperatures can get down to -50F in the winter and we get a handful of days in the 80s during the summer. Nobody has air conditioning up here, but everyone has multiple sources of heat. I have four—electric, fuel oil, kerosene, and pellets, with the fuel oil boiler doing the heavy lifting. The pellet stove saves some money when we run it.

Otherwise, it's a beautiful time of year right now. Stanley, our pitbull, and I spend a lot of time in the woods beside our home. Also, we've had some great northern lights already this year. We can watch them from the privacy of our own driveway. We don't have any light pollution where I live. When the sky is clear, we're rewarded with a great view.

We have to watch out for the porcupine that has been hanging out around our house. I've got some great security video of the fat beastie waddling around the outside.

As a reminder, https://www.omnicalculator.com/physics/acceleration —need to keep that acceleration calculator close at hand. That's it, a bunch of rambling thoughts and a finished book, but far from a finished story. More coming very soon.

Peace, fellow humans.

If you liked this story, you might like some of my other books. You can join my mailing list by dropping by my website at craigmartelle.com, or if you have any comments, shoot me a note at craig@craigmartelle.com. I am always happy to hear from people who've read my work. I try to answer every email I receive.

If you liked the story, please write a short review for me on Amazon. I greatly appreciate any kind words; even one or two sentences go a long way. The number of reviews an ebook receives greatly improves how well it does on Amazon.

Amazon—www.amazon.com/author/craigmartelle

Facebook—www.facebook.com/authorcraigmartelle

BookBub—https://www.bookbub.com/authors/craig-martelle

My web page—https://craigmartelle.com

Thank you for joining me on this incredible journey.

THANK YOU FOR READING CONFRONTATION

We hope you enjoyed it as much as we enjoyed bringing it to you. We just wanted to take a moment to encourage you to review the book. Follow this link: **Confrontation** to be directed to the book's Amazon product page to leave your review.

Every review helps further the author's reach and, ultimately, helps them continue writing fantastic books for us all to enjoy.

Also in series:
Starship Lost
The Return
Primacy
Confrontation

Fallacy Engagement

Check out the entire series here! (Tap or scan)

Want to discuss our books with other readers and even the authors? Join our Discord server today and be a part of the Aethon community.

Facebook | Instagram | Twitter | Website

You can also join our non-spam mailing list by visiting www.subscribepage.com/AethonReadersGroup and never miss out on future releases. You'll also receive three full books completely Free as our thanks to you.

Looking for more great books?

ROGUE STARS
PURGATORY
BOOK ONE OF THE ROGUE STARS SERIES
JAIME CASTLE

Abandon ship, or go down in a blaze of glory. Commander Predaxes, former Marine in the Lazaab military, has been recommissioned to Prison Station 12, known colloquially as Purgatory. On the outskirts of the Centridium, PS12 relies solely on a wormhole for contact with the government -- not to mention supplies. His newest inmate, Samea Malik, is more than a bit of trouble. Son to the Minister of Justice, Malik is the target of both assassination and recovery. When the station is attacked and chaos rains down upon them all, those onboard must abandon their posts for the closest habitable planet, Faebos. With what little planning they could do, Predaxes and crew discover an old, defunct mining colony and quickly discover why the project was deserted. Faebos is home to violent and nasty creatures, but also great beauty. Survival will mean cooperation between PS12's captives and captors. But will it be enough? Faced with hardship no one expected, needing to tap into old skills and new, Predaxes and Malik find themselves in their own form of Purgatory. *Rogue Stars* **is a brand new Military Space Opera series by #1 Audible and Washington Post bestseller Jaime Castle, creator of the** *Black Badge* **series. Perfect for fans of David Weber, Larry Correia, JN Chaney, and Rick Partlow.**

Get Purgatory Now!

What if there was a war raging for one million years, but it was kept secret? Sargis is an upper middle class man living in Prime City, basking in the glow of the Techno King's so-called "Millenia of Peace." As far as he, or anyone else knows, humanity has no army, no weapons, and no wars. The people of Earth have been expanding into the stars for as long as anyone remembers, free of conflict while the Techno King and his Royal Cabal enrich themselves on the backs of their labor. All was as it always has been. Then, Sargis dies. Unbeknownst to him, an app he used every single day of his life hijacks his consciousness and uploads it into a synthetic engine of war known as a *sleeve*. Along with countless others, he has been conscripted into the Undying Legion, charged with fighting a secret, unending war in the name of humanity. **Experience the start of the next explosive Military Sci-Fi series from Joe Kassabian, author of the** *Liberty of Death* **Series. This boots-on-the-ground twist on being a soldier is perfect for fans of** *Rick Partlow, Galaxy's Edge: Legionnaire,* **and** *Starship Troopers.*

Get Invisible War Now!

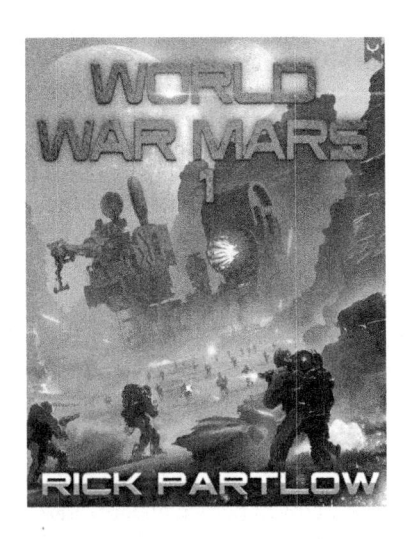

Alien tech discovered. The race to claim it could spark a new kind of War. When a derelict alien starship appears in the solar system and crash-lands on Mars, it ignites a desperate race to be the first to reach the Red Planet to claim the mysterious technological treasures of the Visitor. Space Force General Tom Bradstreet, ace Air Force fighter pilot and the only active-duty officer with actual space combat experience, is given control of the *Morrigan*, the first manned mission to Mars — and the first space warship. He and his elite team know their mission. In fact, it should be simple. The US is the only nation with a spaceship capable of making it to Mars. Or so they think… Maverick Russian General Mikhail Antonov has been handed the insane, desperate gamble of building an Orion-style spaceship powered by nuclear warheads. Launching it from the heart of Russia could be the spark that touches off a nuclear war but it's the only way the Russians and Chinese can hope to reach Mars before the Americans. The scene is set for a devastating world war, and the first shots may be fired on another world… **Don't miss the next action-packed, gritty military sci-fi series from Rick Partlow, the bestselling author of the *Drop Trooper* Series and *Taken to the Stars*.**

Get World War Mars Now!

For all of our science fiction titles, check out
www.aethonbooks.com/science-fiction

OTHER SERIES BY CRAIG MARTELLE

 # - available in audio, too

Battleship Leviathan (#)– a military sci-fi spectacle published by Aethon Books

Terry Henry Walton Chronicles (#) (co-written with Michael Anderle)—a post-apocalyptic paranormal adventure

Gateway to the Universe (#) (co-written with Justin Sloan & Michael Anderle)—this book transitions the characters from the Terry Henry Walton Chronicles to The Bad Company

The Bad Company (#) (co-written with Michael Anderle)—a military science fiction space opera

Judge, Jury, & Executioner (#)—a space opera adventure legal thriller

Shadow Vanguard—a Tom Dublin space adventure series

Superdreadnought (#)—an AI military space opera

Metal Legion (#)—a military space opera

The Free Trader (#)—a young adult science fiction action-adventure

Cygnus Space Opera (#)—a young adult space opera (set in the Free Trader universe)

Darklanding (#) (co-written with Scott Moon)—a space western

Mystically Engineered (co-written with Valerie Emerson)—mystics, dragons, & spaceships

Metamorphosis Alpha—stories from the world's first science fiction RPG
The Expanding Universe—science fiction anthologies

Krimson Empire (co-written with Julia Huni)—a galactic race for justice

OTHER SERIES BY CRAIG MARTELLE

Zenophobia (#) (co-written with Brad Torgersen)—a space archaeological adventure

Glory (co-written with Ira Heinichen)—hard-hitting military sci-fi

Black Heart of the Dragon God (co-written with Jean Rabe)—a sword & sorcery novel

End Times Alaska (#)—a post-apocalyptic survivalist adventure published by Permuted Press

Nightwalker (a Frank Roderus series)—A post-apocalyptic western adventure

End Days (#) (co-written with E.E. Isherwood)—a post-apocalyptic adventure

Successful Indie Author (#)—a non-fiction series to help self-published authors

Monster Case Files (co-written with Kathryn Hearst)—A Warner twins mystery adventure

Rick Banik (#)—Spy & terrorism action-adventure

Ian Bragg Thrillers (#)—a hitman with a conscience

Not Enough (co-written with Eden Wolfe)—A coming-of-age contemporary fantasy

OTHER SERIES BY CRAIG MARTELLE

<u>Published exclusively by Craig Martelle, Inc</u>
The Dragon's Call by Angelique Anderson & Craig A. Price, Jr.—an epic fantasy quest

A Couples Travels—a non-fiction travel series

Love-Haight Case Files by Jean Rabe & Donald J. Bingle—the dead/undead have rights, too, a supernatural legal thriller

Mischief Maker by Bruce Nesmith—the creator of Elder Scrolls V: Skyrim brings you Loki in the modern day, staying true to Norse Mythology (not a superhero version)

Mark of the Assassins by Landri Johnson—a coming-of-age fantasy.
For a complete list of Craig's books, stop by his website—
https://craigmartelle.com

Printed in Great Britain
by Amazon